Canyon

A Post-Apocalyptic/Dystopian Adventure

The Traveler Series Book Two

Tom Abrahams

A PITON PRESS BOOK
Canyon
The Traveler Series Book Two
© Tom Abrahams 2016. All Rights Reserved

Cover Design by Hristo Kovatliev
Edited by Felicia A. Sullivan
Proofread by Pauline Nolet
Formatted by Stef McDaid at WriteIntoPrint.com

PITON PRESS

http://tomabrahamsbooks.com

Visit my website to join the PREFERRED READER'S CLUB

WORKS BY TOM ABRAHAMS

THE TRAVELER POST APOCALYPTIC/DYSTOPIAN SERIES
HOME
CANYON
WALL

POLITICAL CONSPIRACIES
SEDITION
INTENTION

JACKSON QUICK ADVENTURES
ALLEGIANCE
ALLEGIANCE BURNED
HIDDEN ALLEGIANCE

PERSEID COLLAPSE: PILGRIMAGE SERIES NOVELLAS
CROSSING
REFUGE
ADVENT

For Courtney, Samantha, & Luke;
My bright, shining lights

"Those to whom evil is done do evil in return."

—W.H. Auden, Poet

CHAPTER 1

JANUARY 3, 2020, 2:31 PM
SCOURGE -12 YEARS, 9 MONTHS
ALEPPO, SYRIA

The IED ruptured without warning, blasting pieces of pipe, shards of glass, ball bearings, red fur, and carpenter screws into three of the six soldiers on patrol near Abdul Wahhab Agha Hospital on the city's western edge.

The concussion blew Captain Marcus Battle from his feet, slapping the back of his helmet on the cratered pavement of Assultan Suliaman Alqunoony Avenue. He was dazed, a sharp ringing in his ears overpowering his thoughts.

For an instant, as he stared into the cloudless pale blue sky, he thought he was in Killeen, lying in the grass with Sylvia.

Almost as quickly as the delusion formed, it evaporated. The muted sounds of shrieks and pained screams accompanied the high-pitched tone of the ringing.

He rolled over onto his side, facing the spot where the tattered Elmo doll had exploded. Two of his comrades were on their feet, tending to what was left of the other three. Then he saw one of them spasm. He shuddered, his head snapped backward, and he went limp in a spray of red.

The second soldier dropped to his chest, quickly engaging his HK416 rifle, thumping random targets as he searched for the source of the gunfire and took two shots in his left leg.

Battle, still dazed, rolled over and found his HK416 on the ground next to him. He dragged it into position, pulled himself to one knee, and started firing.

He couldn't hear and could barely focus, he didn't know who was dead or alive, but he stood and started moving toward the gunfire. Bullets whizzed past his head and ricocheted off the ground around him. He took one in the side that slugged his Kevlar. It knocked him back for a second and felt like a thick punch to his gut. Battle kept moving forward, fully exposed, until he emptied the thirty-round magazine and found some protection behind the overturned charred frame of a pickup truck.

"Battle!" the wounded soldier called during a momentary lapse in gunfire. He'd managed to find adequate protection behind a concrete road barrier, having dragged himself there with one good leg. "I'm pinned. The others are gone. Get out of here. Try to find us help."

Battle couldn't hear him. The dog whistle piercing his ears hadn't subsided. At least his vision was clearing. He exchanged magazines and looked through the holes in the truck's frame. Behind him was a three-story building. Most of the windows were shattered or cracked, but he couldn't tell from which spot the sniper was taking shots. Battle looked back toward his patrol partner. It was only a matter of minutes and he'd be dead. He couldn't leave him.

Battle, his back pressed against the underside of the truck frame, said a prayer and spun around free of the truck. He aimed up at the building and pulled the trigger, releasing a quick burst for cover. He dashed across a short field of debris to the building's entrance and bolted through. He found himself inside a narrow concrete stairwell that stank of urine. Battle bounced up the first flight of stairs, and feeling the vibration of gunfire against the stair rail, he knew it was coming from a higher floor. He pressed his eyes closed against a searing headache and clenched his jaw as he climbed the second flight of steps. He stood still and felt the vibrations of the gunfire, unable to distinguish from which direction they were coming.

He was about to move to the third floor when, through the ringing, he heard a garbled, guttural-sounding discussion between two men. They were on the second floor. No doubt. Battle stood to the left of the door, his back against the wall, and with his left hand pulled on the handle to swing the door wide open. He guessed he had maybe twenty-five rounds left in the magazine. He took a deep breath, spun the handle, and moved into the open doorway with his HK416 leveled at whatever waited on the other side.

Nobody was there. It was an empty hallway. It was dark, except at the far left end. From the corner of his eyes, he saw movement in that light. An open door led to the two men unleashing the barrage onto his fellow soldier.

The men were preoccupied with reloading what looked to Battle like a Kalashnikov AK-103-4. One of them was pacing back and forth with a pair of binoculars. He was pointing wildly and yelling at the other man, who was manually loading a new clip. That explained the long pauses between volleys. Behind them was a window devoid of glass and an armoire pressed up against it they were using for cover.

This was his chance.

Battle took another deep breath and took off in a full sprint. As he bounded along the hallway, yelling at the top of his lungs, he tapped the trigger.

Thump! Thump! Thump! Thump!

The spotter turned to face Battle as the bullets slapped into his chest. He dropped the binoculars and stumbled backward. Battle pressed the trigger again as he reached the open doorway.

Thump! Thump! Thump! Thump!

The second volley found the man's neck, throwing him against the corner of the room in a violent heap. Battle burst into the room, shifted his momentum, and slid toward the dead spotter. To his right, the shooter was still on one knee, trying to engage the magazine. He was too late. Battle held down the trigger.

Thump! Thump! Thump! Thump! Thump! Thump! Thump! Thump!

The bullets tore through the shooter, rattling his body as they knocked him onto his back. Battle lowered his weapon, aiming it directly at the shooter's head, and tapped the trigger for good measure.

Thump! Thump! Thump! Thump!

Battle checked the rest of the room, which he figured was once a dorm room for the medical school or nearby university. There was a mattress on the floor. A desk was on its side. The bullet-riddled armoire blocked half of the open-air window. On top of it, Battle saw what looked like a crude detonator. He looked to his right. The wall was adorned with Arabic graffiti he couldn't read and bullet holes he imagined were from return fire.

Battle pinched the bridge of his nose and loosened his helmet's chin strap. The ringing was subsiding. He could hear yelling from across the street, but he resisted the urge to move to the window. It could subject him to friendly fire.

He fished around the back of his neck for his earpiece and found it, plugging it into his right ear. He pushed the button on his comms. It didn't work. So he yelled from inside the building, hoping his voice would carry far enough.

"This is Battle! All clear! Threat neutralized!"

"Battle, this is Buck. I'm injured. Need assistance."

Buck. Rufus Buck. That was who survived. The men liked him. He was a natural leader. He was a fellow Texan, though he wasn't one of Battle's favorite people. He didn't always adhere to the rules of engagement, as they were. He liked to bend them in his favor. Still, he was American, he was a soldier, and he needed help.

"On my way." Battle cleared the room, found his way back down the stairwell, and maneuvered through smoking debris into the street.

He crossed the crumbling asphalt to its opposite side, for the first time seeing the full impact of the IED Elmo. Bile rose in his throat. He couldn't distinguish arms from legs or one man from another. Only the names on the ragged, bloodied strips of the digital camouflage uniforms told him who was who.

"You're it?" Battle asked Sergeant First Class Buck. He was an enlisted man, an E-7 NCO who didn't always play well with the commissioned officers who he considered fast-trackers.

"Roger that." Buck was still leaning against the concrete barrier. "I don't know for how much longer, though."

Battle stepped to the other side of the barrier and saw the extent of the sergeant's injuries. He had a tourniquet tied above his knee. Below his knee was a bloody mess. His foot was wonky, turned at an unnatural angle.

"I'm gonna need your help." The sergeant was pale, his eyes sunken. Battle knew he'd lost a lot of blood. "I've called for help. Nobody's coming. Our comms are busted."

"I know. Can you walk?"

"What do you think?"

"Had to ask." Battle scanned the debris field. "I'm guessing the medic's kit is gone."

"Good guess."

Battle put his rifle on the ground and stepped over Buck. "I'm gonna carry you."

"You're what?"

"We've got no choice. I'm gonna put you on my back and carry you back to the checkpoint. Then we can get help."

"That's gotta be an hour away."

"At least."

"You're not gonna make it. I'm gonna bleed out."

"Give me a better option."

"Go get help. Come back for me."

"That'll take too long," Battle argued. "And clearly, the faction we thought was controlling this part of the city isn't really in control. You'll be dead before I get back."

Buck was pointing behind Battle with a trembling, blood-soaked finger. "What about that?"

Battle turned around and saw a small wheelbarrow. It was on its side, its load of rice spilled onto the ground. He ran over and uprighted it, tested the wobbly, loose wheel, and rolled it back to Buck.

"Hang on a second," Battle said, moving toward the remains of their fellow soldiers. For all of them, he tugged the dog tags from their necks. He carefully placed one from each set in the mouth of its corresponding soldier. He stuffed the duplicates into his pockets.

"Let's give it a go," Battle said, having completed the morbid but necessary task. He helped Buck into the tray, his injured leg dangling off the side.

Buck unstrapped his helmet and tossed it to the ground. "All right." He grimaced. "Let's do this."

CHAPTER 2

OCTOBER 15, 2037, 4:48 AM
SCOURGE + 5 YEARS
ABILENE, TEXAS

"We're gonna leave the bodies here?" Lola asked. "Out in the open?"

Battle looked at his handiwork, his hands on his hips. "Yeah. We don't have time to drag them outside and bury them."

There were four bodies. All of them were grunts who'd overplayed their hands. In a matter of seconds, Battle had unloaded his 9mm Sig Sauer nicknamed McDunnough. They'd never had a chance. Their low-level existence in the Cartel's hierarchy came to a sudden, bloody end.

He looked at the glazed, vacant stare frozen into the eyes of one of the grunts, a cheating card shark named Hedgepath, and remembered he hadn't prayed before pulling the trigger. There hadn't been time.

Battle stepped over to the dead man and knelt down, pulled his cowboy hat from his head, and held it to his chest.

"As far as the east is from the west," he whispered to himself, "so far has He removed our transgressions from us." He repeated the brief offering at each of the three remaining bodies.

"Seriously?" Lola called out. "You're praying for them?"

Lola was on the arena floor between the card table and the motor pool.

"I was praying for myself," he said. "It's too late to pray for them." He put his hat back on his head and reached down to take the weapons the dead men wouldn't need anymore.

Lola looked past him at the bodies and then refocused on Battle. She folded her arms across her chest, rubbing her arms with her hands.

"You cold?" Battle took the last of the grunts' weapons and walked past her to toss them into the back of the Humvee. She shook her head. "No. Just wondering."

"What?" He reached the Humvee, placed the weapon inside it, and slammed the driver's side door of the Humvee shut. "How did you do this?"

"What?"

Her eyes widened with incredulity and she opened her arms to reference the carnage on the arena floor. "This. How did you kill four men like that? How did you do everything you did at your home?"

"I dunno." He shrugged. "I just did."

"I've seen a lot of bad things," she said, lowering her voice. "I've seen a lot of bad people. They did horrible things. They were horrible people. None of them could do what you do."

"I was in the Army," he answered. "I was—"

Salomon Pico emerged from a wide vehicle entrance at the far end of the arena, behind the motor pool. "I found the loading exit," he said. We can get out of here pretty quick. Get our bags from the horses and do what we need to do."

"Good," Battle said. "Let's go."

"Why are we taking this one?" asked Pico. "Why not the box truck? We could carry more. Lola and I could hide."

Battle rolled his eyes. "This isn't a democracy. We're taking the Humvee because that's what we're taking."

Pico frowned. "I was just asking. I thought the truck was—"

Battle waved him silent. "The Humvee is armored. The box truck isn't. The Humvee is a four-speed automatic. The box truck is a stick. The Humvee has all-terrain, cross-country tires on it. They can go for thirty miles with a flat. The box truck doesn't and can't."

Pico raised his hands in surrender. "Okay. Okay. Fine," he huffed. "The Humvee's better. I get it."

"Lola, hop in," said Battle. "Pico, you guide me out. I'm driving. Once we clear the building and get to the horses, you'll drive and I'll ride in the back. Got it?" Battle climbed into the driver's seat as Lola buckled herself into the front passenger seat of the desert tan vehicle.

The Humvee, nicknamed for its High Mobility Multipurpose Wheeled Vehicle designation, was the Army's workhorse in Syria. For close to fifty years, the United States military and some of its allies had deployed the HMMWV into the worst places on Earth. If he'd attempted to add them up, Battle figured he'd probably spent more hours in a Humvee than he had in any car he'd owned. They were as safe as any personnel carrier available, they were reconfigurable based on the mission, and they could move at a pretty good clip for something that weighed anywhere from six to eight thousand pounds. The official top speed was seventy miles per hour. Battle knew they could exceed that in the right conditions. He hoped he wouldn't need those conditions.

He reached to the left side of the dash to the rotary start switch and looked at the three-position switch, turning the key to "run". A "wait-to-start" lamp above the switch blinked off, and Battle turned the switch to the "start" position. He released the switch lever and it popped back to the "run" position automatically. He waited for the glow plugs to activate, and the six-and-a-half-liter, eight-cylinder turbo engine rumbled to life.

He looked at Lola. "You ready?"

"As I'm going to be."

Battle shifted into drive and rolled the Humvee toward Pico, who started back toward the wide loading entrance.

The Humvee was utilitarian and not built for comfort. Despite its wide front compartment, Battle shifted as he would in the worst coach seat in a commuter plane.

He rode the brake, slowly trailing Pico through the loading entrance and down a slight decline to a concrete ramp. Pico raised his hands, stopping the Humvee short of a large rolling galvanized door. He reached up and tugged on a chain at the side of the door, raising the door as it coiled upward.

Once Pico had the door fully raised, he waved Battle through the opening. Battle let his foot off the brake and accelerated out of the arena and up an incline onto a gravel road that ran along the loading side of the arena.

"We've still got a couple of hours until daylight," said Battle. He spun the wheel to the left, driving around the southern side of the complex to avoid driving near Highway 36. "I think sunrise is around oh-seven-thirty."

"So we're hitting them before sunrise?" Lola asked.

"That's the plan," said Battle. "We'll have the advantage."

"How so?"

"They won't see us coming. It's always best to initiate a direct action under the relative protection of darkness."

"Direct action?"

"A quick operation in hostile territory."

"So this will be quick? We'll have Sawyer back quick?"

"I don't know about that," Battle admitted. "We don't know exactly where they have your son."

Lola blinked back tears and turned away from him to stare out the window.

The Humvee, rumbling with its lights off, crossed over a narrow strip of parallel roads and rolled to a stop a few feet from the trio of horses tied to the exterior fence near the airport's runway.

The horses grunted against the noise of the Humvee and pulled against their reins. Their discomfort strained the already weakened fence. Battle quickly turned off the engine to calm them and slid out of the vehicle.

Pico walked across the road and trudged to the horses. "Load everything?"

"Yep." Battle loosened the saddlebags on his Appaloosa. "Everything can go in the back."

Lola joined the men and began working on her bags. "What do we do with the horses?" asked Lola. "Are we leaving them here?"

"No," Battle said. He rubbed his hand along the horse's mane. It nickered. "We're letting them go."

"What? Why?"

"We don't have a need for them," Battle said, running his fingers through the animal's coarse black hair. "We don't know where we're headed or how long we'll be gone. We keep them tied up here and they could die."

Pico waved his hands in the air. "So we just free 'em?"

Battle pulled his hand from the horse and swung around to face the dissenters. "Is this going to be a repeated issue?" He pointed at Lola and then moved his aim to Pico. "The two of you?"

Lola and Pico exchanged glances. Neither answered the question.

"Because I'm not putting up with it." Battle's hands were at his sides. He was flexing his fingers in and out of a tight ball. "Salomon Pico, I know you took a risk riding with me. I appreciate that. You really had no choice. And Lola, I know you're desperate. You want your son back, I got it. However, you both have to understand that you need me. It's not the other way around. I'll survive out here without either of you." Battle released the saddlebags from his horse. He carried one of them over to the Humvee and dropped it into the open bed in the back. "So I'm not having this conversation again. You both do what I say, you live by my rules, you follow my plan. Otherwise we'll part ways."

Lola's eyes hawked him as he walked back to the horse for the second bag. Pico was looking at the ground, mumbling to himself, kicking at the weeds.

Battle grabbed the bag and heaved it over his shoulder. "We good?"

Lola nodded. Pico did the same.

"I need verbal confirmation," Battle insisted. "Yes or no?"

Lola ran her fingers through her hair and rolled her eyes. "Yes."

Pico shrugged. "Yes?"

"That a question, Salomon Pico?"

"No," he replied. "It's a yes. Yes."

"All right then," Battle said. "Let's load up, let the horses loose, and hit the HQ. We're running out of time."

CHAPTER 3

JANUARY 3, 2020, 3:44 PM
SCOURGE -12 YEARS, 9 MONTHS
ALEPPO, SYRIA

No fewer than twenty factions controlled varying parts of
Aleppo, the most dangerous city in Syria, if not the entirety of
the Middle East.

The one hundred and fifty thousand American soldiers,
Marines, and sailors fighting the war were never quite sure
who was on their side and who wasn't. It seemed to change
from week to week.

One of the factions, the Asala wa al-Tanmiya Front, was
reportedly in control of Western Aleppo near the university
and the hospital. It was one of the largest sections of the city
controlled by a singular group. They called for help patrolling
the zone between their checkpoint and one controlled by the
hardline Syrian Islamic Front, a coalition of smaller factions
that kept assimilating like-minded groups to increase its reach
and power.

Battle and his men were the last of three teams tasked with a
daylong, triple-shift effort to check weaknesses along the
sector's boundaries. They'd unwittingly found one when the
IED exploded under their feet.

Now, Battle was burdened with carrying the lone surviving
member of the patrol more than four miles back to the
friendly checkpoint. The wheelbarrow had lasted exactly
seven minutes before the front brace collapsed, the axle broke,
and the wheel fell off. It was nice while it lasted.

While Buck wasn't a small man, Battle wasn't either. He held Buck over his shoulders like a fireman, one armed draped around the backs of Buck's thighs and the other around the injured soldier's back. The slog was slow and Battle took a break every ten minutes, resting in the relative protection of abandoned cars or behind the remnants of decimated structures.

"We're exposed," Buck said in between sips of water from Battle's canteen. "We run into any opposition, we're both dead. Every time I see a burka or a kid carrying a backpack, I freak."

Battle adjusted a makeshift splint on Buck's leg that ran from his ankle halfway up his calf. He looked up at the sergeant. "How's the pain?"

"Bad. I feel like I'm gonna puke."

"I can't give you more morphine. I've got Phenergan. It might help the nausea and amplify the morphine."

"Where'd you get it?" Buck accepted the circular orange pill Battle held out and tongued it into his mouth, finishing it off with another swig of water. "The medic kit was obliterated."

"I have my own stash," Battle said. "I like to stay ahead of the game."

Buck laughed and then coughed. "It's a game, is it?"

"Everything is a game one way or the other, Sergeant." Battle stood and scanned the surrounding area. "You stay here for a minute. I'm gonna check the path forward."

Battle picked up his HK and stepped over a rusting wheel frame, walking north. It was late afternoon, he was drenched in sweat, and they were maybe halfway to the checkpoint. He pulled out a handheld GPS and tried to orient himself. The sun set early in Aleppo; he had maybe forty minutes of sunlight.

They were near the intersection of Handaseh Street and Kher
Eddin Al Asadi. Behind him was what was left of the
university's civil engineering faculty building. A block north
was a bank building and the Alrazi Hospital.

He knew the hospital was on the edge of Asala wa al-Tanmiya
Front control. The latest intelligence was a month old. It could
have flipped hands. He couldn't risk showing up there for
help and being shot on sight or, worse yet, taken prisoner.

The checkpoint was between the old Aleppo Railway station
and Aziziya Square on the eastern side of the narrow Queiq
River near an amusement park. It was about two and a half
kilometers. In the best conditions it would take him twenty-
five to thirty minutes to walk it. He had two options. He could
walk north and skirt a public park. Though it would be faster,
it would leave them exposed all the way to the checkpoint.

He was better off taking a straight line route east along Al
Bohtory Street and then jogging north at Saadallah Al Jabri
Square. If he took fire, he had places to hide. Either way, it
probably was a crapshoot.

Battle turned back south toward Buck when he heard the
familiar zip of a semiautomatic rifle coming from the east near
the railroad track.

Pop! Pop! Pop! Pop! Pop!

A pair of shots whizzed past his head, and he dove behind the
corner of a building for cover. He was maybe fifty yards from
Buck.

"Buck! I've got incoming. Are you good?"

Pop! Pop! Pop! Pop! Pop!

"I'm good!"

Pop! Pop! Pop! Pop! Pop!

Battle adjusted his grip on his rifle. His butt was resting on his heels, his weight on the balls of his feet as he leaned against the building in a narrow alleyway leading onto the main street. He couldn't pinpoint the location of the rifle fire. Another volley zipped past him, a pair of bullets crumbling the clay brick a foot above his head.

Pop! Pop! Pop! Pop! Pop! Pop! Pop! Pop! Pop! Pop!

Battle backed further into the alley. He knew somebody was spotting him and relaying location information to the shooter. The shots were too accurate for the random sniper fire they encountered.

Battle stayed low, moving back to Buck's position. Once he'd disappeared from the alley, the gunfire stopped.

"We're pinned?" Buck asked, the color gone from his face. His skin looked almost translucent.

Battle nodded. "Yeah. And we're about to lose daylight. I've got to find another way out of here."

CHAPTER 4

OCTOBER 15, 2037, 5:09 AM
SCOURGE + 5 YEARS
ABILENE, TEXAS

Cyrus Skinner blinked his eyes open. His leg was dangling off the edge of his bed and his toes were cold. A nightlight he kept plugged into the outlet closest to the bed was dark. The power was out again.

Skinner slid his leg back under the sheet and rolled onto his back. He stared into the dark at the ceiling and sighed, rolling back onto his stomach. It was more than twenty-four hours since he'd sent Queho southeast to take care of the rancher he knew as Mad Max.

The reclusive rancher had already killed at least three of his men. He knew that for sure. There was a good chance the posse boss Rudabaugh and his posse were buzzard food. And now, Queho hadn't come back.

Skinner grunted and reached over to a nightstand, dragging his lighter and cigarettes into bed with him. He turned onto his back and scooted up on his elbows. With a half-empty feather pillow propped between his back and the headboard, he shook a cigarette free of its package and lit it with a couple of puffs. He drew in a deep breath and held it. The familiar buzz filtered into his bloodstream and he exhaled through his nose. Smoke plumed around him. He sucked in another drag; the bright orange glow hanging from his lips intensified. It was the only light in the room.

Skinner rubbed his jaw, scratching the three-day-old growth. He had a decision to make.

Clearly Mad Max, and the woman he was keeping from them, was far more of a problem than he'd anticipated.

Skinner was an area captain, a job which came with certain privileges and responsibilities. Being a captain meant all of the bosses in his area, which stretched from east of Abilene, west to Midland, and then north to Lubbock and Amarillo, reported to him. It was a triangular territory that had as many roadrunners as people, strategically important to the Cartel's hold on power.

In the months after the Scourge, a coalition of previously warring criminal organizations had seen the mutual benefit of joining forces. They'd inflicted heavy casualties on a less-than-inspired US military.

Rather than engage in a bloody war with its own people during a time when there was no appetite for more death, what was left of the United States military and border patrol had retreated. It had given up control to the coalition of gangs, drug traffickers, and ex-cons, abdicating its claim to roughly two hundred and seventy thousand miles between Louisiana, Oklahoma, and New Mexico. The Cartel had been quick to establish a wide area of influence, forming a paramilitary hierarchy to control and oppress those who lived within their staked claim.

The Cartel's highest levels of leadership, who called themselves generals, chose the nastiest of the nasty to lead four key areas. They were called captains. Those captains then chose their bosses. Bosses recruited grunts. Grunts harassed, robbed, beat, tortured, raped, or killed whoever didn't submit to their will. Sometimes they did those things regardless. Among a mean lot of captains, Skinner was the meanest. He was the least likely to suffer fools. He was the perfect man to tame what his superiors called the Wild West. As long as he kept his bosses in line, his people under his thumb, and made sure the spoils made it to the generals in Dallas and Houston, the leadership left him alone.

With a rogue killer on land he didn't control, Skinner was restless. He slid out of bed, his feet slapping on the cold wood floors of his bedroom as the nightlight flickered to life. He crushed the cigarette into a full ashtray and tapped out a replacement from the box.

He lit it, the paper sizzling, and took another healthy drag. Skinner stretched and walked across his room to a large monitor on the wall opposite his bed.

He cleared his throat. "Computer on," he said. The screen blinked to life and the operating system cycled. He squinted against the bright light of the display.

"Computer, open email."

The computer's home screen gave way to an email program. Though Internet access in the Cartel's territory was limited and slow, it worked. For most, the filters prevented most communication beyond what the generals approved. The captains, however, had unfettered access.

"New email message," said Skinner. "Address to generals. Subject is…" Skinner paused. He didn't know what to call the message. He didn't really want to send it.

"Subject is Wild West," he decided. The computer entered the email addresses for the generals, filled in the subject line, and presented a flashing cursor at the top line of a blank message. Skinner sucked the cigarette. He pinched it between his fingers and pulled it from his lips. "Generals," he began, "I've got a problem here in the Wild West. Long and short of it is a runaway thief wandered into some land we hadn't secured. We chased her there but didn't get her. The owner of that land killed some of our men and helped the thief."

Skinner looked at what he'd dictated so far. He didn't like it, and changed course.

"Computer, open live chat," he said. "Call generals."

The email program closed on the screen and a new application opened. Four windows appeared on the display. In the lower right, Skinner saw a delayed, choppy mirror image of himself, smoke trailing upward from the cigarette dangling from his lips.

The other boxes flashed the word "connecting" while the computer dialed the extensions for three generals. The first to answer was in Houston. His image appeared in the upper right box.

"Skinner?" he asked, rubbing his hands over his bald head. "What do you want?"

Another general answered the call from Dallas. His digitally distorted face filled the box in the upper left corner. "Skinner? Why are you waking me up?"

"I got a problem I need fixed," Skinner said to the two of them. The box in the lower right was still dialing. The general on the other end wasn't answering.

"You can't fix it yourself?" asked the bald general. "This isn't about the problems we keep having up near Amarillo, is it? Those people up there give me fits."

"No," Skinner said. "No problems in Amarillo. No problems with Palo Duro Canyon."

"That's a first," chimed the second general. The resolution on his call was improving, revealing the general's leathery face and neck. He was shirtless. "What's the problem?"

Skinner took another drag and then thumped the ashes into a tray next to the monitor. "I'll try to make a long story short."

"You do that," offered the bald general. "Otherwise I'm likely to hang up and go back to sleep."

"We had a couple of thieves, a woman and her boy, working for us here in Abilene," Skinner explained. "They ran away. We caught the boy. The woman found her way to some land we hadn't cleared."

"We know about the boy," said the bald general. "General Roof told us about your plan to send him to Lubbock. We didn't know about the woman. She's still missing?"

"Yes," said Skinner. "She is. I'm calling you because—"

"Stop there." The leathery general stroked his unshaven chin. "Why was there uncleared land? Didn't your bosses clear everything months ago? I thought I remembered you telling us that."

"Yeah," added the bald general. "He told us that. Skinner, you told us you'd acquired all of the outstanding land in your triangle."

"I thought we had," Skinner said. He pushed the cigarette into the ashtray and put it out. "There was this one plot, maybe forty or fifty acres near Rising Star that we ain't got."

The leathery general scratched his head. "So what's the problem? Go get the land and get the woman."

"That's the thing." Skinner looked at his reflection. He pulled his shoulders back and lifted his chin. "We done gone there. We sent a posse to get the woman and kill the man who owns the land. He killed 'em."

"So send more men," said the bald general, scratching his scalp.

"We did."

The leathery general picked his front teeth, digging at the space between the center two. "And?"

"He killed them," said Skinner. "Well, I think he killed 'em. So I personally sent one of my bosses to clean it up. He took a half dozen or so men. They been gone a day now. I ain't heard from them. I'm thinking he got them too."

The bald general leaned in, staring into his camera. "One man?"

Skinner nodded.

"Is that an answer, Skinner?" the bald general asked. "My signal's choppy. Did you give me an answer?"

The leathery general chuckled. "He gave you an answer."

The bald general tapped on his screen. "Who is this one man?"

Skinner cleared his throat. "We call him Mad Max."

"Mad Max."

"From the movie."

"I know what it's from." The bald general raised his voice. "It's stupid. You're stupid. You've wasted who knows how many men on some woman thief. Then you call us at the butt crack of dawn to ask us how to handle it."

"I'm not asking for advice." Skinner stuck out his chin, his eyes unblinking. "I don't need your advice. I'm giving you a heads-up about what's going on."

The bald general grimaced. "Sounds to me like you need advice," he grunted. "You can't kill one man? I'm disappointed in you, Skinner."

"I can't say I'm too impressed neither," added the leathery general with a digitized shake of his head. "You best clean up this mess right quick. And you better make an example out of this Mad Max."

"Understood. I'll let you know as soon as it's done." Skinner glanced at the empty box on the screen. "You'll fill in General Roof?"

"We'll tell him what an incompetent you've become, if that's what you're asking," replied the bald general before he punched out of the call.

"He's on his way to Lubbock already," said the leathery general. "He said you already made the arrangements."

"Yes," said Skinner. "He had to go there anyhow, I'm told, to check on inventory. I figured we could send a message by having the boy there and letting everyone know—"

The leathery general frowned and ended his call without saying anything further.

"Computer, off," Skinner said. He pulled on a pair of jeans, his boots, and a long-sleeved T-shirt. He slid his hat, cigarettes, and lighter from the bedside table and walked toward his kitchen. The pale pink light of predawn hadn't yet begun to peek through the windows. It was still dark. Skinner knew this was going to be a long day. He needed some coffee and another cigarette.

CHAPTER 5

JANUARY 3, 2020, 4:27 PM
SCOURGE -12 YEARS, 9 MONTHS
ALEPPO, SYRIA

It was dark, which Battle tried to sell to Buck as a mixed blessing. True, it was harder to see their enemies. It also was harder for their enemies to see them.

The intermittent pop and rattle of gunfire was steadier now. Battle could see the flashes in the distance as the percussion bounced off the densely packed buildings.

"We're screwed," Buck said. He was slurring his words. His eyes were barely open. "I'm screwed. It's like I can feel the life oozing from my body."

"That's the drugs," said Battle. "You'll be fine."

"If I survive this," Buck said, "I'm getting out. I'm done fighting other people's wars. I'll fight my own."

Battle checked his GPS, hoping he'd find a new, alternative route he hadn't discovered the previous fifteen times he'd checked. "Your own war? What does that even mean?"

"I know people. They know people. I'm getting mine when I get back. That's all I'm saying."

"You're not making any sense," Battle said. "Shut up and let me focus on how to get us out of here."

The two were tucked in a narrow alley near Ofra Avenue. Despite having the GPS, Battle took them too far north. Now they were faced with having to dart across an exposed train yard to head straight east to the checkpoint.

In the alley, it was dark. They were hidden. Once they left the security of the high-walled alley, they'd be bathed in the orange glow of the train yard lights. They'd be a target for anyone perched on either side of the tracks.

"You know what the markup is for Mexican meth?" Buck asked. "And black tar heroin? It's ridiculous. So cheap. I'm taking my check from Uncle Sam and I'm buying a bar." Buck sounded delirious. "I'm buying a bar. Everything's cash in a bar. So easy to wash money in a bar."

"Dude." Battle held his finger up to his mouth. "Be quiet. I don't want to hear this."

"I'm gonna be the rich dude, Battle," he said. "Right now we're fighting other people's wars. When we're the rich dudes, we have people fighting our wars. That's how the world works. Old rich men send young poor men to fight. It's always been that way. Now we're here. They're in bed with their young, hot wives drinking caviar and eating champagne."

"All right." Battle took Buck's collar and yanked him forward. "Shut up. We can talk about this later. We need to get out of here."

Buck chuckled and mocked Battle, holding a finger up to his own lips. Battle let go a huff. "Whatever, man."

He looked back at the GPS. There were no options. He couldn't wait until daylight. Buck would be dead by then. It might already be too late for him, but Battle wasn't going to give up. They had to cut across the train tracks. That was their only option.

He helped Buck to his feet, slung him over his back, and inched from the alley. If he took incoming fire, the best he could do was run. He'd crossed Ofra and run along Kinda Street, which ran east until it ended at the train yard. Battle stopped at the dead end, which, thankfully, was out of reach of the orange lights perched high above the tracks. There was a high chain-link fence separating them from the yard.

Battle set Buck and his rifle on the ground, pulled the sweat rag from around his neck, and wrapped it around a link closest to the ground near a metal post. Resting on his kneepads, he pulled a set of wire cutters from one of his vest pockets and cranked it onto the cloth-covered link. He felt a snap and removed the cloth, working the half-cut link back and forth. A few pulls and tugs and it snapped. He methodically repeated the process five more times.

"What's with the rag?" Buck asked.

"It keeps the noise down," Battle answered. "We don't know where the enemy is."

Buck laughed, his eyes wide. "They're everywhere."

Battle worked the fence from the ground up and folded back the links to create a gap high enough for the two of them to crawl under. Battle went first, using his elbows and knees to slip under the fence.

"Scoot over here," he whispered to Buck. "On your stomach. I'm pulling you through."

To Battle's surprise, Buck complied and positioned himself at the edge of the fence opening. He reached under the chain link with his hands, stretching for Battle.

"Take this and stuff it in your mouth."

"No way."

"Do it. It's an order."

Buck took the rag and stuffed it into his mouth, gagging on it as he repositioned himself, extending both hands again.

"Not that way." Battle sat up and braced his feet on the fence post. He leaned on his side, reached back under the fence, and grabbed Buck's vest at the shoulders. "This is gonna hurt your leg. Bite down on that rag."

Buck shook his head in protest as Battle was already tugging, yanking him under the fence. The injured soldier was essentially dead weight, and Battle was already exhausted from carrying him as far as he had. He found something deep inside that helped him propel Buck through the opening. Even as Buck screamed in pain, his voice muffled by the rag, Battle pulled him clear of the chain link.

Once he was through, Battle rolled onto his back. His chest was heaving, his arms and lower back thickened with exhaustion. He took deep breaths in through his nose, trying not to make too much noise.

Buck was whimpering next to him until he reached over and pulled out the rag. Buck cursed at him, at his injuries, at God. "There ain't enough morphine in the world for what you did to me."

"Sorry," Battle said, looking at the clear sky above them. "Had to get you through there."

Buck lifted his shaky hand and offered Battle a one-fingered salute. He was grunting through clenched teeth.

Battle surveyed the open valley of the tracks. Directly in front of them, there was a steep decline into the valley. There were four sets of tracks, two of which had train cars on them, and a shed on the opposite side. A sharp incline led to the opposite edge and another fence.

Beyond that, it was too dark for Battle to see much of anything. He knew there was a wall of tall buildings behind them. On the far side, there was a cluster of lights, which Battle assumed were buildings. There didn't appear to be the concentration of threats they faced from behind and from the open tracks. Once they crossed the valley and cut their way through the fence on the opposite side, they'd only be a few hundred yards from the checkpoint and relative safety. Battle wished he'd recovered an XM25 from one of his dead compatriots. It was a tactical mistake. He'd been too consumed with helping Buck and hadn't thought with enough clarity.

The XM25 was a smart weapon that fired up to twenty-five rounds of laser-guided grenades. If Battle had it, he could aim it into the darkness at a perceived threat and fire with ridiculous accuracy. Even if he missed a target, the grenades would explode in the air at the designated distance. Despite its relatively heavy weight, every patrol that wanted one had one of them as a backstop. Battle cursed himself and calculated what he needed to do to escape with an injured soldier, a sidearm, and an HK416. He came to a difficult conclusion.

Battle reached out and put his hand on Buck's shoulder. "I think you're going to have to walk from here."

Buck coughed out a laugh. "Funny."

"I'm serious. I can't carry you and return fire. It would take me too long to get you off my back and then reposition into a defensive posture. Can't use the fireman's carry. Can't do the pack strap. You've got to walk."

"How the hell am I supposed to walk? I barely have the energy to keep breathing."

"Your heart rate is slow because of the morphine and the Phenergan. You've lost blood. You're *not* dying."

"If I weren't dying," Buck answered, "you wouldn't be in such a hurry to get us out of here. You'd be holed up in that alley back there, waiting for daylight."

Buck was right, of course, though Battle wasn't going to admit it. "Not true. The longer we stay here, the more vulnerable we are. The daylight isn't necessarily our friend. We got blown up in daylight, remember?"

Buck sighed. "How are we going to do this?"

"Walk assist. I'll put your arm around my shoulder and then hold it with my hand. My body will be your crutch. You shouldn't have to put any weight on your injured leg. I'll have my other arm around your back. I can hold my rifle. If we take fire, I can let go of you quickly and defend us."

"I don't know if—"

"You don't have a choice. It's what we're doing. I want you to take my sidearm. That'll give us two weapons ready to return fire."

Buck cursed and gritted his teeth. "Fine. Let's do this."

CHAPTER 6

OCTOBER 15, 2037, 5:57 AM
SCOURGE + 5 YEARS
ABILENE, TEXAS

Battle stood in the back of the Humvee, his legs working to keep balance while Pico drove toward the center of town. He had his Prairie Panther rifle at his shoulder. After considering the Browning as an option, he'd thought better of it. The Inspector, as he called 5.56 caliber semiautomatic, was a far superior weapon at long range.

He adjusted his hat when Pico picked up speed out of a turn. The hat, Battle hoped, would give any hostiles pause. They'd think he was a posse boss until they realized he wasn't. That was more than enough time for Battle to set, aim, and fire.

Pico was rolling dark. The Humvee's light array was off. They were as stealthy as they could be in a large armored vehicle. Battle scanned the road ahead of them and swiveled from side to side, sweeping the streets with his eyes and the rifle. They still had about ninety minutes until sunrise. The streets were empty. Most of the houses and buildings were dark.

The air was cold and the wind swept past Battle as the Humvee pressed forward. His ears stung; his nose ran. He ignored both.

The Humvee turned off of Fourth Street and rolled onto Walnut Street. For the first time, he recognized where they were. He remembered the wide street, the old buildings, and the green awning that hung from Bible Hardware.

It wasn't Bible Hardware anymore, though. It was the Cartel's Abilene headquarters.

Pico slowed to a stop in front of the awning. Battle looked across the street to a large fenced lot that surrounded the old post office. There was concertina wire wrapped around the top of the fence. He didn't remember that. He rubbed his chin and looked back at the awning. A lone streetlight strobed above them.

"Battle." Pico was standing outside the idling Humvee. "We're here. What next?"

Battle looked down at Pico and handed him his rifle. He pulled a backpack from the supplies littering the vehicle's open bed and slung it over both shoulders. He climbed from the Humvee and took the rifle back from Pico.

Battle pointed to the post office. "What's that over there?"

Pico shrugged. "I think they keep a lot of weapons and such inside that building. It was a post office."

"It was." Battle took a step toward the middle of the road. "You're saying it's an armory now?"

"I think so," Pico said. "I ain't never been in there, so I can't be sure. I heard talk about that, though."

"Anybody in the HQ?" Battle adjusted the pack on his back and walked back to the curb in front of the old hardware store.

"Shouldn't be," Pico said.

Lola rounded the bed of the Humvee. "Sawyer could be in there." Her hands were stuffed into her pants pockets, her shoulders raised to her ears. Her teeth chattered. "They could be holding my son in there, right?"

"I don't know. Guess I need to find out." Battle stepped to the front glass doors. He took the butt of his rifle and jammed it into the door. Glass shattered and Battle used the rifle stock to clean out the remaining shards hanging to the frame.

"That was kinda loud," said Pico. "I thought you were trying to surprise 'em."

Battle looked back at Pico and shrugged. He stepped across the threshold and disappeared into the darkness.

He flipped on the night-vision scope mounted onto his rifle and pulled it to his eye, carefully working his way around the main space of the building. He bumped into a table on one side of the room and then crossed the room to a bar. On the far side of the room past the bar, he found a locked door. He stepped back and punched through it with his foot, blowing past the lock. The door shot open and bounced off the wall behind it, almost hitting Battle as he slid into the hallway behind the door. There was another door to the left and a side exit at the end of the hall. He stepped to the door and tried the handle. It was unlocked. He opened the door and stepped into an office. He checked closets, a bathroom, a storage locker. The place was empty.

Battle started to leave when he thought better of it. This was a private office in the HQ. There had to be some actionable intelligence lying around. He quickly crossed the room to the desk. He leaned the rifle against it and sat down, his pack hitting the back of the chair. There was a stack of papers on the desk and a tablet computer in one of the drawers.

Battle stood, slipped off his pack, and set it on the desk. He unzipped it, pulled out four grenades, and replaced them with the papers and tablet computer.

Battle closed the pack, slid it on to his shoulders along with his rifle, and took two grenades with each hand. When he reached the doorway of the office, he turned around, pulled a grenade pin with his teeth, and tossed it toward the desk. That gave him five seconds.

He marched up the hall to the second doorway, pulled a second pin, and rolled another grenade down the hall. Battle hustled into the main room, yanked out the pin on the third grenade, and tossed it as the first grenade exploded in the office.

Battle was using MK3A2 concussion grenades. Unlike fragmentation grenades, the MK3 was designed for blasting and demolition. The overpressurization it produced was far greater and was effective inside buildings or bunkers. The resulting blast wave produced external shrapnel from ripping apart anything hit within its effective radius.

The eight ounces of TNT exploded, destroying the office and shaking Battle's balance. He nearly tripped as he bolted to the entrance. The second grenade detonated, blasting debris into the main room as Battle leapt through the glassless front door. He spun, pulled the pin, and the noiseless fuse activated. He heaved the final grenade through the door. "Run!" he yelled to Lola and Pico, not aware they'd already crossed the street to the post office fencing after the first explosion.

Battle was halfway across the street when the final two grenades blasted shrapnel through the HQ. He looked over his shoulder, the backpack bouncing against his body as he ran to join the others. The Humvee rattled against the explosion.

Lola gripped Battle's arm. "Sawyer wasn't in there?"

Battle coughed and cleared the phlegm from his throat. "I wouldn't have blown up the place if he had been."

"So that was a big wake-up call," Pico said. "I guess you wanted to invite them out to play?"

"No. We're not sticking around." Battle started back across the street and waved for Pico and Lola to join him. Thick gray smoke plumed from inside the HQ and through its aged flat roof. Battle slid off his pack, tossed it into the Humvee's bed, and climbed in. He took the Inspector by the forestock and checked it for damage.

"Let's go," he said. "Pico, you're driving."

"Where?"

"Who's the big boss?"

"The captain?"

"Whatever. Captain. Boss. Who is it?"

"His name is Cyrus Skinner," Pico said, pulling open the driver's side door. "I don't think —"
"You know where he lives?"
"Yes. But —"
"Drive."

***

Cyrus Skinner heard the series of explosions and felt them vibrate the water glass in his hand. He dropped the glass and ran out to his front stoop. In the distance, a couple of blocks away, thin wisps of gray smoke spiraled into the air against the faint glow of a flickering streetlight.
Skinner tensed and he stomped his foot on a wooden plank of the stoop. "Son of a b —"
"Captain Skinner," called a posse boss named Tom Horn. He lived in the house next door and was standing on his stoop. He was dressed in cargo pants, a faded Pink Floyd T-shirt, and his brown boss hat. One hand was wrapped around a coffee mug. "You think that's the HQ?"
"It's the HQ," Skinner sneered. "Get your posse together now and meet me over there pronto. You see any others on your way, you tell 'em the same."
Horn slipped back into his house. Skinner punched a wooden column that ran from the stoop's wooden floor to the low-hanging ceiling. He punched it a second time and cursed Mad Max.
Skinner marched back into his kitchen and retrieved his Browning. He checked his revolver, assuring it was fully loaded, and dropped it into his hip holster.
He exited the house through the back door and found his horse cribbing on the wooden fence to which it was tied. Its teeth were clamped onto the top rail, its back was arched, and it was pulling against the rail, sucking in air.

"Cut it out." Skinner yanked on the bridle's throatlatch and unloosed the reins from the fence. "You're gonna suck in a splinter and kill yourself." He shoved the Browning into a saddle scabbard, stuck a foot into a stirrup iron, and heaved himself into the thick leather saddle. He gripped the saddle horn with one hand and looped the reins around the other. "Git," he said to the horse, digging his boot heels into its sides. "C'mon, let's go."

The horse trotted to the front of the house and picked up its pace. Others emerged from their homes, pointing toward the dissipating smoke. Skinner's horse was nearing a full gallop when he tugged on the reins and stopped in the middle of the street.

He rubbed his eyes, not sure of what was moving toward him. It was still dark and he could only make out the roughest outline of the approaching machine. The sound, though, was unmistakable. A Humvee, with its lights turned off, was rolling at him.

He reached for the scabbard but decided against pulling his rifle. If he took aim now, he'd waste ammunition. He directed his horse to the side of the road. He stopped in front of a ramshackle house and hopped off his horse. He tied it to the leg of a rusted swing set in the yard, took his rifle, and crouched down behind it.

As the Humvee neared, a light flipped on inside the house and a man swung through the front screen door, standing there in his underwear. He wasn't Cartel.

Skinner stayed low, hiding from the man. He squatted lower and leaned forward on his knees, careful not to make a sound. The Humvee slowed in front of the house. Skinner got a good look at it. Aside from the driver, he could see an armed man standing in the bed, wearing a dark cowboy hat. Skinner couldn't place the man's face, at least not in the little ambient light the moon provided.

"Hey!" the man called from the Humvee. Skinner shrank lower to the ground. "You know where Cyrus Skinner lives? I hear it's on this street."

Skinner glanced over at the man in his underwear. The man hesitated and extended his left arm outward and pointed down the street. "Five houses down. Got a covered wooden stoop."

"Thanks." The man in the Humvee rapped on the top of the Humvee's cabin and the vehicle rolled along.

Skinner stood up, his hands on the shotgun. "Psst," he said to the homeowner. "Hey, you."

The man spun around, his face contorted with confusion until recognition washed over his expression. The man started waving his hands and stammering.

Skinner kept the Browning at waist level, hidden from the man's view. He stood there silently, listening to the man apologize and grovel. Midsentence, Skinner pulled the trigger. The man dropped in a heap.

Skinner turned toward a red light to his left. The Humvee's brake lights cast a glow. It was stopped in front of his house. He left his horse and started running toward the Humvee, staying along the edge of the street in the knee-high weeds and grass.

Others were leaving their stoops and yards to fall in behind the Humvee. Skinner couldn't tell how many of them were Cartel and how many were civilians. There were maybe a dozen total.

Skinner stopped two houses from his own and crouched low. He scanned the crowd again. None of them were Cartel. None was armed. None was wearing a hat. None was doing anything other than standing around looking dumfounded by the machine in the street.

The man in the back of the Humvee jumped out. He reached back into the bed and pulled out another weapon, bigger than a rifle, though it wasn't something Skinner recognized.

"Y'all are going to want to step back," the man called out to the crowd. He pulled the weapon up to his shoulder, his silhouette giving away how large a man he was, tall and muscular.

Skinner pulled his rifle up and leveled it against his own shoulder. He knew the distance wasn't good for the Browning, but he wasn't going to let someone shoot holes into his house.

He drew the man into his sight and pulled the trigger at the exact moment an explosion of light and the percussion of a cannon blast tore through the air.

Skinner couldn't tell where his shot hit. His eyes were focused on the instantaneous inferno his house had become.

His eyes wide, his breathing quickened, Skinner stood and started marching toward the Humvee. The man wasn't looking for him. He'd hit him by surprise.

A loud, skin-crawling scream came from the crowd. Skinner instinctively looked to his right. The crowd was gathered around a body on the ground. A woman was screaming and moaning as she held the body. Another woman tried to console her. A couple of others turned toward Skinner and pointed at him.

The Humvee was already on the move, speeding away. Skinner stopped and took a second shot, aiming at the man standing in the bed.

"You killed him!" the moaning woman wailed. The crowd parted and Skinner saw her face. Even in the dark, he could see the anger. "You shot my husband. Why did you shoot him? I don't—"

Skinner leveled the shotgun at her head and snapped the trigger. The blast silenced her and sent the crowd running back to their homes.

He looked at the mess. He wasn't happy about it. While he didn't want her dead, he'd learned a long time ago not to leave an angry person alive. It could only come back to haunt him. Revenge, he knew, was a powerful motivator. It made good people do bad things and bad people do worse.

The heat of his burning home took the chill from the air. It was hot on his neck. He turned around to look at the flames.

The fire devoured his home, crackling and popping as it chewed through the wood frame. He didn't recognize the man in the back of the Humvee. Still, he knew who he was.

"Captain Skinner," a voice called from his left.

Skinner swiveled with the Browning in position to fire. It was Tom Horn, the posse boss. He was running toward him with a half dozen grunts trailing behind him. Skinner lowered the shotgun, holding it with one hand where the stock met the receiver.

"Where the hell you been?" Skinner asked when Horn was close enough to hear him above the fire.

"I did what you asked," Horn said breathlessly. "I went and gathered some men." He nodded at the house. "What happened?"

"Mad Max."

"The guy from Rising Star?" Horn tugged at his brown cowboy hat. "The one who took the woman?"

"That'd be the one," Skinner said. He reached into his pocket and pulled out a cigarette. He lit it and slid it between his pursed lips. "You see a Humvee pass you on your way?"

Horn shook his head. "No. I think I heard it though. Must have turned off the street."

Skinner drew the cigarette from his mouth and slowly exhaled. He closed his eyes and listened to his house burn.

"You seem kinda calm," said Horn. "I mean, ain't you upset? I'd be madder than a wet hen and fixin' to whoop somebody good."

Skinner chuckled. "Oh, I ain't calm," he said. "I'm simmering here while I think of the best way to deal with Mad Max. In a second here, I'll be at a boil."

CHAPTER 7

JANUARY 3, 2020, 4:45 PM
SCOURGE -12 YEARS, 9 MONTHS
ALEPPO, SYRIA

"This is already a bad idea," Buck protested.
Battle helped him inch down the concrete embankment into the track valley. They were exposed in the orange light illuminating the rails.
Battle didn't answer him. He was too focused on each step. If they slipped on the steep decline, they'd make too much noise, Buck could aggravate his injury, they could lose their weapons.
"Did you hear me?" Buck pressed. He was hopping more than walking. His bad leg was useless.
"Shut up, Buck," Battle said, sliding his boot downward. "Focus."
Buck grunted and adjusted his grip on Battle. They were halfway down the slope when they took fire.
Pop! Pop! Pop!
The shooter missed to their left. The bullets smacked into the concrete mere feet from them.
Pop! Pop! Pop!
Another volley was closer to them. The shooter was finding his aim. Battle knew the next round of slugs would hit them. He yanked on Buck, eliciting a howl from the sergeant, and pulled him flat to the concrete.
"Roll!" he said and cradled his HK against his chest. He turned his body sideways and began rolling down the embankment to the tracks, Buck's body slapping against his. He knew the sergeant was rolling with him. Each time he spun, he could see Buck right behind him.
Pop! Pop! Pop!

Battle heard the rifle cracks and felt a punch to his lower back as he slowed near the bottom of the slope. He rolled to a stop near the first of the four sets of tracks, got to his feet, and grabbed the back collar of Buck's Kevlar vest. He crouched low and dragged the sergeant behind one of the two series of train cars. They were flatcars, absent walls or a roof, so they weren't the best protection, but they were enough to stop the incoming fire for the moment.

"You okay?" Battle scrambled to his knees and shuffled over to Buck, who was lying on his back.

Buck nodded. His eyes were squeezed shut and he was holding his breath.

"We're okay here for the moment," Battle said. He reached around to his back and felt where a bullet had embedded itself into his vest.

Buck exhaled. "I lost the sidearm," he said. "I dropped it somewhere."

"Don't worry about it," Battle said. "I'm good. I've got plenty of ammo. Lie there until I find us a path out of here."

Battle grasped his HK at its sling and let the front hand guard rest on his forearm. Keeping the muzzle off of the ground and dragging the butt, he dropped to a low crawl position. He pushed his arms forward underneath the flatcar in front of him and then pulled his firing-side leg forward. He pulled again with his arms and pushed with his leg until his body was entirely under the car on the tracks.

The rock ballast was digging into his legs, and his thighs were draped uncomfortably across one of the rails. He was hidden. Battle pulled his rifle around to his front and set it into a firing position, the butt against his shoulder. He peeked out from underneath the flatcar and scanned the opposite end of the valley for the sniper. He didn't see anything.

He inched forward, trying to see up the incline on the far side of the tracks. On the edge of the orange glow, against the fence, he caught a slight flicker of light. It looked like a reflection off of a mirror.

Battle kept his eyes on the spot and waited. Again, there was a quick flash of reflected light. The sniper was there. The flashes of light were from his scope.

Battle tried to figure if he could accurately hit the sniper from his position. The HK416 had a short barrel and the velocity of its 5.56x45mm NATO rounds were relatively low.

He knew within fifty yards, maybe seventy-five, he could unleash a tight pattern. Beyond that, without the hollow-point bullets he wished he carried, he'd be taking a huge chance. If he missed or winged the sniper, he'd expose his new position. Battle closed his eyes and tried to calculate the distance in his head. He guessed it was between seventy-five and one hundred yards. It was worth the risk.

He popped up both sights and took aim. He'd wait for another flash and then he'd fire. Battle lay on his stomach, his elbows propping him up. This wasn't ideal. Nothing about war ever was.

He exhaled twice and slowed his breathing. He steadied his left hand and rewrapped his fingers around the barrel shroud. Battle was targeting the spot where he'd last seen the flash. He waited. Waited. Waited. His finger was pressed to the trigger.

There it was. A brief, slight orange flicker.

Battle pulled, holding the trigger long enough to release an effective burst of five-and-a-half-millimeter rounds.

Thump! Thump! Thump! Thump! Thump!

He lay still, his eye still focused beyond the twin metal sights. If he'd missed, he'd be taking incoming fire. There was nothing. Then, in the distance, from the direction of those brief flashes, he could hear men yelling in Arabic.

There were at least two distinct voices. The only word Battle
recognized in the loud chatter was *qutil*, which meant killed.
He could assume he'd hit the sniper. There were at least two
other men in their way.

Battle couldn't see them. He pressed the trigger again anyway,
sweeping the barrel infinitesimally from the left to the right,
sending another half dozen shots screaming across the valley
and up the embankment.

Thump! Thump! Thump! Thump! Thump! Thump!

The thunder of the shots was followed by the thud and crack
of a body hitting the concrete embankment. There were no
voices following the shots this time.

Battle slid back under the flatcar and pulled himself back to
Buck's side. The sergeant was still lying on his back. His eyes
were closed, trails of sweat on his forehead glistening in the
orange glow.

"You get 'em?" Buck slurred.

"Yeah. I'm sure there'll be more. We've got to find a way to
get out of this light. It's too much of a disadvantage."

Buck laughed and then coughed. "I've been saying that."

Battle looked at the row of flatcars and counted them. There
were five. To the north, the first of the five was hooked to a
long chain of freight wagons. Those wagons stretched beyond
the lighted portion of the rail yard. If he could get to them, he
could travel from car to car without anyone seeing him move.
He could emerge beyond in the darkness on the far northern
edge of the valley. It would mean tracking back south once
they'd reached the eastern fence line. It was a far better
alternative than an exposed rush across the shortest distance.

"I've got a plan," he said. "We're gonna get out of here."

"You've been saying that," Buck mumbled through a film of
drool. "I'll believe you when you do it."

CHAPTER 8

OCTOBER 15, 2037, 7:04 AM
SCOURGE + 5 YEARS
ABILENE, TEXAS

The Humvee screeched to a stop. Battle jumped from the bed and met Lola on the passenger side. She was standing by the open door. Even in the dim light of predawn he could see her brows were furrowed and she looked ready to pounce.

"What are you doing?" She shoved him with both hands. "I want my son back and you're playing vigilante." She shoved him again and then pounded his chest with both fists.

"You're gonna get us killed," said Pico. He was leering at them from across the Humvee and waving his hands above his head. He'd left the Humvee running. "You use grenades to blow up the HQ and then you use…whatever that is…to set Skinner's house on fire. She's right, you're not helping her boy."

Battle glanced over at Pico and then back at Lola. "We need to get into the post office," he said and nodded at the ten-foot chain-link fence in front of them.

"Answer me." Lola glared at him. "Don't ignore me. Don't tell me it's your way or nothing. What would you do if it were your son?"

Battle's eyes narrowed and he stuck a finger in Lola's face. "Don't talk about my son," he spat. "You don't have that right. I know what I'm doing."

Lola stepped back from his finger. "It would help if you shared whatever it is you're doing with us. Our lives are at stake too. We're not soldiers. We're not the animal you are."

Battle took a step forward, his finger still jabbing at the air in front of Lola's nose. "If I tell you everything about what's coming, you'll argue. You'll fight. You'll question. You can't do that."

"I know these people better than you do," Pico said. "What you're doing, the bombing, the burning, it's gonna get us killed. I'm telling you."

Battle faked a smile, grinning widely. "Okay then. I'll fill you in on why I'm doing what I'm doing, but we're wasting time. Every second I spend explaining myself is another second these people get closer to us."

Lola and Pico stood silently. Lola folded her arms across her chest. She raised her eyebrows expectantly.

Battle huffed. "I want their attention. I'm want them hurried. I want them panicking. We use grenades to blow up the HQ and then a totally different weapon to set fire to Skinner's house. It tells them we're well supplied. It gives them pause."

"What about the element of surprise?" Pico asked. "That's gone."

"Given that we don't know where her son is," Battle argued, "I don't know how much that would have helped us."

"Your plan hasn't found him so far," Lola chided.

"So far," Battle said. "We've been here for less than an hour. They'll be coming for us. They know we're in a Humvee. They'll see it parked here. We'll be fine. I need to get into that post office."

"This is no plan," mocked Lola. "This is suicide, that's all it is."

Battle took a deep breath. "You're impatient. I get it. You want your son. No matter how we approach this, it's dangerous. Trust me."

"Battle!" Pico snapped. "They're already here."

Battle looked over his shoulder. A platoon of men was racing toward them on horses from the east. He cursed and leapt into the back of the Humvee. "Get in," he instructed and tore open his pack. He yanked out a flash-bang grenade and clipped it to his belt. He pulled out a new scope and a thirty-round magazine for Inspector. He affixed the scope to a mount on the top of the semiautomatic rifle and then replaced the current magazine with the fresh thirty round mag.

He banged on the top of the Humvee and Pico threw it into drive, peeling away from the curb to move west. Battle pulled the rifle sling over his head and adjusted it with his thumb. He dropped to his knee for balance and turned to face the back of the bed.

Battle counted at least six horses. They were gaining.

"You should have found the boy already," a voice in Battle's head said, shaking his focus. "Lola was right," Sylvia counseled. "You're distracted from the purpose and you're going to get everyone killed."

Battle shook his head, disagreeing, trying to free his mind of his wife's criticism. "I'm not getting anyone killed." He crawled on all fours to the back of the Humvee's bed. He braced himself with one hand and then set himself between a supply bag and a pair of large ten-gallon gasoline canisters.

"You're plotting this as a direct action instead of a simple hostage rescue," Sylvia's voice argued. "And you're sanitizing it. This isn't some high-value extraction, Marcus. You're trying to return a son to his mother."

Battle clenched his jaw and swung Inspector into position. He looked through the scope, adjusting the focal length to get a good look at the pursuing horsemen. They were armed with Brownings and revolvers. One of them, on the left of the formation, was carrying an AR assault rifle. That one was wearing a brown hat. He was a posse boss.

Battle lost his focus when Pico swung the Humvee north and took the turn too quickly. The rear wheels drifted and Battle slammed into the left side of the bed. He held onto the rifle and squared himself.

"I know what I'm doing," he told the voice.

The horsemen cut the corner and shortened the distance between their detachment and the Humvee.

"If you have to tell me that—" she laughed "—then you don't. You haven't been active duty in more than a decade, Marcus. You need to think of this like a father, not like the soldier you aren't anymore."

"I'm not a father anymore either," he snapped and immediately regretted it as he reset his position at the back of the bed. The voice didn't respond. Sylvia was gone.

Battle swallowed the lump in his throat and drew the rifle to his shoulder. He picked the lead horseman, exhaled, and tapped the trigger.

Thump!

He lifted his eye from the scope in time to see the horseman jerk and slump forward on the horse. His hands, still wrapped around the reins, yanked the animal's head down and to the right, guiding it straight into the path of another horse. The two collided and tumbled over each other. The second horse threw its rider forward over its head and landed on him.

Battle exhaled and dropped his eye to the scope. He picked the boss, aimed at his head, and tapped the trigger again.

Thump!

Battle kept his eye at the scope this time. The bullet missed its mark, drilling into the brown hat atop the boss's head and knocking it off. The boss reached for it and missed.

Battle took aim again. He pulled the trigger, holding it a beat longer, and Pico took another hard turn to the right, this time heading west away from town. Battle lost his balance as he fired.

Thump! Thump!

Both shots went wide and missed everything until they sank into the vinyl siding of a long-closed cafe. Battle grabbed the side of the Humvee and regained his balance. He looked back to see the four horsemen of the post-apocalypse cut another corner. Somehow, they were keeping up with the Humvee. Battle checked his hip and tugged at the flash-bang grenade. He held the long black cylinder tight in his hand as the Humvee passed a faded yellow clapboard house. Battle kept his eyes on the house and counted out loud until the horses passed the same house.

"Four seconds," he said. "That'll work."

He pulled the pin on the grenade, held his hand over the Humvee's tailgate for one second, and dropped it into the middle of the road. He ducked down into the bed, covering his ears.

Three seconds later the flash-bang detonated just as the group of horses reached it. The loud explosion and bright flash of light stunned the animals and their riders. Battle peeked over the back of the Humvee in time to see the panic. The horses were running in different directions. One of them was on its side in the street, having fallen. Another was on its hind legs, roaring and snorting. The resulting cloud of thick white smoke plumed quickly and enveloped them before dissipating.

Pico kept the Humvee speeding west for another couple of minutes, and Battle climbed to the front of the bed to bang on the cab. The Humvee slowed to a stop and Battle hopped out. He looked at the sun-bleached green street signs. They were at the intersection of Victoria and Ninth Streets. There was a church on the southwest corner. The sun was peeking above the horizon to the east. The sepia tone of early morning was giving way to orange and red.

Pico opened his door, remaining in his seat. "Why are we stopping?"

"We lost them," Battle said. "For now."

"So what do we do?"

"We need to head back. Not in this. There's a big carport over there next to that church. Go park it there. We'll get what we need and head back into town."

Battle shut the door and directed Pico to the carport. He trailed behind and then met Pico and Lola as they were exiting the vehicle.

"If I remember correctly, we walk east about a mile and then turn south," said Battle. "We'll find them at the HQ. That's where they'll be."

"You think?" Lola asked.

"Yeah." Battle nodded. "It's a natural gathering place for them. And it's across the street from the post office." He looked down at Lola's ankle still wrapped in an Ace bandage. She'd injured it the night they met. "How's your ankle?"

"Better," she said. "The swelling is going down. I can put my weight on it. I'm good to walk, if that's what you're asking."

"Good to hear. You can make it to the post office?"

Lola nodded. "Yeah," she said. "Then what?"

"We'll talk about it on the way," Battle said, slugging a large pack onto his back. "And, Lola?"

"Yeah?"

"I'm sorry." Battle looked at Lola's feet. "If it were my son, I'd have handled it differently. I made a mistake."

"Thank you," Lola said softly and hooked her pack at her waist. She looked at Battle, trying to draw his eyes to hers. "We better find him. He better be okay."

CHAPTER 9

OCTOBER 15, 2037, 7:15 AM
SCOURGE + 5 YEARS
SNYDER, TEXAS

Sawyer gripped the bars of his cell, rubbing his palms on the roughness of the rusted iron. He had no concept of time or place. All he knew was that he was alone and in trouble. His mop of red hair hung over his eyes, and he leaned his forehead against the cold bars. He was tall for thirteen, and bone thin like his mother. His stomach groaned from hunger, interrupting him from any semblance of good sleep.

Sawyer couldn't remember the last time he'd really slept. It certainly hadn't been since the Scourge. His eyes were always encircled with darkness, his legs always tingled on the verge of weakness. He suffered a headache so consistently he didn't even notice it anymore except when it drew blurriness and light sensitivity in his right eye.

He squeezed the bars, tried rattling them, and let go. He sulked back to a lone metal bed that hung from the concrete wall by a pair of metal chain links and rubbed his hands free of the rust. Sawyer plopped down and leaned against the wall. He closed his eyes and was drifting into an uneasy twilight until a loud metallic bang caught his attention. He opened his eyes to see a pair of grunts standing at his cell.

"You know your momma's dead," the shorter of the two said. "Ain't no way you're gonna see her again." He laughed and backhanded the chest of the larger grunt, who answered the thump with his own chuckle.

"You shoulda never ran off," said the taller grunt. "You found yourself a world of hurt now. It ain't gonna end good fer ya."

Sawyer pulled his knees up to his chest and wrapped his arms around his legs. His eyes danced between the grunts. He didn't say anything. He knew better.

"You hear me?" asked the shorter grunt. "Things are about to get real bad and your momma ain't gonna be around to kiss it and make it better." He offered a greasy smile and laughed. "Real bad."

"I think he asked you a question." The taller grunt banged his fists against the bars.

Sawyer shook from the noise and trembled. "I heard him," he said.

"You heard what?"

"I heard he said it's about to get hard." Sawyer wiped the back of his nose with his arm. "And my mom's not gonna be around to help me."

"You ever heard of the Jones?"

Sawyer shook his head. Sawyer hadn't heard of a lot of things. He was eight when the Scourge had taken hold. He and his parents had been living in a small riverfront house in Jacksonville, Florida. Both of them had worked. Sawyer would go to a day care after school. They would eat a lot of fast food and takeout for dinner. They'd spend weekends together on the beach or fishing on the river.

He didn't remember much of his life pre-Scourge. He'd blocked it out or forgotten it. There were occasional flashes, snapshots of what life had been. He couldn't put them in context or be certain whether they were real memories or images from dreams.

It didn't really matter. Neither existed in the post-Scourge world in which Sawyer had lived nearly half his life. It was a life spent on the run, in hiding, full of fear.

His mother, he knew, had done everything she could to keep him safe and provide food and shelter. She'd done unthinkable, selfless things for his sake. All of her sacrifices, he thought, were worthless. She was dead. He would be soon. Sawyer was thirteen and he'd already lived the lives of five men. That was penance lost on Sawyer; those who survived the Scourge were damned to live their remaining years in a painful slow motion.

"What's the Jones?" Sawyer bit. He could sense from the grunts they weren't going to make anything easy for him. The taller grunt answered Sawyer's question with another question. "You like games?"

Sawyer shrugged. "I guess."

"It's like a game, then." The grunt chuckled.

"You could call it a game," said the shorter grunt. He pressed his face against the bars and stuck out his tongue to wiggle it. "It's no dominos or nothing."

Both men laughed. "It's no dominos," they echoed one another.

Sawyer shifted his back against the cinder-block wall. "What is it, then?"

The taller grunt stopped laughing and cleared his throat. "I want you to imagine the worst day of your life. Can you do that?"

Sawyer blinked. He swallowed hard. He pulled his knees tighter against his chest. The bad days were always close to the surface. It was the good ones that took time to render.

"I'm guessing you got a bad day all conjured up?" the shorter one sneered. "Now double it and add the boogie monster."

"The boogie monster!" hollered the tall one, his words bouncing off the walls of the cell. "The damn boogie monster. I love it!"

Sawyer had no idea what they meant. He'd never heard of the boogie monster. He concluded it wasn't good. He bit the inside of his cheek, working hard to keep the tears at bay. The harder he bit, the more his eyes welled. He shuddered and the tears spilled down his cheeks.

"You got a few more hours here," said the shorter one once he'd stopped laughing. "You can cry like a baby till then. After that, you're on the move."

"Yeah," the taller one chimed. "You're on the move to the Jones."

Both of them slammed their fists against the bars and followed each other away from the cell and down a narrow hallway. They turned a corner and disappeared. There was a loud buzzing sound, a click, and the sound of a door opening and closing. The echo of the door dissipated and left Sawyer sitting alone again in silence.

He buried his head in between his chest and his knees. He gripped his hands tightly, squeezing his fingers too hard, and he sobbed. Whatever or whoever the Jones was, he was afraid of it.

Sawyer's mother had always told him to be positive. She'd told him that there was always hope. And with hope there was the possibility that tomorrow would be better than today. She was gone now. She was dead. She was with his father. At thirteen years old, Sawyer sat on a metal bench in a central Texas jail cell, certain he would die a death worse than the Scourge.

There was no hope.

CHAPTER 10

OCTOBER 15, 2037, 7:15 AM
SCOURGE + 5 YEARS
ABILENE, TEXAS

Skinner stood amongst a cadre of bosses and grunts in the middle of Walnut Street, an unlit cigarette dangling from his dry lips as he spoke. "I think it's safe to assume Rudabaugh and Queho are dead. Their men are gone too. This here" — he pointed to the smoking shell of the HQ and pushed his white hat back on his head — "this is Mad Max. And he's got help."

"Who's helping him?" asked a boss named Pony Diehl. "The redheaded woman?"

"Maybe." Skinner took a deep breath through his nose, inhaling the acrid, metallic odor hanging in the air. "Somebody had to be driving that Humvee."

"Where'd they get it?" asked Diehl.

"I'm gonna make another assumption," Skinner said, the cigarette dancing on his lower lip. "He stole it from the convention center. Looks exactly like one we got stored over there."

"Want me to go check it out?" asked Diehl. "I can take a couple of men and take a look."

Skinner nodded. "Yeah," he said. "You do that. Get back here quick, though. I gotta feeling I'm gonna need you 'fore it's all said and done."

Diehl pointed to two grunts. The trio hopped on their horses and rode south and east toward the convention center.

Skinner lit the cigarette, relishing the hiss and crackle of it burning as the embers grew. He sucked on it and closed his eyes until the sound of a galloping horse to the west caught his attention. It was Tom Horn. His hat was missing. His blond hair was matted with so much sweat it stuck flat against his head even as he bounced in the horse's saddle.

Skinner flicked the ashes from his cigarette. His face turned red. He gnashed his teeth. "Where are your men?"

Horn swung his leg over the saddle and tugged on the reins to stop his horse. He dropped to the ground, his AK in one hand, and bent over at his waist. "I don't know. I mean, I know three of them are dead. The other two are hurt. Or dead. I can't be sure."

Skinner stepped to Horn, his boots scraping the asphalt. "What do you mean you can't be sure?"

"We got close to him." Horn looked up at Skinner. "Real close. He picked off a couple of the guys. One shot. Like an expert or something. One of 'em fell and took out the other."

"You had five men with you, right?"

Horn swallowed hard and nodded. "Yeah. Then Mad Max, I guess it was him, he dropped a grenade or something. It exploded and spooked the horses. One of 'em fell and crushed a grunt. Then there was smoke and gunfire. I don't know what happened. I bolted and came here."

"So you got two men unaccounted for? Three men dead?"

"Yeah."

Skinner dropped the cigarette to the asphalt and put it out with the toe of his boot. "And Mad Max got away?"

Horn nodded and glanced past Skinner at the men gathered behind him. As he caught their eyes, they looked away from him.

"Where is he, you think?"

"I dunno," said Horn. "He might still be around. Or he could be gone. He was heading west. Or north. I can't remember exactly. It was chaotic."

"Chaotic?"

Horn nodded.

"Chaotic," Skinner repeated. "That's a big word for you, Tommy. A mighty big word. I'm so sorry you were put in the middle of a chaotic situation. I'm sorry the chaos was too much for you and your men."

Horn ran his hands through his matted hair and wiped the sweat on his jeans. His forehead was drenched, despite the brisk October morning.

"Give me your rifle," Skinner said.

Horn's eyes popped wide. "What?"

"Give it to me," Skinner repeated and motioned with his hand.

Horn looked down at the AK in his hand and slowly extended his arm. Skinner took the rifle from him.

"You know, this rifle is what they'd call an engineering marvel." Skinner gripped the Russian semiautomatic Kalashnikov in his hands, testing its weight. "It's been around since after World War II. It's cheap, and it's reliable even in rough conditions. Did you know that, Tommy?"

Horn shook his head.

Skinner laughed and pulled the weapon to his shoulder. He checked the sights. "I even jump-started a car with one once," he said. "I connected the cleaning rod and the metal parts of the AK to the battery terminals. I didn't have jumper cables." Skinner lowered the weapon and snapped his fingers in Horn's face. "Worked like a charm."

Horn took a step back toward his horse. He looked over his shoulder at the empty street. There was no help.

"Of course—" Skinner laughed "—this is a killing machine most of all. It can kill a man from three hundred yards." Skinner shook the rifle with one hand, the business end pointed at Tom Horn. "How many rounds you got in this magazine, Tommy?"

Horn shrugged. "Thirty?"

"You ain't fired a shot, then?"

"No."

Skinner turned around to the men behind him and laughed. "You believe that? Two men. Maybe four men. He don't know how many. He lost all those men and he ain't fired a single shot at Mad Max?"

None of the men responded and Skinner turned back around.
"Start running, Tommy."

"What?"

"Start running," Skinner repeated. "Remember I told you I
was about to boil? I'm bubbling over right now. I can't have a
boss who fails to fire off a single shot and lets who knows how
many of his men die or get hurt or whatever. So start
running."

Horn took a couple of steps, walking backwards, until he
stumbled. He turned on his boot heel and started running.
Every step or two he'd look over his shoulder, his eyes wide.

"We're gonna test the accuracy of this here AK," Skinner said
over his shoulder, leveling the AK and raising the sight to his
eye. "Three hundred, maybe four hundred yards. That's what
they say."

Skinner found Horn's back in the sights and pulled the
trigger, holding it as the AK rattled a barrage of 7.62×39mm
M67 bullets. A half dozen of them penciled through Horn's
lower back. The farther he ran, the more the butts yawed,
lodging deep within Horn's muscles, lungs, and kidneys.

The volley dropped Horn immediately and he slammed face-
first into the street, some hundred yards from Skinner. He
twitched, his legs and arms swimming against the asphalt
with decreasingly intense spasms until he stopped.

Skinner turned and looked at his men. Without exception they
lowered their eyes.

"That" — Skinner pointed back at the dead boss and the
spooked horse galloping west — "is a lesson to all of you. I
ain't gonna let this Mad Max beat us. I ain't gonna tolerate any
more incompetence."

"He's one man!" Skinner yelled at the top of his lungs. "One man!" He tossed the AK-47 to the ground. He stepped closer to his men, drawing their attention to him, making eye contact with them as he walked amongst them. "I want him," he said, grabbing one of the grunts by the shoulder. "I want him alive. You bring him to me alive."

CHAPTER 11

JANUARY 3, 2020, 5:15 PM
SCOURGE -12 YEARS, 9 MONTHS
ALEPPO, SYRIA

Buck wasn't much help. The drugs had taken hold, adding to his inability to effectively move or communicate.

Battle managed through sheer will to drag Buck's injured body underneath the flatcar and pull him along the railroad ties until they'd reached the last of the five flatcars.

Aside from scattered pops of gunfire echoing in the distance, and the rolling, rusty whine of a train on the last set of tracks, it was quiet.

"Stay here," he whispered to Buck and checked his HK to make sure it was loaded. "I'll be right back."

Buck groaned, either acknowledging or protesting.

Battle used the protection on the rolling train to emerge from underneath the flatcar and open the end door of the first freight wagon. He cranked it wide enough to squeeze inside the wagon. The slatted sides allowed the orange glow of the train yard to leak inside. Ribbons of light revealed an empty wagon.

He stepped purposefully to the opposite end of the empty car, groped for the handle, and pushed it open to move to the next wagon. It too was empty.

Battle repeated the inspection through eight identical wagons. At the ninth, he found pallets of what looked like Ukrainian military rations.

Battle couldn't read the language and thought they were Russian. He did recognize the word *Ukraine*.

He pulled a utility knife from his breast pocket and ripped open the Visqueen packaging surrounding the pallet. He picked up one of the containers and moved closer to the light at the edge of the wagon.

Battle tried to recall the last time he'd eaten and couldn't. It might have been that morning. Maybe it was an energy bar a few minutes before the IED detonated. He wasn't sure. He'd not even thought about food or recognized the pangs of hunger in his gut until he opened the K rations.

The cans of meat and fish were labeled, but he didn't know which was which. Along with the cans there were a half dozen plastic bags filled with dry goods, plastic spoons, napkins, disinfectant wipes, powdered bouillon, and some vitamins.

He carried the open package back to the pallet and spread out the bounty. Battle looked at the variety of offerings and cursed himself for having left his pack behind. He'd decided against slinging it with him in favor of carrying Buck. Now, as he looked at the amount of food he couldn't carry with him, he recognized his mistake.

He ripped open a package of millet-flour biscuits and stuffed a couple deep into his mouth, chewing them quickly so as to pack his mouth full with another one.

They were awful, and they were also the best thing Battle'd ever tasted in his life. He licked the remnants from his gums and the roof of his mouth. He then took the vitamins, tore open the packet with his teeth, and swallowed all three of them dry.

He took a couple of plastic spoons, the antiseptic wipes, and the bouillon. He stuffed them into one of his shirt pockets and knifed open another ration.

He took duplicates of the wipes and powder for Buck. He also plucked another bag of biscuits and the package of vitamins.

If nothing else, the rations provided two things: nourishment and a much-needed burst of caloric energy, and confirmation that the Ukrainians were involved in the Syrian conflict.

They'd long denied it, despite evidence that hundreds of pro-Russian Ukrainians were training with Russian forces in the long-occupied eastern part of the country. The Syrian conflict, and the war in Iran, had essentially become a world war.

Alliances shifted and changed as rapidly as the Middle Eastern deserts. Oil, nuclear weapons, a Muslim caliphate, and the fight between the east and west to control the metaphorical bridge between Asia, Africa, and Europe combined to make the globe as unstable as it had been since the early 1940s.

The Russians, Chinese, and North Koreans had one idea about how the world should look, the Western world offered a different vision. And though none were publicly enemies in the global fight against Muslim extremism, neither side chose to make the enemy of their enemy their friend.

The Ukrainians, along with the Egyptians, Czechs, and Polish, claimed they were neutral. Ukraine's fragile government claimed it was too busy balancing their own sovereignty with repeated Russian incursions. They were on the verge of collapse. They wouldn't help the United States, despite the Americans' decades-long secret funnel of cash and weapons to keep the Russians at bay. The US asked for troops and tactical support. The Ukrainians said no. Again and again. They'd also refused to accept any Syrian or Iranian refugees, further adding to the overcrowding at the burgeoning camps popping up from Dusseldorf to Donetsk.

Battle had been in mission briefings in which superiors offered intel about Ukrainian detachments working with Russian troops to ingratiate themselves with some of the less moderate factions in Aleppo. Most of the information, however, was anecdotal and not actionable or verifiable.

But here they were, clearly involved. And though it wasn't good for long-term US strategic control, the dry biscuits and vitamins were potentially lifesaving battlefield provisions in the short term.

Battle put the politics of the newly gained intelligence out of his head. None of it mattered if he died in the train yard.

Finished pilfering what he needed from the pallet, he stepped through the door at the front end of the wagon. Standing between the ninth and tenth cars, he looked east. He was beyond the orange glow of the yard. And there was no steep incline opposite him. Instead there was a long slope leading into the darkness. Battle nodded and pumped his fist.

He slipped back into the wagon and marched through it to the eighth, seventh, sixth, and fifth empty wagons. He was moving swiftly, anxious to get back to Buck and help him retrace the path to the end of the train yard.

When he opened the door to the fourth wagon and stepped inside, he wasn't alone. He stopped short and raised his hands above his head. There were two armed men standing shoulder to shoulder in the center of the empty cargo hold. In the slivers of orange light, Battle could see their rifles were pointed straight at him.

CHAPTER 12

OCTOBER 15, 2037, 7:28 AM
SCOURGE + 5 YEARS
ABILENE, TEXAS

"We should split up," Pico said, adjusting the pack on his back. "You and Lola go one way. I'll go another."

Battle shot a glance at Lola. She was on his right, walking faster to keep pace with the men, her cheeks puffed with air.

"I'm just sayin' they don't know I'm with you," Pico said. "They got no idea about what happened with Queho. I could roll up on 'em and find out where they're keeping the boy while you and Lola go do whatever it is you gotta do."

Lola skipped ahead a couple of steps and walked backwards to face them. "I like that idea."

Battle nodded. "It's a good idea," he said. "Where would you go to find out?"

"I think I go to the HQ," Pico said. "If that's where you think everybody is. I mean, I won't come out and ask where the kid is. I'll hint around."

"You need to lose the pack, then," Battle said. "You're gonna have a tough time convincing them to trust you anyway, but it'll be impossible if you have that pack loaded with my gear."

Pico nodded and stroked his mustache with his fingers. "True enough. Where are you gonna be?"

"We're going around the backside of the post office," Battle said. "No need to put ourselves in harm's way any more than necessary. We'll do some recon there. Maybe get some additional artillery or destroy some. Depends on what we find."

"Where do we meet up?" Lola asked, still doing her best to maintain a pace while jogging backward. "When we're done. Where do we go? Where does Pico go?"

"Pico?" Battle asked. "This is your plan. Thoughts?"

"My house," Pico said. "Seventh and Plum near the old Baptist Church."

"How far is that from the post office?" asked Lola, turning around to walk forward again, a limp returning to her gait.

"Four blocks north and four blocks east."

"Okay," said Battle. "Let's do it." Battle stopped walking. "Give me your pack."

Pico shrugged the pack off his shoulders and swung it over to Battle. "See you on the other side," he said. "Seventh and Plum. If I ain't there by sundown, I ain't comin'."

"Don't say that," Lola said. "We'll see you there."

Pico tried smiling. "I'm gonna run east a bit. I don't want 'em seeing me coming from this direction."

"Good idea," Battle said, "and good luck."

Pico waved and jogged ahead. Battle opened up the pack and pulled out some of his food, some additional ammo, a handgun, and a canteen. He pulled off his own pack and set it on the ground, unzipped it, and stuffed it full with Pico's belongings. He rolled up Pico's pack and added it to the mix.

Lola frowned. "What are you doing?"

"I can't carry both bags," Battle said. "I'm bringing what he'll need when we meet up with him. I'll carry it for him."

"Oh."

"What?" Battle cocked his head to the side. "Did you think I was writing him off?"

"I didn't know."

"I'm not that pessimistic, Lola."

"I didn't know."

"We'll do this," he said softly. "We'll find your son. We'll get out of here alive." Battle reached out and put his hands on her shoulders, drawing her eyes to his. "I told you I'd reunite you with Sawyer. It'll happen."

Lola's eyes glazed, but she held back her tears. "I…believe you."

There was doubt in her eyes. Battle understood it. He'd seen the same uneasy gaze from his wife, Sylvia, in the days before their son died. He'd tried to assure her the illness wouldn't take hold and that the medicine would work. He'd taken too many precautions and forced his family into too many sacrifices for Wesson to die in the earliest days of the Scourge. Maybe it was that she'd known he was trying to convince himself. Maybe she'd known the truth before he did. Either way, she'd been right to doubt him. He'd been wrong. Their son had died. And days later Sylvia had too.

"She doesn't believe you." Sylvia's voice echoed in his head. "Look at her. She knows the odds aren't good. She's not an idiot, Marcus. Be honest with her."

"I am," Battle said aloud.

Lola looked at him sideways. "What?"

Battle shook Sylvia's voice from his head. "Nothing."

Lola pulled away from his hold. "Let's go."

***

Pico turned north off of Third Street onto Walnut. It was as if he tripped an alarm. Every one of the two dozen men gathered in front of the HQ's remnants spun to look at him. Half of them raised their weapons in a synchronized chorus of suspicion.

Pico had walked farther west than needed so he could approach from the south and east, as if he'd limped in from Rising Star. Two blocks east of Walnut, he'd rolled around in the dirt and ripped his shirt at the collar and along one of the shoulder seams. He pulled at his cracked lips with his fingers, aggravating the hairline splits in the skin to produce thin tendrils of blood around his mouth. He favored his right leg, which was actually bruised, and held out his arms.

"It's me," he croaked, "Salomon Pico." He waved his hands as he held them high. It's me. Don't shoot." He limped another half dozen steps and dropped to his knees.

Cyrus Skinner flicked a cigarette to the street and walked towards Pico. "Put down your guns," he said, motioning with his head toward Pico. "He's one of ours."

"You got water?" Pico asked, looking up at Skinner when the captain neared. "I need some water."

"Bring me a canteen," Skinner called over his shoulder. "Pico here needs some water." Skinner squatted down onto the toes of his boots, resting his forearms on his thighs. He squinted and held Pico's gaze.

Pico blinked first but kept his eyes on Skinner. He knew this was a test. Skinner was trying to read him.

"So," Skinner said and peppered Pico with questions. "What happened? Where is everybody? Didn't you leave with Rudabaugh? Did you ever see Queho?"

Pico swallowed hard. He was about to speak when a grunt appeared over Skinner's shoulder, holding out the canteen so the captain could grab it.

"Hand it to him," Skinner said, his eyes still trained on Pico. "I ain't the one who's thirsty."

The grunt reached across Skinner's shoulder and stretched the canteen to Pico as if he might bite. Pico took it, flipped the cap with his thumb, and chugged the warm water.

"Whoa," Skinner cautioned. "You drink too fast, you're gonna make yourself sick. We wouldn't want that."

Pico slugged back another swallow and wiped his mouth with the back of his hand. He handed the canteen back to the grunt. Skinner motioned with his head for the grunt to go back and join the others. He did.

"So you were about to tell me what happened to my men?"

Pico was matter of fact. "They're dead."

"All of 'em?"

Pico nodded. "All of 'em. I couldn't tell you the number. They're all dead."

"How do you know that, seein' as how you got yourself back here without a scratch?"

Pico's eyes narrowed with indignation. "I don't know what you're saying, but I'm hurt. I barely made it out of that...hell."

"That so?"

Pico smoothed his mustache and swallowed. "Yeah, that's so. I nearly died. Took everything in me to get back here to warn you."

"Warn me?"

"He's coming for us," Pico said. "Mad Max. He's coming. He wants the boy."

"What boy?"

"That redheaded woman. Her boy. He's coming to get him."

"That so?"

Pico nodded.

Skinner leaned in, his face inches from Pico's. "How do you know that? I mean, if you was running for your life. If you nearly died and everyone else did, how would you know what his plans are?"

"I heard him," said Pico. "I was playing dead. He was only a few feet from me. I heard him talking to the woman. They said they was coming here."

"They ain't gonna find him. He's gonna be headed to the Jones." Skinner licked his teeth. "Tell me how everybody died."

Pico shook his head. "I don't know. I know there was a lot of gunfire. There were booby traps everywhere."

"So you were with Rud, right?"

Pico nodded and wiped the sweat beaded on his forehead.

"You survived the booby traps and gunshots," said Skinner, his voice low like an idling engine. "And then what did you do until Queho got there?"

Pico searched Skinner's face for an answer. He ran his fingers through his hair. "It's such a blur," he rambled. "I hid near an oak tree for what was hours, I reckon. I lost my shotgun. I was afraid of stepping into one of the traps, so I hid. Then Queho showed up. He and his men attacked, but Mad Max was ready."

Skinner nodded slowly. "Huh." He stood and spun on his boot heels. "I need some help over here," he called to the grunts. "My man Pico needs some water and some food." Skinner turned back and offered his hand to Pico. Pico reached up and took it with both of his and heaved himself to his feet. Skinner nodded toward his men, motioning for Pico to follow him.

"Thanks." Pico followed Skinner, favoring his left leg as he limped to the group.

Skinner walked ahead, his feet kicking up dust as he moved, then halfway to the men he stopped. He cocked his head to the side and put his right hand on the revolver at his hip.

"Pico," he said without turning around, "tell me something."

Pico limped another step and stopped. "Yeah?"

"How come you're favoring the wrong leg?"

A chill ran through Pico's slender frame. "What?"

"You was limping on your right leg when I seen you coming here," Skinner said. His head was turned now so that Pico could see his sharp profile. "Now it's your left."

Pico froze. He didn't move either leg. Skinner rapped his fingertips on the handle of his revolver.

"I shoulda known that Mad Max fella wouldn't have found our Humvee on his own. Even if he did, he wouldn't have figured out where I live. Ain't that right?"

Pico tried to speak. He couldn't find the words. There *were* no words.

"So then," Skinner hissed, "seems we got ourselves a real problem."

Gravity pulled on Pico's legs, cementing them to the asphalt. He stopped breathing. His eyes focused on Skinner's long, nicotine-stained fingers as they trilled atop the gun.

"Now I could let you live, Pico," Skinner spat. "I really could. And I could pick you clean for every bit of information you got about Mad Max. That ain't what I feel like doing."

An involuntary shudder racked Pico's body. Every bit of him trembled.

"'Cause I got a stinkin' feeling you either don't know much, or you wouldn't tell me," Skinner said. He was flexing his fingers above the revolver. In and out. In and out. "Any man who'd cheat on his own, find comfort with the enemy, then come back here as a traitor looking for something ain't worth the time."

Pico found enough control of his body to speak. "I ain't a traitor," he said. "I ain't done nothing wrong. I came back to tell you all about Mad Max. I can tell you everything you want to know."

Skinner's eyes narrowed. He snorted and then spat a thick glob of phlegm onto the street in front of him. "That so?"

"His name is Battle," said Pico, the words pouring from his mouth as fast as he could form them with his lips. "He's got the woman with him. They want the boy. They're armed."

Skinner chuckled. "Battle, huh?" He cracked his neck and rolled his shoulders. "Good name, I reckon. That other stuff, I coulda told you that. Ain't no news in what you're selling, Pico."

Pico waved his shivering hands in protest. "I got more," he said. His body was beginning to tire from the shivers coursing through his body, wave after wave. "Let me live and I'll prove it. I got more."

Skinner closed his eyes and took a deep breath, his chest filling with air. He slowly exhaled and his eyes opened. He looked at Pico, a smile worming its way across his stubbled face. "Boys," he called to the grunts over his shoulder, "never mind the grub. Our friend Pico here ain't gonna be needing nothing to eat."

Pico's vision blurred. His arms tingled from his shoulders to his fingers. Fresh beads of sweat bloomed on his forehead and on the nape of his neck, streaming into the folds of his cheeks above his mustache and down his back. A flood of nausea washed over him when Skinner turned to face him. The grunts coalesced into a single mob behind their captain. Pico knew he was done. His play hadn't worked.

***

Battle was moving toward Pine and Third Streets on the western corner of the post office. He and Lola were walking south from Fourth Street, scouting the best entrance along the building's front entrance. Along the top of the facade, the lettering read FEDER LDING ST OFFI E AND RTHOU E.

"This was more than a post office," Battle said, surveying the brick exterior. Most of the tall narrow glass windows were intact. Those that weren't were covered with pressed plywood boards. "It was the federal building and courthouse too, built in the 1930s. It's more than a hundred years old. Kinda funny."

"How's that?" Lola's limp was more pronounced as she worked hard to keep pace with Battle's long stride.

"This was the place scum like the Cartel would meet their makers," he said, nodding at the wheat-colored brick. "Figuratively, I mean. They'd find justice here. Now it's where they store their ill-gotten arsenal. Good thing they're not smarter."

Lola moved a step ahead and then slowed. "How so?"

"If they were smart," Battle said, "they'd have consolidated everything inside that building. It's much better fortified than the hardware store across the street. That was too soft a target."

Battle reached the corner and stepped to the building. He motioned for Lola to join him and hugged its southwestern corner to peer east toward Walnut Street. Lola tapped him on his shoulder as he inched along the southern wall step by step. "What are you doing?" she mouthed.

"Pico should be here," he whispered. "I'm just checking to see if there's any action on this side before we go back and pry one of those loose plywood boards from the ground-floor window."

Lola tapped his shoulder again. "I don't know if that's —"

Battle raised his hand, his arm bent ninety degrees at his elbow. His fist was tightly closed. He was at the eastern edge of the southern side of the building. He had a good look north around the corner of the building. He leaned around the brick edge and then whipped back to Lola.

"Pico's in trouble," he said. "Stay still. No matter what, stay hidden right here."

Lola's eyes popped wide. "What?"

"If things go bad," he whispered, his eyes boring into hers, "you run. Got me? You run back to my place. You run north. You run south. Just run."

"But —"

Battle crouched low and leveled his rifle in front of him. He inched around the corner and pulled the scope to his eye. Pico had found himself in a gunfight with no knife. It looked to Battle like a high-noon duel at thirty paces.

Pico's back was to Battle, a dark sweat stripe running down his shirt. Opposite Pico was a tall man in a white hat. He had an incredibly thick, muscular neck with a broad chest to match. His right hand was hovering above a pistol on his hip, his legs less than shoulder width apart.

A white hat. *Skinner!*

Battle dropped the pack from his shoulders and lowered one knee to the ground to set himself. He drew Inspector tight against his shoulder and set his finger on the trigger, ready to apply pressure.

Skinner was talking to Pico. Pico waved his hands in front of his face and said something Battle couldn't hear. The throng of grunts behind the white hat moved closer.

Battle took another glance at Skinner's hand and then moved the scope along with Inspector's barrel to the center of his target's face, above the bridge of his nose.

"As far as the east is from the west, so far has He removed our transgressions from us."

He exhaled, let his breathing settle, and pulled the trigger. The instant Battle applied gentle pressure, the rifle's hammer slammed against the firing pin. It struck the cartridge primer and the powder charge ignited. That explosion thrust the bullet from the muzzle. The recoil thumped the rifle deeper against Battle's shoulder and the single round ripped through the damp early morning Texas air at a blistering twenty-nine hundred feet per second. Less than a second after Battle engaged the trigger, the 5.56 caliber shot tore past Skinner's head, snagging the edge of his right ear as it zipped past him and struck the neck of a grunt standing twenty feet behind him.

It was that same grunt who'd seen Battle the millisecond before he fired. That grunt pointed at Battle and yelled a warning to Skinner, who shifted his weight and turned his head enough to escape the incoming volley.

The grunt sank to the ground, holding his neck as he died there in the street. Skinner found his pistol and returned fire. He quickly unloaded his six shots and yelled for the grunts to take aim at the intruder. "Get him!" he yelled, the anger contorting his face into a monstrous mask. The veins in his neck bulged and he yanked the Browning from the hands of the grunt closest to him.

Battle held his ground, picking off grunts one at a time. He worked his way from left to right.

Thump! Thump! Thump!

It was like a shooting gallery. Grunts trying to take aim and return fire, only to find themselves contorting from the impact and searing heat of the hollow-point rounds.

Thump! Thump! Thump!

Another three grunts joined the macabre dance, clutching the sucking wounds and collapsing to the asphalt. Battle scanned right and then left again, searching for Skinner. He didn't see him.

Pop! Pop!

A pair of shots whizzed past Battle, blasting the brick wall above his head. Battle found the shooter and sent a shot zipping into his chest. Battle swung back to the right. Skinner was hiding behind a pair of dead bodies. The captain was reloading.

From the edge of his vision, beyond the boundary of the scope, he saw a figure running toward him. Battle swiveled and met the approaching grunt with his rifle. He applied pressure to the trigger, picked up his head, and recognized the man as Pico. He was huffing, his cheeks full of air as he hustled to safety.

Battle waved him to the corner of the building. "Hurry! Get back there with Lola," he called and then focused on the scope. He felt Pico brush by as he scurried for cover.

Pop! Pop!

A pair of shots missed to the right, and Battle found the spot he'd last seen Skinner hidden behind that pair of fresh corpses. There was no movement. Skinner wasn't there. Battle looked over the scope, searching for the barrel-chested captain. He found him retreating into the HQ with a dozen grunts. Battle quickly focused, aimed, exhaled, and pulled. He held the trigger and released a trio of shots.

Thump! Thump! Thump!

The first blistered what was left of the door frame leading into the HQ, spraying a burst of wood and plaster. The second two each found marks.

One of them drilled squarely between the shoulder blades of a grunt trying to slip past the crowd collapsing into the building. He arched his back, dropped his shotgun, reached for an itch he couldn't scratch, and fell awkwardly against the cockeyed door frame.

The second hit a posse boss in the back of the head. He was a full head shorter than the grunt next to him and without much of his brain by the time he dropped to the concrete sidewalk. His brown hat flew off as he tumbled, revealing the circular, dark red hole bored into the back of his shaved scalp.

Battle unconsciously adjusted the hat on his own head, watched the last of the Cartel disappear into the building, and hopped to his feet. He looked over his shoulder at Pico and Lola. They were crouched low, their backs pressed flat against the brick building. They were pale, their eyes filled by their enlarged pupils.

"We should go after them," Battle said, pointing toward the tattered HQ with Inspector. He was holding it with one hand around its handguard. The magazine rattled as he shook the weapon. "They're in one spot. We can end this now."

Both of his companions shook their heads.

"They're not the only ones in Abilene," said Pico. There are so many more. This is only one group of them."

"Skinner's with them," Battle said. "You said he's the leader."

"He's *a* leader," said Pico. "You kill him and another one's gonna rise up. I told you we can't kill them all."

Lola pushed herself to her feet, remaining against the wall. "What about Sawyer? If you kill them, we won't know where Sawyer is. We'll never find him."

"Did you find out where the kid is?" asked Battle. "Before they tried to kill you for whatever reason."

"I don't know where he is now," Pico said. "But I know where he's headed."

Lola gasped. "Really? So he's alive?"

"I'm guessing he's alive," said Pico. "Otherwise he wouldn't be headed to the Jones."

"The Jones?" Lola echoed.

"Yeah," Pico said. "It's in Lubbock."

Battle looked over his shoulder at the bodies in the street, tracing them to the HQ's entrance. He knew the Cartel was regrouping. In a matter of minutes, Battle knew he'd lose his advantage. He turned back to Pico. "Lubbock? That's gotta be one hundred fifty miles from here. At least. We're talking a three-day hike."

"We can take the Humvee," Lola said, "as far as the gas will take us."

"We should take care of Skinner and those men first," said Battle. "We leave them here, it'll come back to haunt us. I'm telling you."

"That's suicidal," Lola said. "They outnumber us four or five to one."

"I've got a plan."

Lola and Pico exchanged glances and then nodded in agreement. "Fine," they said in unison.

"Good," said Battle. "Let's get 'em. Then we go get the boy."

CHAPTER 13

JANUARY 3, 2020, 5:24 PM
SCOURGE -12 YEARS, 9 MONTHS
ALEPPO, SYRIA

The men were yelling at Battle in Arabic. He understood a couple of words and immediately regretted not springing for Rosetta Stone when so many of his fellow officers had.

He tried calming them by speaking softly, using a couple of the Arabic phrases he had learned. He didn't move and remained standing with his hands raised above his head. Dressed in tight-fitting paramilitary uniforms and wearing thick black beards on their faces, the men alternated jabbing their weapons toward him and screaming either instructions or obscenities. Maybe it was both.

"Min 'anta? Madha tarida? Hal 'ant al'amrikiatu?"

Battle recognized the word *American*. He started to say something in English, but stopped himself and instead offered what little Russian he knew. He couldn't read it, but he knew a few phrases.

"Я русский." He told them he was Russian.

"Alrrusiat?" one of the men said and lowered his gun. The other man looked at him, the barrel of his AK-15 dipping low enough that Battle felt comfortable taking an enormous risk. In one swift move, he lowered his right hand into his breast pocket and drew out the utility knife. Before the men could react, Battle slung the knife at the second man. The blade tumbled end over end until it sliced across the man's wrist. The target dropped the weapon, giving Battle time to draw his HK and fire a single shot into the man's chest.

As his fellow soldier was dying, the first man was slow to react. Instead of immediately retaliating with gunfire, he watched his friend collapse to the floor, giving Battle the split second he needed to fire a second shot. But the weapon clicked and didn't fire. It was jammed. Battle lunged forward and tackle the surviving soldier. Battle hit him with his shoulder, driving the soldier backward as he executed the tackle with perfect form.

The collision forced the AK from the soldier's hands, and he dropped it harmlessly to the wooden floor of the train car. Battle gained leverage and straddled the soldier, wrapping his large, thick-knuckled fingers around the soldier's bearded neck.

Battle held his breath and squeezed, feeling the man's larynx flex against his grip. The man's eyes widened, the whites glowing in the dimly lit wagon.

The soldier kicked his heels in a tantrum against the floor and pulled at Battle's wrists, trying to loosen the suffocating hold. The veins in his forehead and temples pressed against his skin, filling with the blood that couldn't circulate. His tongue rested on his lower lip as his mouth opened and his nostrils flared. The dying soldier's hold on Battle's wrists weakened. His kicks stopped. His body shuddered then fell limp. His bulging eyes, frozen with the fear of his final violent moments on Earth, were fixed open.

Battle squeezed once more for good measure and fell to the side. He lay on his back, his chest heaving and his eyes stinging with sweat. He inhaled slowly through his nose to catch his breath.

His pulse slowed and a smile snaked across his face. Battle chuckled and mumbled to himself, "I brought a knife to a gunfight."

He rolled over and searched the soldier's pockets, finding nothing of value. He was, however, wearing a tactical belt that held a Makarov PM semiautomatic and an extra eight-round magazine.

The Makarov was Soviet made and for years was the service pistol for the Syrian Army. Since the start of the Syrian civil war, the rise of ISIS, and the decades of a splintered nation controlled by any number of paramilitary groups, the Makarov had fallen into the hands of any temporary Russian ally, so Battle couldn't know to which of the various factions the pair of dead Syrians belonged. They were probably Syrian Islamic Front. Maybe. It didn't matter. He stuffed the spare magazine into a thigh pocket and checked the Makarov. It was loaded and ready to go.

Carrying the 9mm in his right hand, he walked lightly through the final three cargo wagons and slid underneath the coupling that adjoined the last wagon to the flatcar.

Battle crawled on his stomach the short distance to Buck, who was still lying on his back. He rolled onto his side and looked at Buck's face. His eyes were closed and he was drooling, the spittle bubbling with air with every shallow breath. At least he was alive.

"Buck." Battle shook his shoulder. "You awake?"

Buck's eyes fluttered open and then narrowed to slits. He grunted and licked his lips.

"I need you to eat something," Battle said, shaking Buck's eyes open again. "I've got some biscuits, a couple of vitamins. Can you eat?"

Buck nodded, licking his lips again.

"Let's get you fed," Battle said. "We've still got a long way to go. I think I've found an easier way to the checkpoint."

"Easy?"

Battle tore open a pack of crumbled biscuits with his teeth. "Not easy," he said. "*Easier.*"

CHAPTER 14

OCTOBER 15, 2037, 8:56 AM
SCOURGE + 5 YEARS
SNYDER, TEXAS

Sawyer's eyes popped open at the sound of the clanging on his cell bars. He'd finally managed some semblance of sleep. It was nothing solid, but he'd welcomed the dreamless rest nonetheless.

He blinked against the momentary disorientation and then recognized the two men outside his cell. The short and tall grunts were back. The taller one had an Alpine coil of rope over his shoulder. The other was twirling a set of handcuffs. "We're gonna move on out of here a little earlier than planned," said the tall one. "Time to get moving."

The shorter one pulled a key from the pocket of his oversized, mud-stained jeans and slid it into the cell door. He swung open the wide door with a resistant creak.

"Git over here," said the tall one. "Walk slowly and put your hands out in front of you like so." He held his arms out in front of his body, his wrists turned up and pressed together. "We're gonna cuff you, got it?"

Sawyer slid off the cot. He held his arms and hands as instructed and stepped to the smaller grunt, who had moved inside the cell. He winced against the snap and crank of the cuffs. The left one was uncomfortable against his ulna.

The short one tugged on the left cuff. "Too tight?" he asked. Sawyer nodded. "A little."

The short one laughed, a spray of spittle hitting Sawyer in the face. "Good." He turned to the taller grunt and repeated the forced laughter with more intensity. "Little thief don't like his cuffs too tight."

"I'm not a thief," Sawyer said. "I—"

The short grunt shoved the boy in the chest. "Don't you back talk, you hear?"

Sawyer bit his lip and stared into the shorter grunt's eyes until the man blinked. Sawyer believed the end was near. His mother was dead; nobody was going to rescue him. He had little to lose. He smirked.

The short grunt grabbed him by the shoulder and yanked him toward the open cell door. He shoved him from behind, and Sawyer stumbled into the taller grunt.

The teen looked up at the taller grunt and smelled his fetid breath. The man opened his mouth in a sneer, revealing the source of the odor, a pair of rotting teeth at the front of his mouth. "C'mon, boy," he said, "we need to hit the road."

Sawyer held his breath as the words leaked from the man's mouth. He tried hard not to let the sour show on his face, and he walked ahead of the men. The taller one was in control now, guiding Sawyer along a dark hallway and then through a metal door that buzzed open.

On the other side of the door was a third grunt. He was older than the two escorting Sawyer. His eyes were sad, drooping at the outer edges toward his ruddy cheeks.

"I got the horses ready," he said with a deliberate drawl and nodded at the tall one. "There's one for you, Grat, and one for your brother, Emmett, there. Picked good ones for you," he added. He was in front of them now, looking over his shoulder as he walked and talked. He was decidedly bowlegged. "Can't let the Dalton boys sit on rogue horses, right?" He chuckled and pointed toward the front door. "They're tied up right out here."

"What about the boy?" asked Emmett, the shorter one. "Where's he gonna go?"

"Yeah," said Grat, the taller one, gripping Sawyer's shoulder with more intensity. "You was supposed to have three horses."

"Ohhhh," said the man, drawing out his words. "Don't you worry now, Emmett. I got him a horse too. Though I gotta admit it ain't as pretty as the ones you Daltons will ride." They reached the entry, the early morning light pouring in through the glass sidelights on either side of the oversized six-paneled wood door. The old man reached for the handle to pull it open when Grat Dalton stopped him.

"Hold up," he said. "We got to fix this rope to the young'un here." Grat pulled the looped rope off his shoulder and ran it around Sawyer's narrow waist. He tied a Honda knot, common for lassoing, and pulled it taut. He wrapped the other end around his hand and winked at the boy.

Sawyer quietly followed Grat Dalton and the sad-eyed, ruddy-cheeked, bowlegged grunt into the weed-infested lot in front of the jail. Emmett Dalton pushed Sawyer in the small of his back, shoving him toward the trio of horses tied to a cedar light post near the street.

The older grunt weeble-wobbled toward the horse, his arms outstretched with apparent pride. "Whatcha think, fellas? Good? I got the freshest-looking ones on account'a I know you got a long ride ahead."

Emmett Dalton walked around Sawyer, slapping him on the back of the head when he passed, and marched up to the horses. He inspected each of them and announced his choice. "I'll take this one here," he said, patting the horse's croup. "You good with that, Grat?"

Grat nodded. "Whatever you want, Emmett. Don't much matter to me." He tugged on the rope and led Sawyer to his horse. He helped the boy up onto the saddle and told him to whip his leg over the other side.

Sawyer's legs weren't long enough to reach the stirrup irons. Grat reached down, the rope still wrapped around his hand, and adjusted the straps. He lifted the stirrup until Sawyer's foot slid in without issue and repeated the task on the other side.

He looked up at Sawyer and ran his hand along the horse's crest, trailing his fingers through the thick mane. "I ain't much for kids," he said. "Don't care for 'em. Just giving you that as fair warning."

Sawyer couldn't take his eyes off the rotting teeth in Grat's mouth. They were the color of spoiled bananas, as best the teen could discern. One of them was loose, shifting back and forth as the grunt talked.

Grat tugged on the rope forcefully, forcing Sawyer to grip the reins to prevent himself from falling off the side of the horse. "You hear me?" he spat.

Sawyer took the horn with his cuffed hands and pulled himself upright. "I hear you," he said. "I'll be honest with you. I don't much like grown-ups."

Grat snapped his mouth shut and clenched his jaw. His brow furrowed and he affixed his grip on the rope.

Sawyer braced for another tug of the rope. Instead the taller grunt laughed.

"You're a funny one," Grat sprayed. "A real knee-slapper, you are." Then the forced smile evaporated. "You watch yourself, boy. It's a long ride to the Jones."

The bowlegged grunt helped Grat find his mount and then unhitched the three horses from the light pole. "You should be good. Your saddlebags got some jerky in them, you got canteens full of cold water, and I put some extra ammo in there to go with your shotguns. You got some rounds for your revolvers and shells for the Brownings. Fresh cleaned and all."

"I don't see the guns," said Emmett. "Where'd you put 'em?"

The older grunt's eyes widened. "Oh," he said, his cheeks flushing a deeper red than usual. "They're in the jail. I'll run and get them."

"Hurry up," called Emmett. "We got to get this boy on the road. Places to be and such."

"Places to be is right," echoed Grat. "We got people expecting us."

CHAPTER 15

OCTOBER 15, 2037, 9:01 AM
SCOURGE + 5 YEARS
ABILENE, TEXAS

Battle reloaded Inspector's magazine then checked the nine millimeter Lola had picked from her pack. "You good with this?" he asked.

"Yes," she said. "Remember, I provided cover for you back at your place?"

"True," he said. "With all of your whining, I forget how much of a survivor you are."

Lola frowned and punched Battle in the arm. "Whining? Seriously? My kid is missing."

Battle chuckled. "Sorry," he said. "I'm not laughing at your missing kid. I'm laughing at that punch."

She punched him again in the same spot. "Not funny, no matter why you're laughing."

"You got another gun for me?" Pico asked, stroking the corners of his mustache.

"Your stuff's in my pack," Battle said. "Should be another nine millimeter in there. We each have one. You've got a box of ammo to refill the mag. Help yourself."

Pico was still trembling, his face pale. He squatted next to the pack and rifled through it, removed his bag, and unfolded it. He opened it up and added his share of the supplies. He pulled out an energy bar, ripped the wrapping with his teeth, and shoveled it into his mouth.

"You should have brought that exploding gun with you," Lola said to Battle. "You could have torched them and we could be on our way."

"The XM25? Too heavy," he said. "Not really meant for long hikes. That's why the military never fully embraced it, despite how awesome it can be."

"I didn't need a history lesson," said Lola. She was squinting with her right eye and checking the iron sights on the handgun as she aimed it at the ground. "I thought it would have been nice."

Battle reached into his pack and retrieved a pair of hand grenades. He held them up and shook his hand back and forth. "These'll work too," he said. He stood up and stuffed them in his pants pocket.

"Those are the same things you used in the building?"

"Yep."

Lola uncapped a bottle of water and took a swig. "Okay then."

"I'll carry my pack," Battle said. "You two should leave yours here. We'll come back for them. You don't need the added weight."

Lola stood, leaving her pack on the concrete ground next to the building. She gripped the nine millimeter in her right hand. "Let's go."

Battle exchanged glances with Pico and nodded. "All right. We're gonna move around the opposite side of the post office. If we come at them from this direction, they'll pick us off. Let's hit them from the north. I'll toss in a pair of these grenades; then we'll unload our weapons into the building and be off."

"That doesn't guarantee we kill them," Lola said, hustling around the western side of the building despite her limp. "They could still come after us."

"They won't," Battle said. His urgent march was deliberate and precise. He was focused. His head was clear.

The trio turned right at the northwestern corner of the building and headed east. They walked a block and turned south again on Walnut. Battle was a couple of steps ahead of the other two. He slowed his approach as he moved closer to the HQ and its large green awning. One of the grunts lying in the street wasn't quite dead yet. Battle could hear the rattle of his lungs as he gasped shallow swallows of air. He was facedown in the street.

Battle looked past the grunt toward the front entrance. He was at angle such that anyone looking straight out of the mangled opening of the building would have to crane their necks to the left to see him advancing. The closer he got, the tighter he hugged the eastern side of the street. Without turning around, he motioned to Lola and Pico to follow his lead. They did, trailing directly behind him. When they reached the corner of the HQ, Battle snuck into the narrow alley that bordered the building to the north. It ran east and west along the length of the old structure. About halfway along its length, Battle found his spot. There was a narrow battered doorway that led into the HQ. He knew that door led to the long hallway separating the office from the main room. He'd rolled a grenade along its floor as he made his way out. It was the perfect surprise entrance.

Battle kept to one side of the opening and instructed Lola and Pico to stay behind him. He crouched low and peered into what was left of the hallway. Despite the dim lighting of the fractured corridor, he could see movement. There were a couple of grunts picking their way around the debris. Beyond them, closer to the main hall, he could barely make out the shapes and shadows of more men.

Battle reached awkwardly into his pocket to pull out the first of the two cylindrical MK3A2 concussion grenades.

He offered his whispered prayer again. "As far as the east is from the west, so far has He removed our transgressions from us."

He was about to pull the pin when a voice in his head cautioned him against it.

"This is gratuitous," Sylvia said. "You don't need to do this. You could move on and find the boy."

Battle hesitated with his finger curled inside the pin. He clenched his teeth. Now was not the time for this.

"Consider the covenant," Sylvia said. *"For the dark places of the land are full of the habitation of violence."*

"Psalm 74:20," Battle grumbled. "I know this. I don't need a sermon."

Pico put his hand on Battle's shoulder. "What?"

Battle turned to look up at Pico, his eyes darting to Lola's. He could see she knew what was happening. The pity was evident when she glanced away, pressing her lips together and looking at her feet.

"Nothing," Battle said. "Don't worry about it."

Sylvia's voice, the voice of his conscience, wouldn't be silenced. "You're better than this, Marcus. There is time for killing. This is not it. Go find the boy."

Battle looked at the grenade in his hand. He squeezed it, sighing at the hypocrisy of his existence.

"Do not envy a man of violence," he said. *"And do not choose any of his ways.* Proverbs 3:31." Battle slipped his finger from inside the pin and stood to meet Pico's bewildered stare. "We need to go," he said. "We need to find Sawyer."

Pico drew his features tight, his eyes, nose, and mustache shrinking together in the center of his face. "I—you—but—"

"Don't argue, Pico," Lola interrupted. "Let's go."

Pico shook his head, but he and Lola followed Battle back out onto Walnut Street. They were crossing the street to retrieve their packs when the galloping of hooves grew loud. Fifty yards from them, on the other side of the carnage in the street, were three men on horseback. One of them was a posse boss, the other two were grunts. They were armed with Brownings, and they were coming straight for Battle, Lola, and Pico.

***

Posse Boss Pony Diehl never thought he'd live to see a day like this one: the HQ blown up, Cyrus Skinner's house set on fire, a mess of grunts killed around a card table at the motor pool, and another crushed by an old popcorn machine.

By the time he and his men rode north up Walnut Street, he couldn't comprehend the carnage laid out in his path. Diehl yanked on his reins and pulled his horse to a stop. The grunts followed, slowing their horses and easing alongside Diehl.

"What the hell happened here?" one of them asked.

"Damned if I know," said Diehl. "Looks like a shoot-out."

"Looks like we lost," grunted the other.

Diehl's eyes moved from the dead bodies to the three people crossing the street up ahead. He pulled his pistol and slipped his gloved finger onto the trigger. "Hey!" he called ahead to the trio. "Stop. Who are you?"

Diehl kept his horse still for the moment, but he adjusted his boots in the stirrup irons, ready to slam his heels into the horse's sides. He narrowed his focus and identified two men and a woman. The woman was a redhead. She was vaguely familiar. One of the men was wearing a boss's hat like his though Diehl didn't recognize him. The other man, with a bushy, unkempt mustache, he did know. Salomon Pico.

Diehl lowered his weapon but kept his finger on the trigger. "Hey!" he repeated. "Answer me."

None of the three responded. They picked up their pace, hurrying to the post office fence line running north and south along Walnut.

"Pico," Diehl said. "Salomon Pico? I know you. What are you doing?"

Pico's gait hitched and he looked back at Diehl. He waved but didn't say anything, then quickly disappeared around the corner with the other two.

"That was weird," said one of the grunts.

"You ain't kiddin'," said Diehl. He looked down at the dead in the street and then glanced over at the HQ. There was movement inside the shattered front door, and he raised his pistol again.

"Pony Diehl," a voice called from inside the HQ. It was resonant and full of gravel. "That you?" Cyrus Skinner emerged from the darkness of the building, his boots crunching on broken glass. His ear was bloodied.

"Yeah." Diehl palmed the saddle horn and swung his leg over the horse to dismount. He holstered his pistol and met Skinner where the sidewalk met the street. "Just got back from the Expo Center."

"And?"

Diehl motioned his head toward the bodies in the street. "It looks a lot like this."

"Yeah," said Skinner. "Seems Mad Max is a tough one. And Pico's working for him."

The color sank from Diehl's face. His jaw dropped. "I just saw him," he said, thumbing his hand over his shoulder. "Right there. I just—"

Skinner's face reddened. His body stiffened. "What?"

"He was there…with two other people."

Skinner's bloodshot eyes found the gun at Diehl's hip. "And you didn't kill him?"

Diehl took a step back. "No. I didn't know—"

Skinner's eyes lifted to Diehl's. He spoke through clenched teeth. "You…just…let…him…walk?"

"I—"

Skinner roared, "Go get him!"

Diehl spun back to mount his horse. He wrapped the reins around his glove and kick-started his horse. The two grunts followed him at a gallop. Diehl's heart was pounding, his hands suddenly sweaty inside his gloves.

He looked over his shoulder as he rounded the corner where he'd last seen Pico. Skinner was yelling at the HQ, and men climbed from its hull onto the street. Whatever had happened sent Skinner retreating and forced him to hide.

Diehl was more frightened by that revelation than by Skinner's admonition or the dead bodies strewn on Walnut. In the years since the Scourge, since he'd gone from being a punk kid with a puncture-proof attitude to the day Skinner put the brown hat on his head as posse boss, Pony Diehl had never seen Skinner cower.

Cyrus Skinner was the meanest, toughest, most heartless man he'd ever known. He'd once seen a drunk grunt attack Skinner at a bar. The grunt had a knife. Skinner had been unarmed. The grunt had driven the knife into Skinner's side and let go of it. Skinner, without so much as a whimper or a wince, had slowly, deliberately withdrawn the blade. His gaze had never left the drunk grunt's glassy eyes as he'd turned the knife and slammed it to its hilt through the top of the man's head. Skinner had stitched his own stab wound himself during a round of cards, in between slugs of whisky, while the dead grunt slumped in the chair next to him. Nobody at the table, Pony Diehl included, had said anything about it. They'd played their hands and bet their chips.

This time, Diehl had seen something unfamiliar in Skinner's eyes. It was a glint of fear, of worry. That anger he'd flashed was an attempt to cover it. Diehl was certain of it as he guided the horse to the right, cutting short the corner to ride north on Pine Street away from the federal building.

He turned his head as soon as he completed the turn, looking over his shoulder to the south. There was something in the middle of the road a block back. It took an instant, but he recognized the threat and yelled to the two grunts following him into the intersection and blindly grappled for his pistol at his hip. His muscles tensed. He jerked his reins, trying to redirect the horse as quickly as possible. His gut wrenched. His short, violent life flashed in his mind.

***

Battle was on his back in the middle of the street. He was in what was called the Fulton position. His knees were drawn in front of him in a V-shape and his legs were crossed at the ankles. He'd positioned Inspector's barrel between his crossed legs. His left arm was behind his neck, supporting his head, and his left hand gripped the rifle's butt.

It was an odd-looking position and not altogether comfortable, but it minimized his profile in a way that kneeling or standing couldn't do. Were he lying prone, in a prototypical sniper position, he'd expose his head to oncoming threats.

He was lying in wait for whatever or whoever turned that corner. The rifle was braced and steady. His aim would be true.

Lola and Pico were half a block south. He'd sent them to retrieve the backpacks. He knew the Cartel would come after them. He knew they'd anticipate a northward trek and never expect them to retrace south. It gave them a leg up despite being outnumbered.

He'd instructed them to arm themselves once they'd gathered the packs, and told them to join him in the street. They'd head west and north to find the Humvee at the church.

At least that was the plan he'd spat out to his companions as they ran from the coming onslaught. Battle knew nothing was ever as easy as the plan.

He was breathing in a comfortable rhythm in the street — in through his nose and out through pursed lips. The measured breaths slowed his heart rate and relaxed his muscles.

Even without the scope, he'd focus when a target came into view.

The first horse was followed quickly by two more. The first turned away from him and circled back. By then, the other two were closer targets, one in front of the other. Battle eased his finger onto the trigger. He tilted his head to the right and the world dissolved into a blur beyond the narrow focus of the rider atop the trailing horse. Battle exhaled.

He squeezed the trigger.

Thump!

He quickly adjusted his aim to the left. He exhaled.

Thump!

In succession, the men spasmed and slumped atop their saddles. One of them, his hands wrapped in the reins, fell backward and jerked his horse's head. The horse spooked and fought the reins. It snorted and bucked the rider from his saddle. He fell awkwardly onto his head. The horse trampled him and ran off.

The other fell forward onto the horse's crest, his arms falling limp to the sides, as if hugging its neck. His horse stayed put and blocked Battle's view of the boss who'd first turned the corner.

Pop! Zip! Pop! Zip!

The boss fired twin shots from his revolver. Both of them came close enough to Battle for him to feel them rush past him. The boss and his horse emerged from behind the obstruction. He was riding straight for Battle at full gallop.

Pop! Zip! Pop! Zip!

Battle took another deep breath and exhaled. He knew he was exposed, but this was the best possible position. The boss had only one more shot in that six-shooter.

The boss was high in his saddle, his legs straight as he stood. His hat flew off his head. He leveled the pistol.

Battle knew there was no point in running or rolling over. He was stuck.

The boss drew closer. He was bouncing with the rapid gait of his horse. Battle could see the grit on his face, the determination.

Battle couldn't flinch. He…just…needed…one…more…

Thump!

A single shot found the boss right below his left eye. It whipped his face like a hard slap across the cheek, and the boss twisted in his saddle. He flexed higher for an instant, fell limp, and dropped from the horse. His left foot was stuck in the stirrup iron when his head and shoulders hit the pavement. The horse kept its fast pace directly at Battle.

Battle was transfixed by the disintegration of the boss against the asphalt as the horse drew precariously closer. And closer. And closer.

"Battle!" Lola's voice shook Battle from his momentary trance. He hugged the rifle against his body and rolled to the left as the horse barreled past him. The boss's body flopped against him as he rolled.

From his stomach, Battle looked up at the galloping horse as it clopped southward. The dead boss's face was still grinding against the road. Battle closed his eyes and prayed. He'd forgotten to do it before opening fire on the latest trio of Cartel members to challenge him.

It was becoming more difficult to hold onto his sanity, what made him human. When he was protecting his land and his family, he could justify the violence. He'd pull scripture from the vault in his mind to rationalize what he did.

But now, on the offensive, struggling to resist the easy temptation of revenge and wanton violence against those predisposed to it, he was conflicted. To his surprise, there was no admonition or praise from Sylvia. She was silent. Battle pressed his eyes closed and leaned his head back. He drew in a deep breath and then exhaled with force, pushing the air from his lungs.

Was she leaving him? The thought of not hearing her voice was at the same time frightening and comforting. Battle pushed the thought from his mind. Now was not the time for this.

He got to his knees and picked up his brown cowboy hat from the ground next to him. He checked his rifle for scratches or damage. It was fine.

Lola, with Pico close behind, ran up to Battle. "Are you okay? The horse almost ran you over."

"Yeah." Battle used his rifle to balance himself as he stood. "Thanks for the warning."

Lola's eyes were dancing back and forth with concern. "You were just lying there," she said. "Like you were waiting for the horse to kill you."

"No. There are better ways to die. You both have what you need?" Battle looked past her to Pico.

Pico nodded and shook the pack on his back. He had a nine millimeter in his hand. "We got everything. We should go."

Battle offered to take Lola's pack. "You need to take care of that leg," he said.

She handed him the pack and they started south, turning west onto Third. Battle kept a fast pace, wanting to avoid another street fight until they got to the Humvee.

Lola limped between the men. "So what's the Jones?" she asked Pico.

"It's in Lubbock," he said without looking at her.

"You said that."

"Yeah," Pico said. He cleared his throat and adjusted the pack on his shoulders. He cleared his throat again. "It's a place where the Cartel takes people who've done them wrong. Thieves, runaways, rivals, and such."

"What kind of place?" Lola puffed. She was breathing more heavily than the men, her limp more noticeable.

"It's like a place for entertainment. They don't talk about it much. I mean, you got to be a part of the Cartel to know about it."

Battle guided the other two north on Orange Street and turned right. "I don't follow. It's for secret entertainment and for thieves?"

Lola's voice cracked. "Tell me what it is," she said. "Don't sugarcoat it."

"It's like a gladiator pit," Pico replied. "Like that colosseum they had back in Roman days. They throw the thieves and such into the Jones and then do things to them for an audience. They got lots of Cartel people who go to the Jones and they watch it like it's entertainment, like I said."

The men kept their pace, but Lola stopped cold. She bent over at her waist. Her hands were on her knees and her chest and back were heaving.

Battle heard her gasp and turned around. He marched to her and looped his arm around hers, pulling her upright and forcing her to move. Her face was soaked with tears, her nose running. She was on the verge of hyperventilating.

"We'll get him," Battle assured her, doubling down on his promise. "We'll get to Lubbock; we'll find the arena. We'll save him."

Lola stumbled forward, her body racked with anguish. She held tight to Battle's arm and put one foot in front of the other until the tsunami of emotion ebbed.

"I didn't want to say," Pico offered as some form of apology. "I knew it wouldn't help."

"It helps," Battle said. "It pushes us. Gives us a deadline. We know now where we have to be and how quickly we have to be there."

***

Cyrus Skinner cracked his thick neck and lit a cigarette. He was crouched beside what was left of Pony Diehl. In a post-Scourge world rife with blood, guts, and bone, Diehl's remains were maybe the most disgusting of the things he'd seen.

Skinner held the smoke in his lungs, trying to decipher which parts of Diehl's face were left. It was like a jigsaw puzzle with pieces missing. He exhaled.

He pointed at Diehl's head with the cigarette and tapped the ash from its tip with his thumb. "Is that an eye?"

"I think it's his ear," said a grunt standing over Skinner's shoulder. "Maybe his nose?"

Skinner sucked his front teeth with his tongue. "I think you're right. It's a nose. Well—" he chuckled "—it's where the nose *was*."

"Poor dude," said the grunt. "I liked him. He was a straight-up fella."

Skinner stuck the cigarette in his lips and pushed on his knees with his hands. His knees cracked as he stood, offering a crescendo of pops as nauseating as the remains of Pony Diehl. "Cut him loose," he said to the grunt. "We're gonna need the horse."

"What do I do with him?"

Skinner shrugged. He puckered his lips, sucked in, and the cigarette glowed orange. He pulled it from his mouth and flicked it at Diehl's body. "I don't care," he exhaled, a trail of smoke streaming into the air. "Leave him there. Bury him. Burn him. Whatever. He's dead. He ain't gonna care neither."

Skinner walked away from the grunt toward the rest of the group gathered at Walnut and Third. They'd all seen the horse heading east on Third. Skinner had ordered them to stop it. They had. Then he'd told them to step back while he examined Diehl.

Now they stood together in the middle of the street, awaiting further instructions. They were a motley crew of gunslingers, rapists, and drug dealers. Skinner didn't like men who balanced on the thin line between good and evil. He wanted those who'd jump with both feet into the hellfire. He paced back and forth in front of them, looking into their eyes as he passed. These were tough men. Though they'd seen and done things that would keep good folk awake at night, they slept like babies.

But as Skinner assessed their readiness, there was something in each set of eyes that made him swallow hard. He could see apprehension, fear, weakness. He could see it because he felt it too.

There was something otherworldly about this Mad Max, this *Battle* character. He'd singlehandedly inflicted pain on the Cartel in a way nobody had done since the federal government gave up and pulled out.

Save the small group of nasty holdouts in Palo Duro Canyon, the Cartel had fended off, silenced, and obliterated any challenge to its power. Now, when everything seemed to be rolling along without issue, a single man had spun everything onto its head and then lopped it off with a rusty blade.

Skinner cleared his throat. He wasn't much for pep talks. Threats had always been remarkably more effective, but he knew his men needed incentive.

He stopped pacing and spread his boots shoulder-width apart. He cracked his muscled neck and peacocked his chest.

"All right then, we're gonna mount up and head north. Mad Max, or Battle as Pico called him, is heading to Lubbock. He's looking for that redhead's kid. The kid is already on his way. We had him in the old Scurry County Sheriff's Office in Snyder about eighty miles from here. I got the Dalton boys with him."

One of the grunts raised his hand. Skinner pointed at him. "Lubbock?" the grunt asked. "Why Lubbock?"

"I'm putting the boy in the Jones."

A hushed murmur ran through the men. They mumbled to one another, but none of them said anything directly to Skinner.

"We're gonna catch up with Mad Max," he said. "We're gonna make him think he's got a safe path to Lubbock and that boy. We're gonna let him go for a bit. Then we're gonna pounce." Skinner slapped his right fist into his open left palm. "We're gonna pounce and we're gonna crush them."

The same grunt raised his hand again. Skinner begrudgingly gave him the floor.

"How do we know he's heading to Lubbock?" he asked. "Why not go get him now while he's close?"

"I know he's headed to Lubbock 'cause I told Pico about it," he said. "And we ain't hitting him now because he's hot. He's expecting it."

Skinner motioned toward the federal building with the brim of his hat. "With all these buildings, he's got places to hide. On the road, he won't see it coming. He won't have nowhere to hide. We're gonna get more men. We're gonna trail him. Then we'll get him."

CHAPTER 16

JANUARY 3, 2020, 6:52 PM
SCOURGE -12 YEARS, 9 MONTHS
ALEPPO, SYRIA

The second trip through the railcars was much more difficult than the first. Buck was little help, and Battle's legs were enervated, the lactic acid thick in his muscles by the time they reached the final car.

They were in the ninth wagon, the one with the food. Battle leaned Buck up against the slatted wall, assuring he wouldn't tip over or jar his injured leg, and trudged to the pallet of Ukrainian MREs.

He tore open another package and replenished what he and Buck had eaten. Battle's hope was that they'd be out of danger and at the checkpoint before they grew hungry again. It wasn't worth taking the risk with the bounty afforded him. Satisfied with his haul, Battle stepped out to look east between the ninth and tenth cars. It was darker outside than an hour earlier. That was good. The orange light dissipated more definitely with the sharper contrast of the deepening night. There was enough of a pale haze to help him clear the tracks and disappear onto that slope up the other side.

He stood silently on the platform between the two cars and closed his eyes. In the distance he could hear the pecking echo of semiautomatic gunfire. There was a car alarm chirping. The orange lights hummed. There was nothing else. The air was still and growing noticeably cold. It was an uncommonly warm January, so the chill was recognizable. He felt it in his nostrils as he inhaled.

He stepped back into the car and found Buck in the same place he'd left him. His breathing was rapid and shallow, like a dog panting. At least he was breathing.

Battle checked his watch. It was nineteen hundred hours local. If he'd calculated correctly, he could have Buck past the checkpoint and in friendly hands by twenty-one hundred hours. It was probably less than a thousand yards and, under normal circumstances, might only take ten minutes to walk. This wasn't normal circumstances.

He knelt in front of Buck and gently shook his shoulders. "Hey, Buck. Brother, we gotta move."

Buck grimaced. "Gotta move," he mumbled. Spittle drooled from the corners of his mouth. Battle could tell he was trying to open his eyes. The trek through the train wagons had taken its toll, and Buck had already paid heavily in the journey to get to the tracks.

Battle squeezed Buck's shoulders with his fingers. "Can you get up?"

"Up?"

Battle reconciled he wasn't going to get any more help from Buck, who'd already fought as hard as he could to get to this point. He checked his watch again. He had the luxury of a long night, but with the dead militia in a nearby railcar, he figured that luxury was mitigated by what was probably a regular patrol.

Soon enough, somebody would find the dead men and call for help. The train yard would be swarming with malicious opposition, making it impossible to escape.

Battle holstered his nine millimeter. Sitting in a baseball catcher's crouch, he took a deep breath and pulled on Buck's arms until he'd draped him over his shoulders. Once he'd regained his balance, he shifted Buck's body and wrapped his left arm behind Buck's neck. He wrapped his right arm around his thighs. He lightly bounced up and down, gaining confidence and momentum until he slowly pressed himself upright, carrying Buck like a competition weightlifting barbell.

Buck groaned as Battle started his slow stomp to the exit. Battle's exhaustion was momentarily overcome by the adrenaline of knowing he had little time to find safety. Essentially unarmed despite having the HK in one hand, he pushed his way into the open between cars nine and ten. Bracing himself against the side of car nine, he stepped down gingerly to the tracks. He was at the edge of the orange light and quickly short stepped his way north and into the darkness.

Ahead of him was an overpass for a four-lane street. Battle's thighs and back burned from the effort, and he turned right. He headed east, parallel to the overpass.

Buck was dead weight on his shoulders and neck. It was good because it meant he wasn't moving or shifting. It was bad because Buck was a thickly muscular soldier. Muscle weighed more than fat. And the tough part was coming.

Battle crossed the last of the tracks, almost slipping, but he kept his balance and found the lower edge of the long slope upward. His pace slowed when he hit the incline, his quadriceps and calves straining with each upward step. He leaned forward as he climbed, trying to balance the awkward weight of Buck on his back.

He was halfway up the slope when he heard voices behind him and to his right. The echo made it difficult to know how far away they were. There were three or four different voices, loud and urgent.

Battle couldn't look over his shoulder. He pushed forward, intensifying his effort to reach the top of the incline. As he neared its upper edge, his right boot caught a patch of weeds growing through the concrete. He slipped and fell forward flat onto his chest and elbows. He dropped the HK and it tumbled down the embankment into the darkness below. He had enough sense to turn his head as he dropped. His cheek and ear slapped against the embankment with a thud, and Buck's full weight smashed him into the ground, forcing the air from his lungs.

Battle gasped and flailed under Buck's weight. His lungs stung and his eyes bulged against the pressure and lack of oxygen.

Buck was groaning but otherwise useless. Battle blindly scratched at the concrete and tried shifting his weight to move Buck from atop his shoulders, neck, and head, fighting against the panic of suffocation and claustrophobia. His vision dimmed until Buck rolled off of Battle and onto his back.

Buck coughed against the pressure release, sucking in a welcome gulp of cold air. He worked to control his breathing and regain his wits. He reached for the nine millimeter and sat up. He was in the dark on the incline, a few feet from the top. His face felt bruised. A sting resonated on his cheek and ear where they'd hit and then grated against the concrete. He blinked his eyes into focus.

The voices were growing louder. The echoes were more shallow.

Battle looked to his left, down the embankment and into the orange glow of the train yard. There were four men, all of them dressed in uniforms similar to the pair he'd killed in the wagon. They were armed with AKs and they were scanning the yard, moving north toward Battle and Buck.

Battle knew he could see them, but they couldn't see him. They were in the light. He was in the dark. None of them had night vision as far as he could tell. He also knew he could hit them from the distance between them; however, he risked giving away his lifesaving advantage with the first shot. The fire and light of a muzzle flash from the end of the nine millimeter in the dark would alert the patrol to Battle's location.

He might hit one or two of them before they returned fire with much more powerful weapons. Battle resolved to sit silently in the dark, weapon at the ready. Should he need to open fire, he would. He hoped he could sit silently in the dark, let the patrol pass or give up, and then resume his ascent. He checked his weapon and reloaded it.

It was a good plan. It might have worked.
It didn't.

CHAPTER 17

OCTOBER 15, 2037, 10:45 AM
SCOURGE + 5 YEARS
ABILENE, TEXAS

Battle knelt in the back of the Humvee, reloading the Inspector's magazine. He looked over at Pico, who was standing on the running board with the driver's side door open. "What?" he asked. "You look like you have something to confess."

Pico leaned his elbow on the open door and rubbed his eyes with his thumb and index finger. "I told him."

"Told who what?"

"Skinner," he said. "I told him your name. I told him you were looking for the kid."

Battle dug a canteen out of a bag and spun open the top to take a swig. The water was warm and tasted like spit. He swished it around in his mouth and swallowed it.

Pico took in a deep breath, exhaled, and started talking, as if the words were running downhill. "I told him Lola was with you too and that everyone who showed up on your land was dead. I'm really sorry about it, Battle. I don't really know why I told him. I just did. It came out. I was —"

Battle held up his hand to stop Pico's tumble of explanations. "Don't worry about it. It's not top secret stuff."

Pico's eyes widened. "You're not mad?"

"Not thrilled," Battle said. "But it ain't the end of the world. That already happened, right?"

Pico chuckled with relief. "Yeah."

Battle picked up his rifle. "We need to get going." He cupped a hand around his mouth and called out, "Lola! We gotta go."

"Coming," she called from behind the church. She emerged from behind the building, adjusting her pants. "Girl's gotta go sometimes," she said sheepishly and hopped into the passenger seat.

Battle closed his eyes. It was quiet. There was a subtle breeze that chilled the air as it passed. Nobody was close. They had a minute.

"Let me ask you a question, Salomon Pico," he said. "I want an honest answer. Give me a yes or no. Plop yourself into the seat. Start the engine. Hit the road. In that order. Got it?"

Pico shrugged. "I guess."

"Now, I don't want an explanation," Battle emphasized. "Yes or no. Right?"

Pico nodded and swallowed hard. His eyes danced from the ground to Battle's eyes to the sky and back to the ground. He rapped his fingers on the door frame.

"Before you saved my life and killed Queho at my house," Battle asked, "had you ever killed a man?"

Pico flinched at the question. He scratched his neck and smoothed his mustache.

"Was Queho the first man you killed?"

Pico looked at the ground and nodded. "Yeah."

"Okay, thanks," Battle said. "Let's go."

Pico raised his head and looked at Battle. His eyes welled with tears. He nodded again and got into the Humvee. A minute later the engine rumbled and they were on their way. Battle had instructed Pico to take I-20 west to Highway 84. It wasn't necessarily the safest route, but it was the fastest. Plus, safety was a relative term. They were as likely to run into a collection of bloodthirsty Cartel grunts on a two-lane road as they were on the interstate.

Battle was sitting in the Humvee's open bed, his back pressed against the rear of the cab. He had his knees propped up and his rifle in his lap. The Humvee picked up speed, and Battle fought the urge to fall asleep against the hum and vibration of the tires against the asphalt.

He considered Salomon Pico's admission. It wasn't a surprise to him. He'd watched Pico's reaction to Queho's death. He'd fired three shots into his trail boss: one in the knee, one in the thigh, and one into his stomach.

Queho, the clubfooted thug, had dropped with a shriek. He'd fallen over, squealing through the pain. Pico had shuddered at what he'd done, alternately stroking his mustache and rubbing the back of his neck. Then he'd given up the rifle and crouched down to squat in front of the dying man. He was almost like a child, naively curious about the consequences of his actions.

But it was his reaction to killing the grunt with the popcorn machine that convinced Battle his new friend Pico wasn't among the hardened marauders filling out the Cartel's ranks. Pico's face had been ashen, his eyes glossy with remorse. Battle imagined the former grunt could justify killing Queho. The boss had tried to kill him hours earlier. Crushing a man to death and watching his head pop like a grape was altogether different. There wasn't much reconciling that, even if it wasn't intentional.

The revelation told Battle a couple of things about his companion. He knew he could count on him to react when necessary. The mustachioed grunt had a survival instinct. That was good. He also concluded Pico had some semblance of compassion. He'd quickly discovered that was hard to find in this new world, this Texas he didn't recognize. That wasn't as good. It might cause him to hesitate or twitch in a tight spot.

Lola was a survivor too. Unlike Pico, who reacted out of fear, she was all emotion and grit.

Battle didn't blame her. Her kid was missing and in the hands of people who'd made her life a living hell. She had every right to pout or question or demand action. Battle was almost, though not quite, at the point where he appreciated her devil's advocacy and her sharp, unwavering focus when it came to finding Sawyer.

He braced himself as the Humvee swung to the left and accelerated along the feeder road before merging onto the interstate. The wind whipped past either side of the cab, chilling the air.

Battle reached for a worn olive-colored fleece hoodie from the floor of the bed and slid his arms into the sleeves. He hadn't noticed it before, and it was a little snug, but he was glad to have it. His muscles were already tight, his lungs angry at the cold air. A little warmth was welcome.

He pulled the hood over his head, stretching it atop the Stetson as best he could, and watched the infinite trail of the highway behind the Humvee. The occasional oak or desert willow dotted the flat brown landscape on either side of the wide asphalt strip. A clump of *Vitex* caught Battle's attention. He recognized them despite the lack of distinctive purple flowers. His wife, Sylvia, had loved *Vitex*. They were drought tolerant and offered the same beauty, she'd told him, as a Crepe Myrtle, though they grew faster and appeared less ornamental to Sylvia.

Battle shook free of the daydream, reminding himself of the need to be vigilant. They could run into trouble at any moment. Still, his attention drifted.

The interstate was lined with billboards. Most of them were tattered, the product or place they advertised barely decipherable. Battle found himself trying to piece together the gist of each placard as they zoomed by. The ones he could see best were on the opposite side of the interstate, facing the eastbound traffic.

He smiled at a black and yellow billboard featuring half the face of a cartoon beaver. The board promised clean bathrooms only two hundred and eighteen miles away in Terrell, Texas. That was the closest Buc-ee's.

Buc-ee's was a Texas landmark. Part truck stop, part cafe, part gift store, Buc-ee's made road trips fun. Sylvia had always insisted on stopping at one whenever they passed a location. She'd refused to use the restroom anywhere else. She also loved their fudge and their famous Beaver Nuggets, which their son, Wesson, insisted tasted exactly like Corn Pops cereal.

Battle hadn't thought about Buc-ee's in a long time. There were so many things from the pre-Scourge world he'd forgotten. Then he'd remember them and wish he hadn't.

The smile slid from his face and he tugged the hoodie over his ears. He picked up his rifle and released its magazine. He needed to fill it. Something told him they wouldn't make it to Lubbock without using it.

CHAPTER 18

OCTOBER 15, 2037, 11:30 AM
SCOURGE + 5 YEARS
I-20 BETWEEN DERMOTT AND JUSTICEBURG, TEXAS

Grat Dalton was saddle sore. He hadn't ridden a long distance in weeks. His thighs were chafing. His tailbone felt bruised. They'd been running the horses at a two-beat trot, moving along at about ten miles per hour. Grat didn't think he could handle a gallop.

Emmett Dalton pulled his horse alongside Grat's. "You okay?" he asked above the clop of the metal shoes on the asphalt. "You got a sour look on your face."

"Just sore."

"We're making good time, I reckon," Emmett said. "We hit Dermott a lot earlier than I figured we would. Justiceburg is the next town up ahead."

Grat yanked on the rope that connected him to the boy. "Keep your eyes open," he spat.

Sawyer opened his eyes and looked over at Grat. Grat saw a look on the boy's face he didn't like. He was like a chained dog straining at his collar, ready to pounce if he had the chance.

"How old you say you are?" Grat asked the boy.

Sawyer's body was bouncing along with his horse's gait. His bleeding wrists were cuffed together; his hands gripped the saddle horn. "Thirteen."

"You look older," Emmett said. "He looks older, right, Grat?"

"He does."

Emmett laughed. "He don't look happy neither."

"No. He don't."

"He ain't gonna be feeling any better when we hit Lubbock," Emmett said. "That's for sure."

Grat chuckled an acknowledgement and shifted his weight in his saddle. He grimaced and shifted again.

"You wanna take a break?" asked Emmett. "We could take a few. Stop on the side of the road. Stretch out."

"We did that in Dermott," he said. "The fellas there told us we had a long ride ahead. They said they made the trip plenty. Told us we'd need to keep good time. Weren't you listening?"

Emmett scowled. "I was listening. I heard them boys. They was grunts like you and me. I don't need to take ideas from other grunts. That's not the natural order of things."

"No," Grat said. "But our orders ain't from them grunts in Dermott. They come from the top. You know that."

"Captain Skinner told us the generals was gonna be there in Lubbock. At least one of them. Maybe more."

Grat arched his back and adjusted his feet in the stirrup irons. "He said Roof was gonna be there. He wanted to see the boy. This come from him."

"So?"

"So that means we don't take another break," said Grat. "We do our jobs and get the kid to Lubbock. Then we find ourselves a couple women, some pills, a cheap place to sleep. It's all good then."

A toothy grin spread across Emmett's face. "At least a couple women." He laughed, fidgeting with anticipation in his saddle. "At least a couple."

"And the pills," said Grat. "They got good ones in Lubbock. Lots to choose from."

"Lots of women to choose from," said Emmett. He licked his upper lip and then flicked his tongue like a lizard. "Ooh wee."

Grat felt a tug on the rope and he looked over at Sawyer.

The boy's eyebrows were knitted, his mouth turned down. He suddenly looked his age. "Who's General Roof?"

Emmett cackled. "Boy wants to know who Roof is."

"He's one of the generals," offered Grat. "One of the men who helped put the Cartel together. He's a legend."

Emmett nodded. "A legend."

"What do the generals do?" asked Sawyer. "I know you grunts do all of the hard work, and the posse bosses are in charge of you. And I know there are captains, right?"

Grat turned away from the boy. He was riding between Sawyer and his brother. Emmett shrugged, apparently unsure of how Grat should answer the question. He drew a full canteen of water from his saddlebag and took a sip of the cool liquid. Cold water was a luxury he didn't often enjoy. He took a longer swig and sucked it between the gaps in his rotting teeth, swirling it around in his mouth with his tongue.

Sawyer tugged on the rope again. "What do they do?"

Grat tugged back on the rope, almost jerking Sawyer from the saddle as they trotted north. The boy regained his balance and set his feet back into the stirrup irons.

"They run things," said Grat. "Everything the Cartel does. All over the territory. They're at the top of the pyramid. That's all you need to know."

"Who are they?" Sawyer asked. "How'd they get to the top of the pyramid?"

"First off," said Grat. "They built the pyramid. Second off, they're the generals. That's who they are."

The kid was persistent. "I mean who *were* they? You know, before the Scourge."

Grat laughed from his belly. "Who knows, boy?" he said. "Ain't none of us what we was *before* the Scourge."

"Yeah," echoed Emmett. "That's a stupid question. None of us is who we was."

They rode for another few minutes in silence, accompanied by the quick tap of the horses' shoes as they pushed forward.

Grat watched Sawyer as they rode. He was intrigued with the kid.

Despite his untenable situation — handcuffed, strapped to a horse, on his way to certain death — he was inquisitive. He was defiant. He was tough. An occasional wind swirled past them, ruffling the collars of the brothers' matching fourth-hand barn jackets. The elbows and cuffs were threadbare.

They were far warmer than Sawyer, whose teeth chattered reflexively with each northerly gust. The wind, when it picked up, came straight at them, dropping the ambient temperature a good twenty degrees. It was cold enough without that wind. The sun was almost straight overhead on what had become a clear day. The sky was ice blue.

Grat noticed the boy shivering. "You cold?"

Sawyer flexed against the metal cuffs on his wrists. He hunched his shoulders forward and drew his arms close to his side. His chin was tucked to his chest. He glanced over at Grat but didn't reply.

Grat forgot about his discomfort in the saddle. He didn't like kids. He never had, even when he was one. They'd picked on him and made him feel small. "Grat the Gnat" they'd called him. He was tall and skinny with narrow shoulders and a bird chest like the boy riding alongside him.

His brother had tried, with a shocking level of futility, to help him when he could. Emmett was small and a half-wit. He wasn't much help with defending Grat physically or verbally. Sometimes he'd made things worse.

Eventually, as they got older and Grat got stronger, the teasing stopped. Grat turned the tables and became the aggressor. His brother tagged along. When Grat hooked up with a biker gang in Montgomery County, Texas, a year before the Scourge, Emmett was allowed to join too.

They fit in. They had friends. They were respected, for the most part, for their proclivities and their willingness to do whatever needed to be done.

"You remind me of me," said Grat. "You're a tough young'un. I respect that. Don't mean I like you. Means I see where you're coming from."

Emmett cackled. "You serious, Grat? You're joking, right? That's a joke."

Grat watched the boy's non-reaction to his admission. Sawyer didn't blink. He turned away and buried his head, trying to avoid the buffeting wind as much as he could.

"I ain't jokin'," Grat said, his eyes still on the boy. Then he turned to Emmett. "What he's probably been through, what he's gonna have to go through at the Jones? I'd be pissin' in my drawers if I was him."

Emmett's face curled into a pout. "That's a joke. Kid's a kid. His momma's dead. He's gonna be dead. Here you are with your pleasantries and whatnot. I don't get you sometimes, Grat."

Grat turned to look at his brother. He sniffed the cold snot dripping at the end of his long, thin nose and then spat a thick wad of it onto the road. "I don't care what you get, Emmett."

CHAPTER 19

OCTOBER 15, 2037, 12:02 PM
SCOURGE +5 YEARS
ABILENE, TEXAS

Cyrus Skinner licked the blood from the tip of his middle finger. He'd sliced it on a shard of wood as he picked his way back through the HQ and into his office.

He checked it for a splinter, spreading open the paper-thin gash until another bloom of blood filled the space. Finding none, he sucked it clean again and found his way to the corner of the unrecognizable room.

He took off his white hat and set it carefully on the floor next to him and lowered himself to his knees. He ran his hands along the wood planks on the floor, occasionally tapping on them with his knuckles. He worked one board and then the next, brushing away debris and dust, until a tap produced a hollow sound.

Skinner looked over his shoulder, assuring none of the hundred men gathering outside the HQ on Walnut Street had slipped inside. Confident nobody was in the room with him, he fished a pocketknife from his pants and slid the two-inch blade into the joint between a pair of hollow planks. He leveraged the blade until one of the planks popped up and he could fit his fingers underneath the gap.

Skinner pulled on the board until the three-foot length of it broke free, cracking into two pieces. He folded the knife, returned it to his pants, and used both hands to free the adjacent boards.

He tossed the boards aside, sucked the sting from his finger, and leaned over to peer into the subfloor compartment. The light filtering in through the window was enough for him to see the treasure buried there.

Skinner reached into the hole and pressed his hand flat against an electronic panel. Nothing happened. He tried again. Nothing. Either the blood on his finger or a dead internal battery rendered the fingerprint recognition useless. Skinner cursed under his breath and searched his memory. "Yes," he hissed when the numbers raced back to his consciousness. He grasped the cylinder, spun it to the left three times, and found the right number. He spun it to the right and again to the left then cranked an adjacent lever to open the Cartel's emergency safe.

Skinner pulled on the heavy iron door and it opened outward. The safe was sitting on its back, its contents placed there neatly. Skinner pulled them out one by one and set them next to his hat.

He looked toward the window and smiled at the dusty sunlight beaming through. Skinner needed sunlight today. He reached one more time into the safe and removed a small black bag. He opened the bag and filled it with the treasure, slung it over his shoulder, and trudged across the debris back to Walnut Street.

A cacophony of gritty, drawling voices met him as he stepped from the wide sidewalk onto the street. He drew his lower lip up toward his nose and nodded. Skinner figured there had to be as many as a hundred fifty, maybe two hundred men crowding the street. Some of them were gathered around a box truck. Others were checking the oil on a rusting black SUV. There was a landscaping trailer draped with a large blue tarp attached to the back of the SUV.

There were countless horses and a couple of motorcycles. Men not preoccupied with prepping their transportation were talking, smoking, checking their weapons. None of them paid Skinner any mind. The grunts and bosses were focused.

This was good. No more child's play. No more special forces scout teams. They needed overkill to handle Mad Max. Skinner tried to remind himself he knew the infidel's real name now. It was Battle. *Battle.* He whispered the name to himself again and again as he walked south on Walnut, away from his army. *Battle.* He cursed the name. He cursed the man. He cursed his predicament.

Skinner looked up at the sky, took the bag from his shoulder, and dropped to a knee in the middle of the street. He opened up the satchel and pulled out a two-pound, eleven-inch, black-fabric-covered square. He carefully unfolded the square, revealing three panels. The panels were coated with solar cells. Skinner laid the portable charger on its back and plugged a long, kinked cord into a port along its bottom edge. A red light illuminated and began flashing.

Skinner adjusted the panels, ensuring they were getting as much light as possible, ran his fingers along the cord, and connected it to a satellite phone. He pushed the power button on the phone, and after a few seconds, the screen on the front of the phone flickered to life.

He looked at the charge indicator on the phone. Three percent. A tiny lightning bolt indicated the solar charger was doing its job.

Skinner pressed a combination to unlock the phone and then pressed a satellite location key. The phone alerted him the search mechanism was working.

He reached back into the bag and pulled out the most important pieces of the treasure: a pack of Marlboro cigarettes and a lighter.

He tore open the box and hungrily slipped a cigarette between his lips. He lit the rarefied treat and inhaled slowly, relishing the taste of a cigarette he'd not enjoyed in years. The crap he regularly smoked might as well have been filled with dirt and sawdust compared to the Marlboro.

The phone trilled with a tone, indicating it had located a satellite and was connected to the network. Skinner took another short drag and cradled the phone in his hands. He carefully dialed the prescribed series of numbers and hit send. He lifted the phone to his ear and listened to a series of clicks, followed by a warbling ring, then someone answered.

"The emergency phone?" asked General Roof. His voice was raspy and hollow. He sounded like someone who'd spent a week in the desert without water.

Skinner pushed the phone against his ear. "No choice."

"This Mad Max fellow is more of a problem than you led me to believe," said the general.

"He's a slippery one," said Skinner. "But we're not taking any chances. We've got a couple hundred men about to track him to Lubbock. We'll get him."

"A couple hundred men?" asked the general. "To stop one man? Is that necessary? That's a lot of rations, wear on horses, and it puts our resources out of position."

"We've tried smaller groups," said Skinner. "It ain't worked. He's too good. I hate to say it, but he is. We *are* taking horses. We're also taking part of the motor pool. He's in a Humvee."

"He's trying to retrieve the boy. That's why he's going to Lubbock?"

"Yes."

"I won't ask how you know this. And I won't ask how he has a Humvee. I don't want to know."

Skinner sucked on the cigarette and then blew out the smoke through his nose. He didn't answer.

The general sighed. "You think you'll get to him before he gets to Lubbock?"

"If we leave now. I got a handful of posses taking different roads. We're bound to find him no matter what path he takes. I'm pretty certain of that."

"Good," said the general. "I'm going to send out a garrison we keep at the southern edge of Lubbock. I want them to squeeze Mad Max as he approaches. It'll leave that edge of town unguarded, but it's tactically smart. You agree?"

"Sure. We'll get to him. One of the posses left twenty minutes ago. They're headed full speed straight up 84."

"Either way," said Roof, "we'll get him. And if you're the one to do it, Cyrus, bring him with you to Lubbock."

Skinner pulled the phone from his ear and looked at the connection indicator. It was solid. "Repeat that," he said. "I don't think I heard you."

"Bring Mad Max to Lubbock."

Skinner was incredulous, and his tone didn't hide it. "You want him *alive*?"

"Yes."

"I don't get it." Skinner looked at the three-quarters of a Marlboro between his fingers and dropped it to the ground. He stomped it out with his boot. It wasn't appetizing anymore. "This man has killed I don't know how many of our men. He's blown up our HQ in Abilene. He set fire to my house with some blowtorch gun. He's got it coming to him. I got plans, Roof."

There was a pause. "Roof?"

Skinner swallowed. "Sorry. General, I meant to say. I got plans, General."

"Those plans will need to wait until I meet our hero," said the general. "I have plans for him too. You get him, and you bring him to Lubbock. Alive."

"I still —"

"Do you understand, Cyrus?"

Skinner rolled his eyes and clenched his jaw. "Yes."

"Say it."

"Say what?"

"Say you understand that you are to bring him to Lubbock alive."

Skinner turned around to see a posse of a couple dozen grunts mount their horses. A pair of bosses were leading them north on Walnut. They were on their way. Skinner had told the posse bosses to leave as soon as possible. He knew they'd need more time.

The horses, even at a full gallop, could only hit twenty-five to thirty miles an hour. They'd be driving twice that fast in the trucks.

Skinner turned back and looked at the crushed Marlboro on the ground. He regretted snuffing it. "I understand I gotta bring Mad Max...uh...*Battle* to Lubbock, and he's gotta be alive when we get there."

General Roof's voice pitched. "What did you say?"

"I said I'd keep him alive."

"No," Roof said. "You said Battle. What's Battle?"

Skinner watched another large posse head north. "Battle is his name, I guess. We've been calling him Mad Max 'cause he won't die. One of my grunts got his name and told me. It's Battle."

"Odd name."

Skinner said, "Fits him, though."

"Perhaps."

"I gotta go," said Skinner. "We're losing time. I don't want him getting to Lubbock before I get a chance to look at him eye to eye."

"Use this line to let me know when you've retrieved him," said General Roof. "I'll let you know then exactly where I want you to deliver him."

"Got it." Skinner disconnected the call and stuffed the treasure into the bag. He marched back to the remaining men. Two more posses were gone. He approached a fat grunt leaning against the black SUV. The grunt pulled up his pants and stood at attention when the white hat headed toward him. Skinner pointed at the grunt, his finger a few inches from the man's pudgy face. "You the driver?"

The grunt's cheeks and lips flapped as he nodded nervously. "Yes, sir. I'm supposed to drive you. I've got the truck ready to go."

Skinner took a good look at the grunt. His waist was hidden behind the girth pouring over his belt. His pants were too short and were frayed at the bottom. His leather boots were stained and scarred with deep scratches. His ill-fitted chambray shirt revealed the need for push-ups. His face looked as though it were squeezed between a closing door and its jamb.

"How in the world does a man get fat after the world goes to hell?" Skinner asked with all seriousness.

The man's eyes dropped to his feet, had he been able to see them, and his shoulders drew inward. He stammered out an apology and Skinner thumped him in the shoulder with a fist. "I'm messing with you, Porky," he said. "More power to you. Just know that if we get stranded without food, I'm eating you first. Let's go."

Porky opened the rear driver's side door. Skinner slid into the SUV and onto the cracked black leather seat. They were cold to the touch. He dropped the bag on the seat next to him. Another grunt jumped into the front passenger seat. A third hopped into the back, next to Skinner's bag. His eyes widened. He was sitting next to the captain.

"The weapons loaded into the back?" Skinner asked, pulling his revolver from his hip and setting it on top of the bag.

Porky looked into the rearview mirror and adjusted it. "Yes, sir. There's a whole stack of shotguns. I got plenty of shells too."

"Let's roll out, then," Skinner said. "Time's a-wastin'."

CHAPTER 20

OCTOBER 15, 2037, 12:31 PM
SCOURGE + 5 YEARS
NEAR DERMOTT, TEXAS

Lola stood on the shoulder of the highway, her hands on her forehead. "How is that possible?"

They were stuck. The Humvee had stalled, or worse, about a half mile south of the town of Dermott along Highway 84.

"Are you sure it's not the gas?" she asked Battle.

Battle pulled off the brown Stetson and wiped the cold sweat from his forehead with the back of his fleece sleeve. "It's not the gas," he said. "I emptied that ten-gallon can we had. Even if the tank were bone dry, ten gallons would get us into town. The engine would start."

"I don't know what it is," said Pico. "Oil maybe? I don't know."

Lola dropped her arms to her sides, planting her hands on her hips. "All right then," she said. "Let's get what we can and go. We're wasting time here. We can be into Dermott in less than fifteen minutes if we walk fast."

Battle motioned at her leg with his head. "Your ankle isn't gonna be able to do that," he said. "It's a mile, right?"

"Yeah," said Pico. "We passed a sign a mile back that said two miles. So I figure that's about right."

"I'll be fine," Lola said.

"Okay," Battle said, reaching into the back of the Humvee for his gear. "Grab your gear. Lola, pick what you need and hand it to me."

Lola frowned. "Why?"

"We need to make good time," Battle said. "The less weight you carry, the better off we are. I'll carry your load."

Lola reluctantly agreed and handed Battle some food, her canteen, and extra ammunition. She tucked a nine millimeter in her front waistband and took a Browning shotgun. "I can carry my own weapon."

The three walked silently, but briskly, toward town. At its peak in the sky, the sun did little to burn off the chill in the air. There was an occasional wind that blew directly into their faces as they marched. Lola worked hard to keep pace and did so without complaint.

In less than twenty minutes they found themselves standing in Dermott. Calling it a town was generous. It was really more of a waypoint between Abilene and Lubbock and consisted of a large steel-framed maintenance barn for Scurry County. It was one of those old Texas towns that had followed the railroads one hundred and thirty years earlier.

The oil boom of 1949 put what was otherwise a farming depot on the map. It went bust two years later. By the 1990s, it had a population of five.

It was, however, one of the few places where the number of residents increased after the Scourge. The Cartel put a permanent crew in Dermott because of its location along one of its drug-running routes. Twenty men were stationed there at any given time. The lowest of the grunts and a couple of unpopular posse bosses rotated two-month shifts. They lived and worked in the maintenance barn, where the Cartel also stored small amounts of rations and bales of its drug supply.

Battle stood on the far eastern edge of Highway 84, looking at the gray metal barn. He, Lola, and Pico were hiding behind a large rusted utility box opposite the barn. They'd approached with caution once they'd seen the sun reflecting off the barn's silver roof from a couple hundred yards away.

Despite Pico's warning that the barn might be a storage depot of some kind for the Cartel, they hadn't seen anybody milling about. It looked, from a distance, as if it might be abandoned.

Up close, Battle could see it had a single door and a lone nine-pane square window facing the highway. To the right of the barn was a cement slab covered with the same tin roof that pitched atop the barn. There were a couple dozen horses tied to the vertical iron posts supporting the roof. Though a three-foot-high barbed fence separated the trio from the building, the gate was unhitched, a looped chain unfastened and hanging free.

The horses told Battle the place wasn't abandoned. The gate told him the occupants weren't particularly vigilant.

"That's convenient," Battle said. "Nice of them to leave the gate unlocked."

"What are we going to do?" asked Pico.

"We need those horses," said Lola.

Battle agreed. "That we do," he said. "Let's go take them." Pico looked at Battle and then searched the property from behind the relative safety of the utility box. "Really?"

Battle shrugged, bouncing the heavy pack on his back. "I'm not going to knock on the door and ask permission."

"We don't know how many of them could be inside," said Lola. "We could get slaughtered."

"I think we take our chances," Battle suggested. "In and out. Find a horse you like. Hop on. Ride off."

"For being a soldier," said Lola, "I really question your strategy."

"He was a soldier?" asked Pico.

"*Was,*" said Battle. "I *was* a soldier. Not anymore." He glared at both of them for good measure and then took off across the road.

He jogged through the gate to the covered area next to the barn, his boots crunching the eroding gravel lot between the highway and the concrete foundation of the barn.

"Pick one and hop on," he said over his shoulder as he moved quickly to the horses. He held his rifle in both hands as he scurried. "Slide your shotguns through the saddle's billet strap if you don't have a scabbard."

He darted onto the concrete and found a horse, but before he mounted it, he helped Lola. He grabbed her thin hips, feeling the sharp crest of her pelvic bone. She was so thin.

She adjusted herself in the saddle. The stirrups were too low for her feet, but she held tight to the saddle horn. Battle slid her shotgun into the billet strap. He turned to look for Pico when he heard a man shouting at them.

"Hey!" the man said. He was standing at the edge of the barn where it met the covered area. "What are y'all doing? Get off those horses."

Battle spun around in time to see the man leveling a shotgun and sending a wide blast of shot in their direction. The sound of the blast echoed against the metal ceiling. That brought six more men running. They appeared from nowhere.

The blast also spooked every one of the horses, initiating a post-apocalyptic carousel of snorting and neighing. The high-pitched chorus was deafening. It also provided confusion and a moving barrier.

"Go!" Battle loosed Lola's horse and it sprinted west, away from the highway, nearly bucking Lola as it galloped.

Pico was already on his way north. He had better control of his horse and was charging hard from the fray.

Battle crouched low amongst the horses and moved away from the barn. He almost took a shoed hoof in his head, but avoided it and ducked lower to the ground.

The men were shouting directions at each other. None had fired another shot after that first blast. Battle figured they knew better than to risk killing their own horses for the sake of stopping thieves.

He moved cautiously to the far northern edge of the open area, dropping to his stomach. He could see the men's boots from underneath the pacing, anxious animals. Battle quickly set himself in the prone position and aimed.

Thump! Thump! Thump! Thump!

His first shot missed. The second hit a grunt in the kneecap, dropping him in what Battle knew was agonizing pain. The third shot hit another man in the ankle. He dropped to the ground too. Battle finished him with the fourth shot, a bullet through the back of his head.

The shots irritated the horses even more. Another round of shrieking neighs pierced the air. Battle winced against the sound drilling his ears but found another target and fired.

Thump!

A bullet sank into the soft flesh of a man's thigh and bored into his femur. He dropped his shotgun and reached for his wounded leg.

Battle scanned right and then left. There were more boots, more men circling him like sharks. They were closing in on him even as he fired. He could make a run for it, but he'd lose the horses as cover.

However, if he stayed on the ground much longer, they'd figure out what he was doing and they'd have him in their sights. He applied pressure to Inspector's trigger again.

Thump! Thump!

The twin shots exploded another pair of kneecaps. Battle shifted to the right.

Thump!

He missed, reset, and fired again.

Thump!

Another miss. This time, the target dropped to the floor with his shotgun in hand. Through the mess of dancing horses, the grunt found Battle's position.

"I see him!" he yelled, struggling to swing around his six-shooter. "He's on the floor by the far —"

Thump! Thump!

Battle silenced him, but it was too late. Others were crouching low, searching underneath the horses for the armed thief. One of them, only fifteen yards away, leveled his revolver.

Thump!

Battle fired first. His shot hit the man on the top of his shoulder near his neck. He was done, but the net was closing.

Pow!

The sudden shotgun blast caught Battle's attention, distracting him for an instant while he panned for another target. It was too far away, its crack echoing too much to be at close range. A man dropped to the floor, his head slapping against the concrete before a horse stepped on it.

The net loosened. The boots were running away from him now, not toward him. He rolled over quickly and got to his feet. Looking east to the gravel lot, Pico was atop his horse. He had a Browning pulled to his eye and was training the muzzle on a grunt.

Pow!

The grunt stumbled forward, falling face-first onto the ground.

Pico kicked the horse and circled back to the highway as Lola galloped into view. She too was taking aim.

Pow!

She hit a posse boss, knocking his hat from his head as he slunk to the ground, the blast peppering his face and neck. Lola's blast gave Battle enough time to spring from the covered area and into the lot.

He knew he had nineteen shots left. As he cleared the horses, he saw nine men.

He drew Inspector to his eye and marched forward purposefully, and set about emptying the magazine into the remaining men.

One by one, they fell, dropped, sank, collapsed, and died at the hands of the man who was once a soldier.

He'd forgotten tactics and made critical errors that had cost him his home. He'd struggled with the carelessness that accompanied the consuming desire for revenge.

Battle wasn't the man who'd graduated West Point or who'd survived tours in Syria and Iran. He wasn't a father or a husband anymore either.

As he laid waste to the Cartel's existence in little, forgotten Dermott, Texas, he was a killing machine. He was Mad Max.

Battle picked the carcasses clean of their ammunition, adding to his supply of shotgun shells. He took a particularly nice Colt revolver from one of the dead men and loaded it with forty-five-caliber bullets, adding it to his saddlebag. Inside the maintenance shed, Pico found bottles of water, which he emptied into their canteens.

Battle mounted a horse alongside Lola and Pico. "Thanks for that," he said. "You saved me."

"You saved us," said Lola. "More than once."

"Still." Battle tipped his hat. "Thanks."

"I ain't never seen anyone as possessed as you, Battle," said Pico. "I mean, the way you mowed down them men."

Battle looked at the bodies strewn about in the gravel lot. He counted eighteen, nineteen, twenty of them. "I don't know," he said. "Something clicked. Like muscle memory or something."

"Or something," Lola said.

Pico sighed and motioned toward the highway. "North?"

"You two start heading north," he said. "I'm going back to the Humvee. I don't want to leave behind that XM25." He gauged their faces and cut them off before either of them could speak. "Don't tell me it's a bad idea. Head north. I'll catch up with you in less than an hour."

Lola and Pico reluctantly agreed and trotted north on Highway 84. Lola turned back and looked over her shoulder. She waved at Battle. He waved back and then swung his horse south.

He needed to get back to that Humvee in a hurry, and something in the back of his mind told him he was already too late.

***

The wind at his back, Battle pushed the horse southeast on Highway 84, rushing past tangled mesquite trees lining both sides of the untended, cracked asphalt. His horse snorted as it galloped, as if it somehow knew the urgency of their mission. Battle's eyes teared from the cold. His lungs, still weak from inhaling smoke at his burning home a day earlier, tightened when he inhaled the chilled air and stopped him from taking a full, deep breath.

Lola was right. He'd made a lot of bad decisions in the past few days. He regretted not having prepared a more thorough defense at his home. A treehouse, some punji sticks, and trip wires weren't enough.

He'd lost tactical advantage more times than he could count. He ran through the possible reasons in his mind, lost in the rhythm of the gallop.

Was it complacency from having handled minor, predictable incursions over the better part of five years? Was it distraction? Did he unconsciously want to die as he had in the days after the Scourge devoured his family? Was he losing his mind?

"You're not losing your mind, Marcus," answered Sylvia's voice without a hint of irony. "You're too strong for that."

"I don't know." He laughed to himself. "I think I'm half gone. I'm answering myself. Whether or not it's your voice is irrelevant."

"You need to err on the side of caution," Sylvia warned. "Remember what it was that made you the man you are. Remember your life before the Scourge."

Battle couldn't remember it. Not really. There were static flashes, like the *Vitex* or the smell of potting soil mixed with Sylvia's jasmine lotion. There was the sound of his son's giggling laughter, which he thought he could remember. Maybe he was confusing it with something or someone else. Maybe he'd manufactured the memory of it as a coping mechanism.

True memories? They were gone.

The sensation of happiness, the satisfaction of a good meal, the pleasure of looking forward to the next day, the contentment of loving and reassurance of being loved wholly were magnetically erased. The only way he could acknowledge they existed at all was the overwhelming sense of loss that never left him. The anxiety was constant.

Battle shook off the voice, rode up to the Humvee, and dismounted. It was as they left it. He searched the horizon and didn't see anyone coming. A roadrunner darted into the road and stopped a few feet away. It pecked its oversized bill and cocked its head at Battle, its distinctive crest fluttering in the breeze. Battle looked more closely and saw a small lizard in the bird's mouth. Its body was limp and flapped as the roadrunner jerked its body.

The bird sprinted from the road and into the dry brush, and Battle turned his attention back to the Humvee and reached in for the XM25. He set it on the ground next to the truck and rummaged around in the bed for the remaining color-coded rounds.

There were four yellow, five red, and five orange. The yellow were the high-explosive air-bursting projectiles. The red were the armor-piercing rounds. The orange were the door busters. He slugged the rounds into an ammo bag and slung it over his head and shoulder. He wore it cross-body, with the ammo bag sitting at his left hip. His neck and shoulders ached already from the weight of the pack on his back. Neither was happy about the addition.

Battle pulled McDunnough, his reliable nine millimeter, from his hip and walked around the front of the Humvee and fired a pair of shots into the radiator. It couldn't hurt. He knew the truck was no good, but didn't want to take the chance of the Cartel making it work.

Battle made sure Inspector was affixed to the side of the horse, held in place by a billet strap. He craned his neck and jumped back onto the horse while holding the XM25.

Battle looked over his shoulder. At first there was nothing. That was good. He turned back to the road ahead and kicked his heels into the horse. The horse accelerated slowly and Battle turned his head one more time to look at where he'd been.

They weren't alone this time. It was hard to tell the exact distance, Battle guessed it was a half mile or more, but there was a black vehicle on the road. Next to it, in the southbound lane, was a large box truck. Despite the distance and the dancing haze on the horizon, Battle recognized both of them from the motor pool. The Cartel was on its way.

Battle took as deep a breath as he could, coughed out the cold air, and urged the horse into a full gallop. He lowered his head against the oncoming wind and worked the reins. They were as good as caught.

***

"That's our Humvee, sir," said Porky. He slowed the SUV to a stop a few feet from the stolen vehicle.

"Stay here," said Skinner. "I'll be right back." He climbed out of the SUV and stomped over to the Humvee. There were bags and various supplies strewn about the open bed. He walked around the front of the vehicle and saw a pair of holes in the radiator.

Skinner cursed aloud and trudged back to the SUV. He slid into his seat and yanked the door shut, slamming it with every bit of force he could muster.

"Let's go," he said. "There's nothing here. They're not far, though. I know it."

"Yes, sir." Porky put the SUV into gear and accelerated. "We should be at the way station in Dermott in less than a minute, sir."

Skinner didn't acknowledge the grunt. He was staring out the window at the mesquite wavering in the wind. He lowered his hat on his brow.

He didn't like his orders. He didn't like competing with some garrison from Lubbock. He didn't like the necessity of keeping Battle alive. Orders were orders, especially when General Roof was the one giving them.

"Sir," said Porky, his voice cracking, "we've got a problem up ahead."

"What?"

Porky stopped the SUV in the middle of the highway, keeping the engine running. Skinner tried to catch Porky's eyes in the rearview mirror, but the grunt wouldn't look at him.

He punched the headrest, jarring Porky. "What?"

"Everybody's dead, sir."

The grunt in the front passenger seat was leaning forward, his hands pressed against the dash so he could look at whatever it was that caught his attention. The one next to Skinner was craning his neck, trying to catch a glimpse too.

Skinner huffed and shouldered the door open. He stepped out of the SUV and into the road. His head was down as he walked forward. When he looked up from under the brim of his white Stetson, it was the blood that first caught his attention. It was everywhere.

Skinner had seen a lot of blood, had spilled much of it himself. This was something different. Someone possessed had accounted for the carnage sprayed before him.

After the blood, it was the eyes. There were too many pairs of dead, vacant eyes fixed with fear. Skinner walked up to the closest body, that of an unshaven older grunt. He was on his back. There was gray stubble on his chin and above his lip. There were deep furrows on either side of his nose and a singular dark red hole at the center of his forehead.

Skinner kicked his side with his boot and cursed the man for dying. He cursed him for failing. He kicked the body again. And again. Each time he pulled his boot back a little farther and drove his toe forward with incrementally more force.

Skinner looked up and started counting the bodies. He quit when he got to thirteen. It was too difficult to tell where one body ended and another began. There was too much blood.

He turned around to see Porky standing behind him. A couple of other grunts from the box truck were also there, their faces ashen and drawn. Even Porky looked thinner somehow.

"This is fresh," Skinner said. "Ain't no smell yet. We're close. We can catch 'em."

"They probably took some horses," Porky offered. He pointed at the open area adjacent to the barn. "Two or three spaces are empty."

"Maybe so," said Skinner. "We'll get 'em before that garrison from Lubbock. They can't be that far ahead. Take some of the weapons, toss 'em into the back of the box truck, and let's go."

Skinner looked up at the sky. There were three blackbirds circling high above. They were riding the currents, their wings fixed as they glided. One of them flapped its wings, dove toward the ground, and swooped back up to join the others.

Skinner followed the bird toward the sun. It was after noon. The sun was past its peak and starting to wane.

"C'mon!" he yelled to the grunts. "Get movin'."

CHAPTER 21

JANUARY 3, 2020, 7:19 PM
SCOURGE -12 YEARS, 9 MONTHS
ALEPPO, SYRIA

Battle had the high ground. He was in the dark. He could see the opposition and they couldn't see him. Advantage: Battle. Then Buck coughed. It was a loud, hacking cough. He gasped for air as if it were his final breath. Then he moaned.

Immediately, like jackals, the four Syrians snapped their attention in Battle's direction. They still couldn't see him, but now they knew he was there.

Battle could see them peering into the darkness. They raised their weapons. All four were aiming directly at him.

Battle saw no downside to a muzzle flash now. He applied pressure to the nine millimeter's sensitive trigger.

Pop! Pop!

Two quick shots downed two of the men, instantly dropping them onto the tracks.

The other two were running up the embankment toward him. Now they had a fix on his position.

One of them opened fire.

Pop! Pop! Pop!

Battle reacted by flinging his body onto Buck's to protect his helpless comrade. He turned his back and ducked his head, hoping a true round would find his Kevlar and nothing else. None of the three shots hit them. One ricocheted off the concrete near Battle's head.

Pop! Pop!

Battle felt a thick punch to his ribs. He bit down on his cheek to suppress a cry and drew blood. The warm, metallic taste filled his mouth, and he rolled away from Buck, unable to catch his breath. He could see the approaching target.

Pop!

The shot tore through Battle's uniform, grazed his left arm, and exploded into the concrete. A shot of searing heat radiated across his bicep. From his back, he leveled the sidearm and pulled the trigger, aiming it directly at the advancing threat.

Pop! Pop! Pop! Pop!

He reflexively pulled the trigger again and again until he saw the Syrian collapse. The second one was still climbing the embankment.

Pop! Pop!

Both shots missed Battle's head to his left. Pieces of concrete sprayed against the side of his face as he found his focus through the metal sights and fired.

Pop! Pop! Pop!

The trio of rounds hit in a tight pattern at the spot where the man's decorations would have been pinned, had he had any. He jerked backward to his left, let out an unearthly wail, and managed one more errant shot with his handgun, toppling over and rolling down the embankment.

Struggling to breathe, Battle dropped his head to the ground and stared up at the sky, trying to gain control of the adrenaline coursing through his body.

His back felt as if somebody had slugged him with an aluminum bat. The burn in his left arm had morphed to a sharp sting and throbbing ache. Buck was next to him, alternately whimpering and coughing.

"You okay?" Battle asked once he'd caught his breath.

Buck mumbled.

"I'll take that as a yes," Battle said and sat up. He tucked the nine millimeter into his utility belt and pushed himself to his feet. He couldn't see how badly his arm was wounded. He stuck his fingers inside his wet, torn sleeve and drew them close to his face. They were dark with blood. He flexed his bicep. It was painful, but he could do it.

He walked up the embankment and stood behind Buck. He turned, exhaled deeply, and bent over to grab Buck underneath his armpits. Step by step he dragged Buck up the rest of the embankment. His sciatic nerve sent an electric sting from his lower back to the back of his right leg. He flinched and his back seized, but he kept pulling and dragging, pulling and dragging.

Battle felt the end of the incline under his boot and he mustered the strength for a final heave onto the wide expanse on the eastern side of the rail yard. He let go of Buck's arms and tried standing upright. He was stiff, and the muscles in his back protested as he stretched upright. He involuntarily laughed at the burst of pain when he managed it.

Buck was on the ground behind him, and he took the dozen steps to the fence line. Beyond the fence they were that much closer to the checkpoint, that much closer to safety.

Battle felt light-headed as he checked for the best spot to cut the chain link. He couldn't take in a full breath. His arm was bleeding; he could feel it trailing down his forearm.

He wrapped his fingers through the fence and leaned his head against it. The night was far from over. For the first time, he questioned his stamina, his ability to finish the job.

He reached into a breast pocket, pulling at the Velcro closure, and removed a photograph. He'd printed it out on cheap photo paper before his deployment. It was creased and faded. He could've drawn the photograph from memory he'd looked at it so many times, but Battle liked seeing it and holding it in his hand.

It was taken on Padre Island National Seashore. Sylvia was standing on the wide, sugary sand with her back to the Gulf of Mexico. Behind her, at the shore break, were clumps of seaweed.

He remembered the dank, salty smell of the seaweed, how it had prevented Sylvia from going into the water. She hadn't wanted to step in it, let alone get nipped by a crab hiding in the green and brown blades.

Still, she was beaming. Her smile was genuine and her white teeth glowed against her sun-kissed skin. She had her hands on her hips in false protest to having her photograph taken in a bikini. Battle loved that bikini. It hid enough to make his mind wander, anticipating the moment late in the day when he'd get to remove it.

He stuffed it back into his pocket and rubbed closed the Velcro. He looked through the diamond-shaped opening in the chain link, trying to assess the landscape.

He knew the checkpoint was about five blocks from where he stood. There were maybe five or six streets to cross before he'd have to navigate the best way to traverse a twenty-foot-wide canal, also known as the Queiq River, that snaked its way through the city. There were three bridges from which to choose.

The northernmost was a wide, popular street that would force him to move past a large mosque once he turned south toward the checkpoint. He checked his watch. It was nine hundred thirty hours local. The nighttime Isha'a prayer was anytime between sunset and sunrise, close to midnight. The mosque might not be busy for the next hour or two. He could risk it. Or he could travel four blocks south and cross the canal. That would put him almost directly in front of the checkpoint between the park and the amusement park. It would, however, require traveling amongst a densely populated neighborhood with high-rise buildings populating every block.

The third option also required traveling through a neighborhood and put him south of the amusement park on Pennsylvania Street. If he chose that route, he'd have to backtrack a block north to the checkpoint. It was the least viable option of the three.

Neither of the remaining two were ideal. And while he didn't like the idea of limping through a high-rise neighborhood, doing the same on a wide-open four-lane road and passing a mosque was the lesser appealing route.

He knelt down on his kneepads and reached into his vest pocket, fishing past a couple of packets of vitamins to remove the wire cutters. Without using a cloth, he cranked down onto a link until he felt the snap. He moved the cutters up one link after another, cranking and snapping, until he'd created a large enough gash in the fence for him and Buck to fit through when pulled apart.

He opened the fence like a tent flap. It was a much larger opening than the one through which they'd squeezed on the western edge of the train yard.

Battle flexed the fingers on his left hand, trying to work out the stiffness. He cupped his hands together and blew into them, warming them with his breath.

He stepped back to Buck and crouched behind his head. "This is the final push, Sergeant. A little more to go and we'll be there."

Battle stood and then bent at his waist. He reached down and grabbed the shoulders of Buck's vest. He leaned back, balancing himself with Buck's weight, and dragged the soldier to the fence.

His back seized again when he reached the opening. He hitched, then dropped onto his backside and kept moving. Battle inched his way backward through the fence while tugging Buck.

Once he'd cleared the fence himself, he used a fence post to brace his boots. That gave him the leverage for the final couple of yanks on Buck's vest.

Though the temperature was dropping, Battle was sweating profusely. He blinked back the sting in his eyes and used the back of his wrist to wipe the perspiration from his cheeks and temples.

He struggled to his feet and looked east. Five blocks had never seemed so far in his life.

CHAPTER 22

OCTOBER 15, 2037, 1:52 PM
SCOURGE + 5 YEARS
SOUTHLAND, TEXAS

"This is supposed to be the warmest part of the day." Grat blew on his hands. He pulled on the rope that linked him to Sawyer, tugging the boy's attention toward him. "You cold?" Sawyer didn't say anything. He hadn't said much in the last four hours of their trek to Lubbock.

Emmett chuckled. "You keep asking that, Grat," he said. "And the boy keeps ignoring you. You should stop asking."

Sawyer adjusted his wrists on the saddle horn and tightened his eyes at the soreness of the cuffs. "I gotta go to the bathroom," he said, his eyes dancing back and forth between the brothers.

"We ain't got time," said Emmett. "You can piss yourself, for all I care."

Sawyer scowled at Emmett and shifted his stare to Grat. "Please."

Grat slowed his horse near an intersection with a four-lane road. Highway 84 ran along the eastern edge of Southland, Texas. A four-square-block town, Southland was home to a handful of farmers who toiled the dry land for subsistence and for the Cartel. A large hay farm on the town's western edge was a major supplier for the Cartel's livestock.

They also grew corn, sorghum, and peanuts. The Cartel kept pushing cotton, but pests had all but made it impossible to harvest a good crop.

Sawyer didn't know any of this, but as they rode north, he could see thin wisps of gray smoke puffing skyward to the east. He recognized it as chimney smoke. It wasn't black or acrid enough to be a controlled burn or a house fire.

There were people in that town. Maybe they could help him.

Grat stopped his horse and dismounted. Emmett sighed and grunted an admonition.

"You're a fool, Grat," said the smaller Dalton brother. "He's playing you. And you're eating it up."

Grat sneered. "Shut your trap, Emmett. I gotta go too." Grat walked over to Sawyer's horse and grabbed the boy around his bicep to help him dismount. He led Sawyer to a clump of leafless, angry-looking oak trees that provided some privacy from the highway.

"Hurry it up, the two of you," said Emmett, watching them disappear behind the thick trunks. "We got to get to Lubbock before dark. Those are the orders."

Grat glared over his shoulder at his brother but didn't say anything. He looked over at Sawyer, who'd already found a relief spot, and then unzipped his drawers. He was still holding the rope with one hand.

Sawyer heard the zip of Grat's pants followed by the splash of his stream hitting the dry dirt. He took in a breath of courage, wound an extra length of rope around his wrists, and yanked as hard as he could.

The short snap of tension gave way, and Sawyer was free of Grat's hold. Surprised by his success, he stood under the tree for a moment and turned to run. His legs were heavy and his rear was tingling with the beginnings of numbness from sitting on the saddle for so many hours, but he churned against the dirt as fast as he could.

The rope trailed like a snake behind him, dusting up the dry earth in a cloud behind Sawyer as he ran to meet the eastbound four-lane road into town. He was careful not to trip on the rope as he chugged. His bound wrists, which he held out in front of himself, were screaming from the friction of the metal cuffs. Sawyer ignored it and focused his attention on the road ahead. He did not look behind him, even as Grat called for him to stop.

"What the—" Grat stood with his fly down, wetting himself as he watched the boy run away from him. "Mother fu—"

Emmett called from the road. "What?"

Grat hesitated. "The boy," he said. "He's running."

Emmett was holding the reins for all three horses. He couldn't leave them. He couldn't give chase without risking the other two horses galloping away. "I told you!" he scolded his brother.

Grat stuffed himself back into his loose jeans and zipped up the fly, then started after Sawyer. "C'mon, boy! This is only gonna make it worse."

Sawyer ignored him. He stumbled a couple of times on the uneven terrain, but once he met the road and veered east, he picked up speed. His long legs strode with surprising ease as he pushed himself closer to the wisps of smoke, the cold air filling his lungs with each breath. Sawyer giggled involuntarily, a nervous smile spreading across his cheeks. His eyes glistened. It was exhilarating. He turned for a quick look over his shoulder.

Sawyer couldn't tell if the grunt was gaining on him. He'd gotten such an unexpectedly good start, there was a good fifty yards between them. Grat's heavy leather boots thumped along the dirt, trying to avoid divots. Sawyer could see him reaching out his arms as if to reel him in as he ran.

Sawyer reached an intersection and turned north, hoping to put more distance between himself and Grat.

There was a large building straight ahead. He guessed it was an old school from the look of it. He couldn't stop there. He'd get caught. When he reached the next street, he rounded the corner and headed east again.

"C'mon. Now!" Grat called out between thick, pained huffs. "You. Can't. Get. Away. Give it. Up."

Sawyer wasn't about to listen to him and ran on. The smoke was getting closer. He could smell a hint of the burning wood. He continued north. He felt the slight ping of a cramp in his right side, but he stretched to the left and eased it as he pushed ahead.

Grat was beginning to gain on the boy. He'd reached his stride and the asphalt road was easier to navigate than the pitted, uneven dirt. "Sawyer," he tried again. "Please, boy. This. Is. Only. Gonna be. Worse. For you."

Grat blinked back the cold as a slight gust of wind hit him in the face and he kept chasing the boy.

Sawyer's eyes widened. Up ahead, maybe a couple of hundred feet away, he spotted someone. At first, he couldn't tell if it was a man or woman, but the closer he got, he could tell it was an older man. He was wearing a wide-brimmed straw hat and overalls. He was pushing a wheelbarrow. Sawyer called out to the man. "Hey!" He pushed harder against the asphalt. "Help me. Please. Help me!"

The man saw him. He had to see him. Sawyer could tell the man was looking straight at him from under the brim of his floppy, ridiculous hat. The man didn't react. He stood there holding the wheelbarrow.

Sawyer looked over his shoulder to see how much time he had to convince the man to help him before the grunt caught up. As he did, his foot caught the front edge of a pothole and he tripped. Sawyer's body flung forward as if he were diving into a pool's shallow end. He pulled his arms up to protect his face as he slid along the asphalt, tearing up his forearms and knees.

Sawyer rolled over, his face squeezed tight with pain. He pursed his lips and blew quickly in and out to mitigate the burn in his arms and legs. One of his wrists felt sprained, maybe broken, from the fall.

Before he could scramble to his feet, Grat was standing over him. The grunt's chest was heaving from a combination of exhaustion and raw ire.

Sawyer laid his head on the asphalt and closed his eyes in resignation. He was so close.

"You didn't see this," Grat said to the man with the wheelbarrow and floppy hat. He reached down to the chain connecting the cuffs and pulled upward.

Sawyer resisted and yanked back. A bolt of pain shot through his right wrist.

"C'mon now," Grat growled, the softness in his eyes gone. "The game is over." He drew his revolver from his hip and, for effect, thumbed back the hammer. "Get up."

Sawyer reluctantly struggled to his feet. Grat wrapped his free hand around the back of Sawyer's neck and put the barrel of the revolver into the small of the boy's back.

Sawyer looked at the farmer. The man caught his glare and then looked away. He put his head down and resumed crossing the street. The wheelbarrow squeaked as he pushed it.

"You aren't gonna help me?" Sawyer asked.

The man blinked, his stride hitched, but he kept moving. He adjusted his grip on the wheelbarrow and disappeared beyond the intersection.

"He knows better," spat the grunt. "He ain't as stupid as you. I told you I hated kids. But I saw something in you." Grat pushed Sawyer by the neck. He didn't bother with the rope, which dragged on the ground as they walked. "I was wrong. My brother was right. You ain't getting any more good treatment."

Sawyer chuckled. "That's funny."

Grat squeezed his neck as they turned west back toward the highway. "Ain't nothing funny."

"Yeah, it is." Sawyer looked up at Grat. His eyes were somehow older than a teenager's. He walked, even in defeat, with the proud gait of an adult. There was no childish bounce or joy. "You said you saw something? Maybe you saw yourself in me? That's what's funny. I had the guts to run. I didn't accept whatever it is you have planned for me. I don't take orders from generals."

Grat let go of Sawyer's neck and then shoved the back of his head hard enough to push the boy to the ground. Sawyer fell forward onto his side and landed awkwardly on his right shoulder. Grat straddled him and squatted. He stuck the revolver in the boy's face, pushing aside his nose with the long, cold barrel.

"You don't talk no more, understand?" Spittle sprayed from his mouth. There were white balls of dried saliva in the corners, which stretched like snot as he berated the boy. "You don't know nothing. You're a punk kid with a dead whore mama. You shut up. Speak again, and I'll let Emmett cut out your tongue."

Sawyer whimpered and nodded his comprehension of the warning. He was again a frightened little boy, beaten and confused. Tears flooded his eyes.

"Get up."

Sawyer obeyed and walked quietly back to the horses. He'd failed. There was no point in fighting again. Lubbock and the horror of the Jones awaited him. He vacantly mounted the horse, with Grat's rough assistance, and reflexively took the horn.

"We got time to make up," announced Emmett. "We need to run. Your boy here cost us time."

"He ain't my boy," said Grat. "He's an orphan punk about to meet his maker."

Emmett reached out and punched Grat in the shoulder.

"That's my brother," he said. "Welcome back."

CHAPTER 23

OCTOBER 15, 2037, 2:15 PM
SCOURGE + 5 YEARS
POST, TEXAS

Highway 84 ran northwest and southeast, cutting diagonally across the region from Sweetwater to Muleshoe. In what was left of Post, Texas, it ran straight north and south through the center of the dirt-gray town.

Battle had caught up with Lola and Pico south of Post. It'd taken him longer than he'd anticipated. The headwind slowed his horse and made it tougher to make up ground.

When he'd galloped alongside them, Lola had offered a warm smile of relief. Her eyes found Battle's and lingered a moment past what was comfortable. Battle felt his face flush. He was, to his own surprise, happy to see her. Her thin angular face, full lips, and fiery red hair were a welcoming familiar sight against the dust and death of a post-apocalyptic life.

He was glad to see Pico. The wrinkled consternation of his brow and the mustache too thick for his face forced the hint of a smile from the stoic warrior.

The silent pleasure of the reunion was short lived. Battle killed it.

"We've got company," he said. "Skinner, I'm guessing, is leading a posse. They've got vehicles. If their box truck hadn't broken down about twenty miles back, they'd have already caught me."

The joy in Lola's eyes evaporated. Pico's mustache curled downward.

"What are our options?" asked Lola, tightening her grip on the reins.

"We need to ride these horses as hard as they'll go," said Battle. "Hopefully we outrun them to Lubbock."

"That's a good forty miles," said Pico. "They'll catch us."

Battle raised his voice above the clop of the horses' shoes. "Are there any alternative routes we can take? Anything that might help us avoid them?"

Pico shook his head and sat forward in his saddle. "I don't think so," he said. "We could take Highway 380, but it meets up again with 84."

The three galloped in silence for another minute. Each of them looked over their shoulder, anticipating Skinner and his posse rolling up behind them.

"How far back are they?" Lola asked.

"I don't know," Battle said. "I think ten or fifteen minutes. At most."

They rode into Post, pushing the tired horses through the empty town. Highway 84 turned into Broadway Street once they entered the heart of it. Up ahead on the right, Battle noticed a large sign that read "Holly's Drive-Inn". It stood above a red and white striped awning that surrounded the former restaurant. He was distracted by the broken windows and spray-painted graffiti on the brick exterior. Lola pulled him back into the moment.

"Battle! Up ahead!"

Riding straight for them, three blocks north, were at least a dozen horses carrying armed men. They were Cartel. A couple of them wore the signature brown hats of posse bosses.

Battle yanked the reins and drove his horse to the left. Lola and Pico followed without instruction.

Pow!

A single shot from a Browning chased them past the intersection as they sped west, racing parallel to the remnants of a drooping phone line, which ran infinitely along the length of the road.

Battle raised up in his saddle and goaded his horse as fast as it could carry him. He lowered his head and looked under his arm to see Lola and Pico a length behind him. The posse wasn't visible yet.

Battle approached a wider intersection and he turned right. Heading north, he bolted between a high school football stadium to his left and a dirt racetrack to his right.

Pow! Pow! Pow!

The posse was behind them. Some of the men were firing off what were no better than warning shots as they gave chase. Battle peeked under his arm again. Pico and Lola were weaving their horses back and forth as they followed. There were no people anywhere. The streets and the houses were empty. It was a ghost town.

Pow! Pow!

While Battle knew the Brownings couldn't hit a barn from the distance between them, the noise rattled his horse. It resisted his pull on the reins and, against his command, turned right back toward Broadway.

Battle tried coaxing the horse, but it didn't want to listen to him. It sped up, which was good. Then it turned again, too quickly, while Battle was adjusting his grip on the reins. He lost his balance in the saddle and was thrown, tumbling to the dirt as Lola and Pico rode past him.

Though he was scraped up and bruised, Battle still had his wits about him. He pulled McDunnough and took aim at the first of the horsemen coming in his direction.

He trained the nine millimeter and tracked the posse boss from left to right.

Pop! Pop! Pop!

He hit the man, sending him from his saddle and into the dirt beside the road. He rolled over, his eyes still open.

Pow! Pow!

The explosion of the Brownings was louder than the approaching thunder of the posse. Battle knew he couldn't fight them by himself. So he turned and ran.

He slid between a pair of shotgun houses and scurried through the narrow space between them. It was too small for a horse to navigate. A pair of errant shots blasted behind him as he emerged on the other side of the homes. He crossed the street and darted down another narrow alleyway, diagonally racing toward an abandoned gas station. He'd eluded the bulk of the posse for the moment and was able to slide under the damaged garage bay door that stood open with a three-foot gap between its bottom and the concrete threshold.

Battle was hit with a familiar, pungently sweet odor that immediately made him gag. He pushed himself to his feet. The only light in the space was coming from underneath the open bay door. It revealed nothing beyond the first couple of feet inside the garage.

Battle stepped into the dark, swallowing against the fetor. He pulled his arm to his face and covered his nose with the crook of his elbow, but he couldn't escape it. He could taste the fruity rot of it. It was the smell of death, human death.

Battle knew from experience that dead people emitted an odor different than other animals. A field medic had told him at the end of a particularly difficult day in Isfahan, Iran, that a unique selection of chemicals was responsible for the distinct odor. That odor had permeated Iran after the death squads eliminated much of the opposition. It was prevalent in Syria too.

That odor, the sour, cringe-inducing odor, was why Battle had been so quick to bury his son and wife after their deaths. He'd have lingered with their bodies for days, lamenting his inability to protect them had it not been for what he knew was coming.

He refused to attach their memories to that smell. He couldn't do it. He didn't want to smell it ever again.

But here he was, the odor enveloping him. He took brief, shallow breaths to avoid vomiting. His gag reflex was in overdrive. He gave in to it, bent over, and heaved. His stomach convulsed, his throat burning as he threw up what little was in his stomach. It was mostly bile. The taste, as awful as it was, muted the odor enough to make it tolerable.

There was a voice outside of the garage. "You see him?"

"I lost him," said another.

A third man cursed. "How'd he get away? We had him."

Battle stood quietly in the dark, his muscles frozen. The men kept talking, but their voices grew more distant.

Battle exhaled, allowing himself to breathe once the men were far enough away. He was reminded of the odor when he inhaled. Slowly, he removed his backpack and set it on the ground in front of him. He knelt down and rummaged through the pack. Near the bottom, he found a Ziploc bag. He pulled it from the pack and blindly opened it, removing a box of waterproof matches.

Battle zipped the plastic bag and stuffed it back into his pack. He pushed open the matchbook, pulled out a stick, and struck it across the rough striking surface, igniting the red phosphorus on the end of the match. It was actually a regular match that Battle had coated with clear nail polish. The polish made the tip essentially waterproof. It lit easily when struck.

Battle held the match up in front of his face, but it didn't do much to help. By the time he'd taken a couple of steps farther into the blackness of the garage, the flame was singeing his finger. He blew it out and lit another. A few more steps. Still nothing. Another match. A few more steps. And—

Battle let the match burn to his finger and snuffed it with a pinch, a flash of what he saw still visible in the afterimage of the dark.

Against the back wall of the garage, stacked like cordwood, were countless bodies.

Battle took another match. He squeezed his eyes closed, popped them open, and struck the match. The gruesome work of the Cartel was as shocking the second time.

Old. Young. Man. Woman. Boy. Girl. Infant. The Cartel's henchmen had not discriminated. Some of the women were nude. So were some of the men.

The match burned to his finger, stinging it again before he put out the flame. He stood there in the dark, welcoming it.

Battle couldn't know what it was the people had done to deserve their fate. Chances were good they'd done nothing. Maybe they'd protested giving up their crops or their land. Maybe they'd mouthed off to the wrong posse boss. Maybe they were executed when they ceased being useful, for whatever purposes. It didn't matter.

Battle clenched his jaw and his fists, inadvertently crushing the matchbook in his left hand. The Cartel was worse than the Scourge. There were those who were immune to the pneumonia, those who were beyond its reach. Nobody, it seemed, was immune from the Cartel.

Battle stuffed the crumpled matchbook into his pocket and found his way to his backpack. He lay down on his stomach and crawled toward the light. He inched toward the support beam that separated the twin garage doors and lay behind it just inside the space.

He peeked out from underneath the open door. There was nobody there. He listened. Nothing. He was safe for the moment.

From his position on the floor, Battle reached into his breast pocket, inside the partially zipped hoodie, and gripped a piece of photographic paper.

On the paper was a picture of a man Battle barely recognized. His eyes shone, his muddy brown hair was neatly cropped. He was tanned and healthy. Filling his cheeks was a broad, genuine smile. His teeth were remarkably white.

To his left was a gorgeous dark-haired woman. Her eyes drilled through him, even from the faded photograph. She was grinning, a hint of devilishness on her face. Her left arm was hidden behind the man's back, her right hand placed lovingly on his chest.

To the man's right was a young boy who was the diminutive clone of the two adults. He was blessed with her eyes. His smile was his father's. His wiry, prepubescent arms were wrapped around his dad's neck. Behind them was a treehouse. He pulled the photograph to his face and inhaled. The photograph smelled of smoke. It was intoxicating.

Battle's eyes welled. A knot tied itself thickly into the base of his throat. He blinked away the tears, swallowed the knot whole, and replaced the paper in his breast pocket. He held his hand at his chest for a moment and exhaled.

Battle slid out from underneath the door and slugged his pack onto both shoulders. He tightened the waist strap and checked McDunnough. He had plenty of ammunition should he need it.

He had no idea where Lola or Pico had gone. He didn't have any clue as to where the posse was or how close Skinner might be getting.

He hoped, for his friends' sakes, they'd kept north to Lubbock, but knew them well enough to believe they'd come back for him. That could be fatal for all of them.

If the Cartel would summarily assassinate a town full of people over what was likely nothing, he could only imagine what they'd do to someone who'd challenged them and threatened them the way he had.

He left the gas station and turned back toward the shotgun houses, hoping he'd find a stray horse. There was the possibility, he reasoned, that his horse had stayed in the area. There was also a chance the dead posse boss's animal was nearby.

He jogged across the street and hurriedly wove his way between two sets of houses, finding himself at the spot where he'd fallen off his horse. As he emerged from the narrow space, he didn't find any horses.

Instead he found a Browning shotgun aimed at his head. At the other end of that muzzle was a man in a white hat leaning against a matching SUV. He was flanked by too many men to count. They too were armed.

"Mad Max, I presume?" he drawled, a sneer snaking across his face as he spoke from behind the shotgun's iron sights. A limp cigarette was dancing on his lips as he spoke.

Battle weighed his options. There weren't any. He dropped McDunnough to the dirt and raised his hands above his head. "Cyrus Skinner, I'm guessing."

The man grumbled out a laugh that sounded like a car failing to start. "What gave me away?"

"The stench."

The sneer on Skinner's face retreated into a frown. He motioned to his men. Four of them marched for Battle. Two of them took him by the arms while the others kept their weapons trained at his face. They forcibly walked him toward the white-hatted heathen in command.

"Despite my better judgment," Skinner said, "I'm gonna have to keep you alive."

Battle struggled against the grunts but didn't say anything. He kept his glare fixed on Skinner, a man whose countenance was different from the other depraved grunts and bosses he'd seen.

There was something missing in his eyes, a conscience, or maybe a soul altogether. Battle studied the lines that ran along the edges of the man's nose, the nasty curl of his mouth, the gaunt, skeletal shape of his cheeks. His right ear was blackened with dried blood. It looked as if a tiny piece might be missing near the lobe.

Skinner lowered his weapon and leaned it against the front of the SUV. He pulled a lighter from his pocket and lit the cigarette. His thick chest broadened as he inhaled deeply, his black eyes narrowing. He exhaled, blowing the smoke directly into Battle's face. "That don't mean I can't rough you up a bit, though," he said.

Battle didn't react. He was stoic.

Skinner pinched the cigarette and drew it from his lips. He stepped toward Battle and, his eyes never leaving Battle's, pressed it into the side of his neck.

Battle flinched at the initial burn, but he bit down on the inside of his cheek to counteract the pain. Even as his eyes watered from the sting, he didn't lose eye contact with Skinner.

Skinner pulled the cigarette from Battle's neck and immediately pressed it to another spot, his face alit with sadistic joy. Battle tensed again and cleared his throat. Still, he remained silent. Skinner twisted the cigarette against Battle's neck, putting it out against his skin. He flicked the butt against Battle's face and leaned back against the SUV with his arms folded.

"Battle's a funny name," he said. The collection of grunts around him laughed. "That a real name, or you come up with it to sound tough?"

Battle said nothing.

Skinner looked over at one of the grunts with a Browning pointed at Battle. He waved his hand at him. "Hand me that gun," he said. "The nine millimeter. I wanna see it."

The grunt handed over McDunnough. Skinner turned it over in his hand, apparently admiring its craftsmanship. He shook it in his hand. "Nice," he said and pointed it at Battle's face, pushing the bushing at the end of the muzzle into his brow. Battle resisted the temptation to close his eyes. He didn't even blink.

"You need to start talking," said Skinner. "Or I'm gonna have to disobey my orders."

"Let me ask a question," Battle said.

"He speaks," Skinner said to the assembled grunts. He laughed. They laughed. "Go ahead, *Battle*."

Battle sighed. "What happened to the people in this town?"

Skinner tilted his head like a dog and squeezed his eyes. "What people?"

"All of them."

Skinner twisted the handgun against Battle's skin. "You're speaking in riddles."

"Everyone in this town is dead," Battle replied. "You killed them."

"So you *know* what happened to them, then." Skinner chuckled.

"Why did you kill all of them?" Battle asked. "What did they do?"

Skinner held up three fingers with his free hand and thumped Battle's forehead with McDunnough three times. "That's three questions."

Battle sniffed. He didn't respond.

"I dunno," Skinner said. "'Cause we could. Ain't nothing in this town we need. Ain't nobody we need. Somebody might have lipped off. Who knows? Why do you care anyhow?"

Battle swallowed. "I didn't say I cared."

"Tough guy." Skinner pulled the gun from Battle's head and stuck it in his empty holster. He motioned at one of the grunts holding Battle by the arm. The grunt reared back and slammed the butt of his shotgun into the side of Battle's head. "Time to go," Skinner said. He slid into his seat and activated the satellite phone. It took a moment to produce a signal. "We got him," he said. "We're on our way."

The men loaded Battle into the back of the SUV. They'd be in Lubbock before sundown.

CHAPTER 24

OCTOBER 15, 2037, 2:35 PM
SCOURGE + 5 YEARS
NORTH OF POST, TEXAS

"We need to go back," Lola called to Pico. "We saved him once. We could do it again."

They were riding north on state Highway 207. It split from Highway 84 on the eastern side of Post. They'd outdistanced the posse chasing them in town and were a good three miles from it.

"We can't," Pico said. "If they got him, we can't help him. There were too many of them. If they didn't get him, he'll be fine. We'll meet him in Lubbock."

Lola gripped the saddle horn and rubbed it with her palm. The constant waves of guilt she felt over losing her son were always roiling beneath the surface. The idea that she'd abandoned the man who was helping her rescue Sawyer was overwhelming. She sank in the saddle as the horse galloped forward. There was something deep within her that told her Sawyer was alive. That same voice was certain Battle was dead. Lola was a realist. She had to be in the dusty, violent hell forged by the plague and its survivors.

Before the Scourge, Lola had lived the life of an eternal optimist. A native Floridian, she'd grown up in Jacksonville. She was an only child. Her father was retired Navy. He was a demanding but loving man who raised her by himself after his wife left him when Lola was nine.

Her father had retreated into a shell, and Lola became the caretaker at a young age. It was her responsibility, she had resolved, to provide the light where she could see only dark. And she had.

Her sunny disposition, and constant belief that tomorrow would be better than today, eventually had drawn her father back to the living. Her love for life, despite its difficulties, was infectious.

It was that ebullience that attracted a fellow student at the University of North Florida. He was on the basketball team. He was popular. And he'd fallen hard for Lola.

They were married a week after graduating. He'd found a job as an accountant at the Mayo Clinic. She'd been hired as a dental hygienist. They'd worked hard during the week and spent their weekends at the beach. Lola had always worn too much sunscreen. Her husband had enjoyed applying it.

Four years after they married, they'd bought a home on the St. Johns River. It was small, but with an incredible view. Lola and her husband had known they were blessed.

Six months after that, while they were still repainting the exterior and improving the landscaping in the tiny front yard, they were expecting their first child. It was a boy.

He was healthy, he was happy and, incredibly, slept through the night. They'd named him Sawyer, after her father.

They'd tried to have more children, but Lola miscarried twice. Despite the heartache, she'd reminded herself daily of her fortune. She had a healthy son, a loving husband, and a beautiful home.

Lola would have liked to stay home with her son, but the house had been expensive and the couple reasoned her income would eventually help pay for college.

Life had been good. Like so many families in 2032, they'd had plans for the future.

Sawyer's eighth birthday had been the beginning of the end of those plans. It was the day Lola's father died of pneumonia. Lola's husband had known the global threat called the Scourge was beginning to take hold in the United States. There had been loud whispers at the Mayo Clinic about failed vaccine trials and increasing patient loads.

It had quickly devolved into a crisis. Lola's father was one of 326 people who died at a Jacksonville hospital on October 2, 2032. Another 417 died the next day. Within two weeks, the city had fallen into chaos.

Lola had kept believing they could stay in their home. Everything would work out for the best. It always had. No darkness was too black from which to find the light.

When a pair of thugs broke into their home, searching for food, and one of them threatened Sawyer at knifepoint, Lola had agreed it was time to leave.

They'd headed west for Louisiana. Her husband had known of a compound there. It belonged to a doctor friend. He was what her husband called a "prepper". Lola didn't really know what that meant. She hadn't cared. She knew he'd developed a rural piece of land. It had several cabins, was stocked with food and supplies, and was hidden from the outside world. The doctor had offered them refuge.

It had taken them nearly a week to find it. Others, with less benevolent intentions, had beaten them there. The doctor and his family were dead. The food, however much of it there had been, was gone. Still, they'd hidden in one of the cabins for close to a month, until they'd run out of the supplies they'd brought with them.

It had only gotten worse from there. Lola, however, had remained hopeful. At least outwardly, she had convinced her family they would find a safe place to call home. The chaos couldn't last forever, she'd believed. Eventually, they'd return home and begin again. Then her husband died and the optimism began to fade. A viral realism took hold, infecting the hope to which she had so long clung.

Now, five years later, the transformation was complete. Her son was missing, and her savior was likely dead. Lola looked over at Pico. He was rubbing his fingers on his mustache. It was his tell. He was nervous and afraid.

"We need to cut west," he said. "If we stay on this highway, it'll lead us straight north, away from Lubbock."

"If we cut back, aren't we in danger of getting caught?"

"Yes. We ain't got a choice."

Lola sighed. They steered the horses from the state highway and onto the dirt. Everything in front of her was gray or brown. The only life she could see was the occasional patch of green weed struggling against the cold.

"We should head straight at the sun," Pico said. "It's west. We'll eventually hit Highway 84. We'll turn right; that'll get us to Lubbock."

Lola's horse seemed to enjoy the soft earth. It was running faster on the dirt. Lola could feel it in the rhythmic bounce of its gallop.

She tightened her grip on the reins and closed her eyes. The wind, though cold, felt good against her face. It reminded her of the Atlantic sea breeze that chilled Jacksonville Beach in the winter. She pictured her husband, the wind tousling his hair. He had Sawyer on his shoulders, his hands wrapped around their son's pudgy feet. For a moment, she forgot where she was.

Pico snapped her from the daydream. "Lola!"

She opened her eyes and saw Pico pointing behind them. She looked over her shoulder. She blinked twice, hoping what she saw was as much a dream as what she'd envisioned with her eyes closed. It wasn't.

There was a cloud of dust and dirt barreling toward them. At least twenty horses were racing in their direction. Atop the horses were armed men.

"How did they find us again?"

"I don't think they're the same men," Pico said, sitting up in his saddle to push his horse faster. "They came from the north."

Lola kicked her heels into her horse and coaxed the animal to quicken its gait and engage a full gallop. The horse responded, pounding away at the dirt. Lola leaned forward, both of her hands working the reins, keeping pace with Pico.

Despite their efforts, the posse was catching up. They were running side by side in a long intimidating line of horses moving at breakneck speed. An impressive cloud of dust trailed behind the posse, framing their advance against the otherwise clear sky. Lola tried not to look back at them, but the temptation was irresistible. Each time she peeked, the line was bigger, closer. They'd be on top of them in no time.

Pico's face was drawn with worry. He too was forward in his saddle. His horse was snorting as it ran, its majestic head bobbing forward and back with effort. Its dark mane was windswept as it worked against the cold swirl that fought against their advance.

The dirt gave way to the rich soil of a plotted farm, and Lola's horse dove straight into seven-foot stalks of ornamental corn ready for harvest. The plants were sown far enough apart for the horse to run clean between the long, tall rows of corn. Lola couldn't see or hear Pico above the rustle of the stalks rushing past. If she sat tall in the saddle, she could see over the top of the tassels adorning the mature green corn silks. Thick leaves slapped her in the face when she tried to look behind her. It was a futile effort regardless. She was swamped in the cornfield. All she could see were the stalks. All she could hear was the brushing and snap of crops, the beat of the horse's hoofs on the soil, and the breathing of the animal.

Lola turned again to look behind her and saw nothing. She swung her body back to face the front and caught a flash of movement to her right.

She glanced to her right and saw the flash again. And again. There was someone riding parallel to her. She pressed her knees against the saddle and raised up to look over the tops of the stalks. The western edge of the field still wasn't visible.

There was a flash to her left. Someone was on her other side. If the rider to the right was Pico, the one to the left most definitely was not. Worse yet, both of them could be Cartel. Lola made a snap decision. She slowed her horse a beat and then pulled him hard to the left. She cut south, racing her horse behind where she imagined the Cartel might be. It was a bad miscalculation.

Her horse, blinded by the thicker density of stalks running north and south, clipped the back end of another animal. The collision sent Lola flying from the saddle. She held onto the reins too long and flipped over the front of the horse, her fall broken by the corn. The horse tumbled too, missing her as it rolled onto its side and slid to a stop.

By the time Lola pushed herself to her feet, she was surrounded by three grunts on horseback. All of them had their Brownings and leering eyes directed at her.

One of them slung his leg over his saddle and dismounted. "We got your little man already," he said. "He ain't talking. I'm fixin' to rip that mustache off his lip."

So they'd caught Pico.

Lola tried not to reveal her disappointment. She rubbed the dirt from her cheeks and tried to pull her hair from in front of her eyes. The man yanked her closer to him. His breath was fetid, as if he'd eaten the fertilizer used to grow the corn.

"We're looking for the big dude," he said, the odor hot and nauseating. "They call him Mad Max. You know where we might find him?"

Lola swallowed, trying to avoid breathing the grunt's air as he spoke. She processed what he was saying.

They didn't have Battle. They believed she could help them find him. *That* was her only value.

She tried to pull free of his grasp. He held tight. She gritted her teeth. "I can help you get him."

The man narrowed his focus and loosened his grip. "How so?"

"He's headed to Lubbock," she said. "You take me there, I'll tell you exactly where to find him."

He licked his teeth with his tongue and then spat a thick green wad of saliva into the soil. "Why would you do that?" he asked. "You was with him in Abilene. You was helping him there. Now you're quick to drop him like a hot iron."

Lola searched his eyes, piecing together a response. "He left us," she said. "Just up and left us."

"Us?"

"Me and my friend with the mustache."

The grunt laughed. "Salomon Pico? He's your friend?"

Lola's eyes widened with surprise.

"We know who he is," said the grunt. "He was one of us. He's a traitor. He ain't nobody's friend. Now what you got going with—"

Lola shook her arm free. "I don't have anything going with him," she snapped. "Now either you want our help or you don't."

The grunt shrugged. "I dunno. Not sure what value you got."

"I tell you the value I *got*," she mocked. "You don't wear a hat. You're a grunt. You tell your boss you had me and let me go—"

"Oh"—he waved his finger at her—"I ain't letting you go. I'm wondering why I shouldn't put a bullet in your head right here and be done with it."

"Because I can help you find Mad Max," she insisted. "He won't suspect me of helping you."

The grunt pursed his lips and took a step back. He folded his arms across his chest and rubbed the sparse curls of hair on his chin. He nodded. "All right then," he said. "We'll take you to Lubbock. Once we're there, I'll let the bosses decide what to do with you."

Lola sighed with relief. She was on her way to Lubbock.

"What about Pico?" she asked.

The grunt laughed. "He's already on the road north. They got plans for him. He ain't gonna die easy."

CHAPTER 25

JANUARY 3, 2020, 8:00 PM
SCOURGE -12 YEARS, 9 MONTHS
ALEPPO, SYRIA

The shots were coming from all directions. Battle was trapped, pinned down with Buck draped across his shoulders in a fireman's carry. He was holding Buck's right wrist with his right hand, his back pressed up against the wall of a four-story stone and brick building. The second and third floors jutted outward, creating an overhang that wrapped around the freestanding mid-rise.

Battle had the nine millimeter in his left hand, but he couldn't return fire. There was no single good target.

Someone had spotted him moving in the shadows along the edge of a narrow street that ran north and south parallel to the canal. They'd shouted first and then fired. Battle recognized the discharge as a Chinese version of the AK-47.

The Type 56, as it was known, was common in the Iranian theatre. It was a leftover from the Iran-Iraq war fifty years earlier. He recognized it by its rapid rate of fire. The Type 56 didn't have a hammer retarder and allowed for the higher rate.

The Type 56 was quickly accompanied by a chorus of gunfire. Together it sounded like fireworks. Because of the buildings' varying constructions and heights, Battle couldn't pinpoint exactly where the multitude of threats originated.

Buck was unconscious and his pulse was weakening. Battle could barely feel it in the sergeant's wrist. There was no way he'd make it the two blocks south needed to cross the bridge to the other side. He couldn't wait it out either.

The percussion of gunfire slowed and then stopped. There were men yelling to each other in Arabic. Battle couldn't decipher it. The echo, the speed with which they spoke, and his exhaustion made it impossible. Regardless, there was a window.

He shrugged Buck up higher on his shoulders. Between his weight and that of his pack, his sciatic nerve was pinging with a constant pulse of sharp pain. His neck was throbbing. His ribs felt abused. His wounded left arm was tingling as if it was asleep.

"Now or never," he mumbled to himself and darted out into the street. He turned south along the street and at the next intersection wove toward the protection of a series of high-rise apartments. He'd advanced maybe one hundred feet without drawing any direct fire.

From his new position he could see one of the shooters. He was shirtless and standing on the narrow balcony of his third-story apartment. The light in his apartment was on, providing a perfect silhouette of his thin frame. Somehow, he'd missed Battle darting across the street.

He had a rifle in his hands, its muzzle resting on the wrought-iron railing at the edge of the balcony. The spinning shadow of a ceiling fan hovered behind his head like a rotating halo. Battle guessed the target was easily forty yards from him. With his right hand, Battle knew he could hit him from that distance. With his left hand, he wasn't as confident.

Add that his sciatic nerve was providing a ridiculous distraction as he planted both feet to evenly distribute his weight, and the odds of a clean hit were greatly diminished. Nonetheless, Battle extended his injured left arm and locked his elbow. He pulled his right hand, along with Buck's, up under his elbow to brace it. He tilted his head to the left and focused through the iron sights.

He found the shadowed target backlit against the apartment, exhaled, and fired. It was an impossible shot given the range, the angle, the weapon, and his fatigue.

Pop! Pop!

The silhouette swayed and fell forward, his body draped over the balcony. The rifle fell from its perch and rattled into the street below.

Battle's shots, however, initiated a newly orchestrated symphony of gunfire. A couple of the shots hit the building against which his body was pressed, though it didn't seem any of the gunfire was well targeted.

Against the echo of gunfire, Battle heard a scream and looked up to where the silhouette had stood. There was a second person there, a woman. She was tugging at the dead body, unsuccessfully trying to pull him free of the balcony.

Her wailing grew louder, and she was waving her hands and crying out in despair before giving up and returning to the apartment. Battle could hear her anguished voice even once she'd disappeared.

His eyes found the rifle on the street. He looked for signs of others shooters and didn't see any. Battle tucked the handgun in his waistband, tightened his grip on Buck, and dashed into the street. He quickly squatted and grabbed the rifle. Rather than retrace his steps, he moved directly underneath the balcony on which he killed the silhouetted rifleman. The woman's shrieks were overhead now.

He leaned back against the cracked stucco wall and checked the rifle for damage. It was the Type 56 he'd heard earlier. It was fitted with the distinctive slant compensator found on the AK-47. That wasn't standard to the Type 56. It had an under folding spike bayonet and a chrome-plated bore chamber. He guessed it weighed eight or nine pounds and was easily heavier than his HK416. It had English control markings on it. It was in the F position.

Battle checked the magazine, which he figured was the midsize box that held thirty rounds. It was half empty.

He'd seen the weapon demonstrated but had never fired it. He had no concept for how sensitive the automatic trigger might be. Regardless, this was better than the handgun. He suddenly felt better about their chances.

Battle held the rifle at his side, the muzzle inches from the ground, edging his way along the side of the building, trying to keep himself in the shadows. He reached the nearest intersection and stopped at the corner. He looked to his left, swinging Buck's body with him, and then looked to his right. He looked back to the left again and a flush of panic washed over him. His pulse quickened. His back tensed again and he shifted his weight to his left leg.

He closed his eyes and tried to retrace his steps, but all he could think about was that he couldn't think. He shook his head and focused. Had he passed two east-west intersections or three? Or was it four? It was three. Or four. How far south had he moved? Was he still north of the bridge? He was north of it. No. He'd gone too far. His breathing accelerated.

In the confusion of the gunfire, despite his efforts to maintain calm, he'd become confused.

Battle was lost.

CHAPTER 26

OCTOBER 15, 2037, 4:20 PM
SCOURGE + 5 YEARS
LUBBOCK, TEXAS

Marcus knew it was a dream. The colors were too bright and his heart too full for it not to be a dream.

He was with Wesson. They were at the back edge of their property, up early enough to see the sun rise and their breath puff in the morning air before the chill burned off.

Marcus sipped hot coffee. It was black and strong. He could taste the caffeine and feel it coursing through his veins, energizing him with each careful slurp.

Sylvia had brewed the pot before they left. She'd also mixed a cup of Swiss Miss for Wesson and poured it into a matching Golden Knights thermos. Wesson insisted they have the same containers, the same hats, the same camouflage bib.

It was their first hunt together. Wesson was talking incessantly. He was fidgeting, snapping dead branches and crunching leaves in his palms. Marcus had to remind him to keep quiet every couple of minutes.

"Buddy," he whispered, wrapping his arm around his son's narrow shoulders, "we've got to be quiet. We don't want to spook the deer."

Wesson nodded like a bobblehead and raised his gloved finger to his lips. He smiled and immediately snapped a dead branch from the sapling next to him.

Marcus could smell the mesquite, the damp oak, and the dirt when they settled into their blind. He pulled a bolt from the quiver and loaded it into his crossbow. He did the same for Wesson, with a much smaller, lighter weapon, and handed it to him.

"You remember what I taught you?" he asked, nuzzling beside his son to make sure Wesson was holding the bow correctly.

The boy nodded and showed his dad the proper form.

"Now we wait," said Marcus, his mind knowing full well it was a dream as he sipped the coffee and inhaled the aroma of Arabica mixed with the smoky air of the central Texas woods. The two Battles sat there in the blind, enjoying one another's company, the elder soaking up the sudden maturity of his son, the younger relishing the bonding time with his idol.

The time came. A young buck appeared behind a fallen oak. It was alone. "Wesson," Marcus whispered, "you see it?"

Wesson nodded and drew his bow's stock to his shoulder. He looked over at his father.

"The limbs are taut," Marcus said of the winged bow pieces that held the tension on the bowstrings. "The bolt is in the flight groove. Check your hand on the foregrip."

Wesson adjusted his left hand. Battle could see the glisten of sweat on the grip.

"Whenever you're ready," said Marcus.

The deer was still. Its large eyes were looking straight at them. It turned its head to the left, exposing the length of its body. It was a nice, wide target.

Wesson kept both eyes open, as his father had instructed, and pulled the trigger.

Clunk! Thooop!

The bolt sailed through the air and into the deer. It hit the perfect spot, above and behind the right leg. The bolt drove through the deer's heart and up into its right lung.

It shuddered, ran a couple of yards, and collapsed into the bed of leaves coating the ground.

Marcus watched the kill and turned to congratulate his son. Instead of the beaming smile he expected, Wesson was gasping for air. His son was coughing and convulsing.

Marcus held his son's shoulders, trying to steady him. The coughing grew more intense. Wesson was bleeding from his nose and ears.

"This is your fault," Sylvia said, appearing from nowhere. She was standing over Marcus's shoulder as he struggled to calm his son. "You promised we would be safe," she said. "You promised we would survive."

Marcus felt cold. Sweat was beading on his forehead and spilling into his eyes. He laid his son down and unzipped the bib. "It'll be okay, son," he told the boy. "It'll be okay."

"It won't be okay," said Sylvia. "You can't make it okay."

"Am I going to die?" Wesson asked between wet hacks. "Dad? Am I—"

Marcus reminded himself it was a dream. He wanted to wake from it. He wanted the dream to end.

Wake up!

"All of your preparation," sneered Sylvia. "All of your promises."

Wake up!

"Dad? Am I going to die?"

Wake up! Wake up!

Battle's eyes popped open. His body twitched. He took a deep, ragged breath. The dream was over. He'd merely traded one nightmare for another.

He was in a dark room, save the fluorescent light above him that was dim and strobing. It gave the space the feeling of a Halloween haunted house.

Battle was on a sofa. There was a large desk, a couple of chairs, a bookshelf, and some plaques on the walls. It looked like someone's office. There weren't any windows.

He sat forward on the sofa and rose to his feet. The room started to wobble and he sat down. His head began throbbing, and he remembered what had happened. Somebody clocked him and knocked him unconscious.

He had no concept of time or place, but he knew he couldn't stay in this room. Slowly, using the sofa's firm arm, he pushed himself back to his feet and walked to the door. It was the only access to the room.

The handle, as he expected it would be, was locked. The door was solid metal.

Battle checked the locking mechanism, but in the dim light he couldn't see anything. He figured they'd be coming for him soon. He needed to figure out as much about where he was as possible before they showed up.

Dizzy and light-headed, he walked slowly to the desk. He inched his way around it to the large wooden chair behind it and sat down. He swiveled in the seat and tried each of the drawers on the desk's face. Only one opened. It was empty. The desk was bare. There was nothing on it but the inlaid cherry pattern running its rectangular perimeter.

Battle spun in the chair and looked at the bookshelf. There were motivational titles, books about strategy, a New International Version Bible. There was nothing that gave away his location. Then he looked at the plaques on the wall.

Each of them was an award for achievement. One was from the Associated Press for 2028 Coach of the Year. Another plaque was for the 2025 Big Twelve Conference Coach of the Year. All of the plaques honored the football coach for Texas Tech University.

Battle nodded his head. He was in Lubbock, likely on the Tech campus. The Cartel brought him here because they knew he was looking for the kid. Maybe that meant the boy was still alive. He reminded himself that Skinner wasn't *allowed* to kill him. Someone higher up on the Cartel food chain wanted him alive.

Battle sat down in the desk chair. His head hurt. He felt the spot where the grunt punched him and hit him with something. There was a large, tender knot behind his ear at the base of his skull.

He leaned forward on the desk with his elbows and lowered his head into his hands. He couldn't think straight enough to process what each of the clues meant. And none of them, even if he had been able to decipher them, would tell him if Lola and Pico were still alive.

He closed his eyes, trying to will away the pain, when the door lock clicked, the handle spun, and the door swung open. Two men walked into the room. Even in the dim, flickering light, he recognized one of them as Cyrus Skinner. He didn't know the other one, a tall, well-built soldier of a man. He was wearing a black hat and black boots. He carried himself with incredible confidence, despite a noticeable limp.

A gray ponytail draped across one shoulder. He had a thick white beard that clung to his cheeks but hung low from his chin. He was more than a posse boss or a captain. Battle was smart enough to know that.

"So you're Mad Max," the man said, "the great warrior who happens to be a major pain in my ass."

Battle pulled his elbows from the desk. He leaned back in the chair. The man approached the desk and planted his thick fingers on it, leaning forward as he spoke.

"Mad Max, huh?" The man's eyes narrowed and he exhaled through his nose. "I hear your real name is Battle. That so?"

Battle folded his arms across his chest. "Yeah."

"Pleased to see you, Battle." The man extended his right hand. "I'm General Roof. You can call me General."

Battle looked at the general's hand and hesitated, but he thought it better not to aggravate the situation with unwarranted defiance. He took his hand and squeezed it as he shook it.

"Nice grip," said General Roof. "That's a soldier's handshake."

Skinner chuckled. He was standing near the sofa, his hands stuffed into his pockets. General Roof turned to look over his shoulder. His hand was still gripping Battle's.

"That's rude," he said to Skinner. "Apologize to the man, Captain Skinner."

Skinner jerked with surprise. "What?"

Roof kept his eyes on Skinner and motioned to Battle with his head. "Apologize for your insolence."

"My ins—"

"You were rude," Roof said. "Apologize to our guest."

Skinner looked at the floor and scratched his chin. He pulled a cigarette from his pocket and dropped it between his lips.

Roof smiled. "I'll apologize for him. That was unnecessary. He's embarrassed that you made a fool of him. From what I understand you burned his house, blew up his HQ, and killed I don't know how many men."

Battle shot Skinner a look. The smirk was long gone from the captain's face.

Roof turned to Skinner. "Don't light that cigarette in here, Cyrus."

Skinner grumbled and mocked Roof like a petulant child when the general turned back to Battle. He licked his lips and stuffed the cigarette back in his pocket.

"Here's my problem, Battle," said Roof, sitting on the edge of the desk. He scratched the scruff on his neck. "As much as I respect you, I can't have you running roughshod over my land."

"This isn't your land," said Battle.

Roof smiled again. "It is until somebody takes it from me," he said. "The Cartel, my carefully pieced together organization, runs everything, you see. Everything. I mean, we earned it fair and square."

"Through muscle and fear," corrected Battle.

"Same thing. That's beside the point. I'd prefer not to digress into the irrelevant facts. You are here on *my* land. You are creating problems for *me*. You are, therefore, not welcome."

Battle swiveled in the chair. He glanced at Skinner, who'd moved to the sofa and was sulking. As nasty as Skinner was, this general was worse. His intelligence and calm demeanor were far more frightening than the obvious bullying of the captain. He was guessing Roof was former military. He had that sense about him, a familiar cadence and quiet confidence. His eyes had seen things he couldn't forget. They were etched in his gaze.

"As much as I'd like to let you walk," said Roof, "I can't do that. It sends the wrong message to the troops. Plus my comrades, the other two generals with whom I run this joint, might have a problem with unilateral clemency."

Battle leaned into the desk and shrugged his shoulders. "So?"

"So—" he chuckled "—I'm going to have to make an example of you. People need to know they cannot challenge the status quo and get away with it. Hell, even the United States government knew to fall in line and leave us alone."

"You do what you need to do," said Battle, looking at Skinner as he spoke to Roof. "I'll deal."

Roof slapped the desk. "I know you will," he said. "We're going to put you into the Jones. It's our Roman Colosseum, our *Thunderdome*, if you will."

"Meaning what?"

Roof stood from the desk. "Meaning we toss you into the stadium with a couple of other haters. Then you die at the hands of some of our better grunts."

"What purpose does that serve?"

"Well," Roof said, "it's a very public way to die. It's fun entertainment for the folks who like us, and it's a darn clear warning for those who don't."

"Fits."

"Fits?"

"Yeah," said Battle. "It fits. You're afraid of losing control. You don't have as strong a hold on your land as you'd like me to believe. Otherwise, there'd be no need to warn anyone. They'd already know."

General Roof nodded. He took a good long look at Battle and then turned to leave. He limped toward the door. "Skinner here will see you get the prep you need," he said without turning around. "We'll move you to the locker room for the night. You'll fight at first light tomorrow."

Roof walked out into what Battle assumed was a hallway. He stopped and stuck his head back into the room. "You're exactly who I thought you were, Battle. You didn't disappoint."

CHAPTER 27

OCTOBER 15, 2037, 5:00 PM
SCOURGE + 5 YEARS
LUBBOCK, TEXAS

The locker room was dank and ripe with the overwhelming smell of mildew. At least there was a light and slow spinning ceiling fan at one end of the long open space.

Battle found a wooden stool, dragged it into the light, and sat on it. He leaned it back onto two of its legs and rested his back against the painted cinder-block wall.

He crossed his arms over his chest and closed his eyes. While he wasn't anxious to fall asleep, given what he'd encountered the last time he dreamt, there wasn't anything else to do other than imagine what he would face in the morning.

Battle never considered himself a warrior or a gladiator. He was simply a smart guy who knew how to take orders and survive. He considered the odds against him and was okay with them.

If his lot was to die on the artificial turf of a football stadium, so be it. He was ready to join his wife and son in heaven. But there was a nagging thought that picked at the peace to which he'd arrived: he'd promised Lola he'd rescue her son.

If he died tomorrow, he'd have failed her. It would be yet another promise he couldn't keep. At least he'd tried. There was that.

Battle had drifted to that odd place between consciousness and sleep when he heard the door to the locker room slam open.

From his spot in the corner of the room, he could only see shadows in the doorway. There were a pair of grunts on either side of a smaller man. They shoved the man inside. He stumbled and fell onto his knees. The grunts laughed at him and pulled the door shut.

The man slowly walked into the light. His head was down, but as soon as Battle saw him, he recognized him. The mustache was unmistakable.

Battle pushed his back from the wall and dropped the stool onto all four legs. "Salomon Pico?"

Pico looked up. One eye was swollen shut, the puffy flesh around it black and deep purple. His nose looked broken. There was a long gash along the top of it, and dried blood caked the edges of his nostrils.

Battle stood from the stool, measured his balance, and then moved to Pico's side. "What did they do?"

"They caught me outside of Post," Pico said. "Right after you disappeared. A whole bunch of them. They knew me. They took it out on me."

"Where's Lola?"

Pico looked up, his open eye searching Battle's. "I dunno," he said. "We got separated. She disappeared into a cornfield. I dunno what happened. I gotta guess it ain't good."

Pico's revelation socked Battle in the gut. He didn't want to think about what might have happened to her. "So you're joining me in the Jones?" he asked, trying to redirect the conversation to the least distasteful of all the nasty possibilities.

"Yeah," Pico said. "They told me I'm getting a traitor's death—public and painful."

Battle snickered. "Surprised they're not hanging you in the town square, then. Seems to be their style."

Pico frowned. "Not funny."

"I'm just saying we could survive this," Battle explained.

"Then what?"

"I don't—"

The door swung open again and the armed grunts tossed in a third gladiator. This one was tall and wiry. His face looked younger than the cynicism in his eyes. His mop of red hair hung over his ears. It was the hair that gave him away.

"Sawyer?" Battle asked as the door slammed shut.

The boy's eyes tightened. He scowled warily at Battle and then at Pico. He kept his distance, standing where the guards left him.

Battle took a step forward; his voice softened. "You're Sawyer, right? Your mother is Lola?"

The boy tensed. His hands balled into fists. His feet spread to shoulder width. "Who are you?"

"I'm Marcus Battle," he said. "You're Sawyer, right?"

The boy nodded almost imperceptibly. "Yeah. I'm Sawyer. You knew my mom?"

Battle took another careful step toward the boy, trying not to spook him. "A bit. She ended up on my land after the Cartel caught you. She's been looking for you. *We've* been looking for you."

Sawyer motioned to Pico. "Who're you?"

"I'm Salomon Pico," he said. "I was trying to help too."

"You look like Cartel."

"I was," Pico admitted. "Not anymore."

The boy took a half step back toward the door. His glassy eyes moved between Battle and Pico. "How did she die?" He lifted his head, apparently bracing himself for the answer.

"I don't know that she's dead."

The boy's eyes widened; his brow lifted. "She's alive?"

"I don't know that either."

The hope on Sawyer's face collapsed into confusion. He shook his head and tried speaking with his hands. Nothing came out. Tears forming in the corners of his eyes streamed along his cheeks.

"She was alive this afternoon," said Pico. "I was with her. We got separated. I don't know where she is now."

"So she *could* be alive?"

"Yes," said Pico. "She could be."

Sawyer stepped forward and swept his bangs from his forehead. "We need to find her," he said. "If she's still alive, we *have* to find her."

Battle stepped closer still and held his hands in front of him, assuring the boy he meant no harm. "Don't take this the wrong way, Sawyer," he said, measuring his words carefully, "but we're not in a position to go looking for your mom right now. We're prisoners here. We're about to be thrown to the lions."

Sawyer's eyes fidgeted. He flexed his fingers and pushed aside his hair again. "We can't just sit here, though. There's gotta be a way..."

Battle indulged him. "A way to what?"

"A way to find out if she's alive," Sawyer explained. "If she is, we can figure out a way to save her. You found me, didn't you?"

Battle chortled. "True, but this isn't exactly ideal."

Pico interjected. "You're not making sense, kid. You're just —"

Sawyer's eyes lit with fire. He clenched his jaw. His face grew red. He started toward Pico, and Battle stepped in front of him. He gently put his hands on the boy's shoulders, noticing how tall the young man was. He was big for thirteen.

"We can try," Battle said softly. "We will try to find out if she's alive. If she is, we'll try to figure out a way to save her. We'll do exactly what you suggested. Okay? We also need to focus on ourselves. We have to devise a plan of action when they throw us onto the field."

Sawyer's glare cooled and his eyes moved from Pico back to Battle. He looked up at Battle and nodded. He rubbed his right shoulder and squinted.

"You hurt?" Battle asked.

"A little. I'll be all right," he said. "I fell on it."

Battle led Sawyer over to a stool and offered him a seat.

"Chill," he said. "It's going to be a long night."

***

The door flung open again with a bang. The familiar grunts were manhandling an unfamiliar man. They shoved him in the back and he fell, catching himself with the flats of his palms. He grunted and then collapsed. He was filthy.

Even in the low light, Battle knew the man hadn't bathed or cleaned himself in days. He could smell it. It was an offensive odor he'd encountered countless times in Syria and Iran and Afghanistan. Both the people in-country and his own men had succumbed to the foul stench after extended engagements.

The man pushed himself to his feet, his head down, and brushed the dirt from his clothing. He was dressed differently than others Battle had seen. He wasn't wearing the ill-fitting pants of a grunt or the overalls the townsfolk wore. He was wearing loose-fitting cotton pants, like sweatpants but thinner. His shirt was reminiscent of a Mexican guayabera. It was distinctive because of the two vertical rows of closely sewn pleats that ran the length of both sides of the shirt. There were tea-colored stains encircling his armpits. Battle hadn't seen anyone wearing clothing like that during his brief trek across central Texas.

The man's head was shaved clean. He was tan, his skin leathery despite what Battle imagined was his relatively young age. He was lanky and the shirt hung wide on his thin build.

"Do you have water?" he asked nobody in particular. "Please."

Battle shook his head. "No. They haven't given us any."

"They want us weak," the man said. He walked across the room to find his own stool, carrying with him a stench-laden breeze that wafted across the room. He pulled it between his legs and sat, leaning forward and dropping his elbows onto his thighs. His long, bony fingers dangled between his legs.

"Who are you?" Sawyer asked. "Are you Cartel?"

The man shook his head without looking up from the floor. "No," he said. "I'm not Cartel."

"Then what are you?" Sawyer pressed.

"I'm Baadal," he said. "I'm a Dweller."

Pico stood from his stool so quickly it toppled over, his face ashen. He pointed at the man, his finger trembling. "That can't be."

The man glared up at Pico. He licked his dry, cracked lips. "It has to be. That's what I am."

Pico paced back and forth, three steps left, three steps right. "There's no such thing," he said. "The Dwellers, they're legend. The Cartel wiped them out."

Battle raised his hands and waved them. "Wait," he said. "I don't understand. What's going on, Pico?"

Pico shook his finger at the man who called himself Baadal, his eyes large beneath his arched brow. "He says he's a Dweller. The Dwellers don't exist. He can't be—"

"Slow down," said Battle. "What's a Dweller?"

"We are a tribe of people who've resisted the Cartel," he said. "We live by our own rules, on our land, without Cartel interference. At least there's not *much* interference."

Battle took a step toward the man to get a better look at him. "And you're called Dwellers?"

"Yes," said Baadal. "We live in Palo Duro Canyon near Amarillo. We control the canyon. The Cartel has no influence there."

"I don't understand," said Battle. "I thought the Cartel controlled everything between Louisiana, New Mexico, and Oklahoma."

"They do," said Pico. "He's lying. The Cartel controls everything."

"Why would I lie?" asked Baadal. "I am a prisoner as you are. What might I gain through dishonesty?"

"Exactly," said Pico, pointing at him. His eyes darted between Battle and Baadal. "Exactly. If you're a Dweller, why are you a prisoner? You said the Cartel can't touch you."

"I am a scout," Baadal said. He sat up and pulled his shoulders back. He raised his chin. "My job is to warn the elders of any Cartel incursion. I was captured and brought here. I would not talk. I am now with you, destined to die in the Jones."

"I'm totally confused," said Battle. "One, I don't get why you're freaked out, Pico. And two, how is it that the Cartel hasn't taken the canyon? Who exactly are the Dwellers?"

"The Dwellers don't exist," said Pico. "If they did, that would mean there's a way out. If there's a way out, that means I've been wasting my life. It's legend."

"A way out? Wait. What?" Battle squeezed his eyes shut with frustration. "You're talking in riddles."

"It is true," said Baadal. "We exist. We live in the canyon. We have fought back the Cartel. We know of ways to leave, a path north of the wall that separates the Cartel from everyone else."

"I'm completely lost," said Sawyer. "Can somebody start from the beginning?"

"Good idea," said Battle.

"In the early days after the Scourge," said Baadal, "the government collapsed. The national guard was deployed. The federal government used active-duty soldiers from military bases to try to restore order. It didn't work. Too many of their resources were dead or dying from disease. Criminal organizations, corrupt politicians, crooked businesses, they joined forces to seize the opportunity provided by the chaos. They formed the Cartel."

Baadal looked at Pico. "Am I correct so far?"

Pico nodded.

"At the same time," Baadal continued, "there were good people who refused to join the Cartel or become subservient to their dictates."

"How many people?" Battle asked.

"Several thousand," said Baadal. "Of course, we weren't as strong in number as the Cartel, but we were smart. We quickly mobilized and found a singular location to consolidate our strengths. Our leader, Paagal, chose Palo Duro Canyon. It provided us with a natural advantage. There is water at its floor and the terrain is difficult to navigate for those unfamiliar with it."

"Living in a canyon is not a tactical advantage," said Battle. "Why not the high ground? The Fort Davis Mountains maybe?"

"The canyon is intimidating," said Baadal. "It is large. Our patrols need only protect the western edge. Over the last five years, we have made it a fortress. Again, it allows for a tight consolidation of people and resources."

"And the Cartel hasn't tried to attack you?" Battle asked.

"Of course they have," said Baadal. "But our scouts have always given plenty of warning. Our defenses are strong. Each time they would attempt to destroy us, we would decimate their posses. Two years ago, after we killed one of their four generals, we reached a truce. They let us live in the canyon. We promised not to help non-Dwellers escape Cartel-controlled territory."

"If there's a truce," Pico sniped, "why are you a scout? Why are you here?"

"We don't trust the Cartel," said Baadal. "That is why we patrol beyond our land and scout their advances. We know, if captured, we are subject to the Jones. It's a risk we take willingly to protect our fellow Dwellers."

"So why does Pico think you're legend?" asked Battle. "Why doesn't he believe you?"

"Because the Cartel has told its people we don't exist." Baadal shrugged. "If people believed they could live in relative peace without the daily fear of the Cartel's indiscriminate evildoings, it could incite an uprising."

Pico rubbed his mustache, his eyes narrowed with doubt.

"Pico doesn't want to believe we exist because it undermines what he's been taught, Baadal said. "It validates his inability to have acted against the totalitarian state. It's an admission of gullibility and weakness. Those are the traits upon which the Cartel feeds. It's how it has devoured what was once a proud state."

"I'm not weak," snapped Pico. "I'm not gullible."

Baadal looked at Pico without responding, then turned to Battle. "We choose to let the Cartel spread the lies about us because it only helps insulate us. If we are legend, nobody tries to find us or seek our help in escaping. It makes it easier for us to hold up our end of the bargain."

"You keep talking about escaping, about finding a way out," said Battle. "What do you mean?"

"There is a wall that surrounds Cartel territory," said Baadal. "The United States, or what is left of it, built an enormous wall that stretches roughly around what used to be the perimeter of Texas."

"A wall?" asked Battle. "On all but the southern border of Texas?"

"Yes," said Baadal. "It is an incredible sight. It rivals the Great Wall of China. It provided those living outside Texas with jobs and rations at a time when there was little of either. It took two years."

"And the Cartel let them build it?" Sawyer asked.

"Of course," answered Baadal. "It kept the United States out as much as it kept the Cartel in. It provided a real barrier, a finite and physical depiction of their influence."

"But you helped people escape?" Battle asked.

"For a while," said Baadal. "But again, the treaty prevents it. The Cartel has sentries on the wall. If we're caught helping someone to the other side, it could reignite the war between us. Nobody wants that."

Battle asked Pico, "You're still not buying this?"

Pico took a deep breath and plopped onto the stool behind him. His reticence was more than enough answer for Battle. He wouldn't press.

"So you know how the Jones works, then?" Battle asked Baadal.

"Yes."

"And you'll tell us?"

"Yes."

"And if we survive, you'll take us to the canyon, to the other Dwellers?"

Baadal's eyes passed from Battle, to Pico, to Sawyer, and back to Battle. "Yes."

CHAPTER 28

JANUARY 3, 2020, 8:16 PM
SCOURGE -12 YEARS, 9 MONTHS
ALEPPO, SYRIA

Battle retraced his steps in his mind. He replayed the crawl under the fence, heaving Buck onto his shoulders as a last resort, and working his way south and east, closer to the middle of the three bridges.

He rewound his movements to the spot where he was pinned by crossfire. He remembered killing the silhouette, hearing the grieving woman, and retrieving the Type 56 Chinese rifle he now held in his left hand.

Crawl. Shoulders. Pinned. Silhouette. Woman. Weapon.

He looked to his left again. He squeezed his eyes shut.

Pinned. Woman. Weapon.

Battle counted one more time as he took shallow breaths to regulate his elevated heartbeat. He knew where he was. He thought he did. He was maybe one block north and one block west of the bridge. A quick zigzag and he'd be at the western edge of the canal. From there he'd be able to see the checkpoint.

He stepped from the edge of the building and rounded the corner to his left. His head down, he turned to head east and didn't see the woman walking toward him until she was a yard from him. Battle looked up before he ran into her. In the dim, flickering yellow light of a dying streetlamp, he could see her eyes peering at him from behind her black hijab. She was with two children: a boy holding her right hand, a girl holding her left. The three of them froze mid-stride, as did Battle. They stared at each other without saying anything. She could call out at any second. Help would come. It would rain lead. He'd be done.

She glanced at the gun. Her son couldn't take his eyes from it. The girl kept tugging on her mother's arm as if she had something important to say.

Battle knew enough about Islam and Sharia law to understand the delicacy of her situation. It wasn't outright illegal, but it was certainly questionable for a woman to be alone, outside, at night without her husband. Even with two children at her side, she could face serious consequences if the wrong jihadis came to her defense.

Their eyes collectively transfixed, Battle greeted her in Arabic with a customary Islamic greeting, *"As-Salaam Alaykum." Peace be unto you.*

The woman blinked for the first time. Because of the hijab, Battle couldn't read her reaction, if there was one. She looked down at her son and then at her daughter. The girl was still squeezing her mother's hand and yanking on her arm. The boy had his gaze locked on the Type 56.

Battle tried to smile and he repeated himself but looked at the boy. *"As-Salaam Alaykum,"* he said and grunted from another seizure in his lower back. He tried again to shift his weight from the nerve pain in his right leg.

The woman bowed her head and replied, *"Wa-Alaykum."* She looked up again and her eyes shifted from Battle's to over his left shoulder and grew wide with panic.

"Afifah," a man's voice called from behind Battle. It was gruff and insistent, demanding she come to him. *"Afifah, tueal 'iilaa huna."*

The woman bowed her head again and pulled her children past Battle, scurrying toward the voice. Battle's muscles tensed. He squeezed his eyes shut and stood as motionless as he could with Buck draped over his shoulders.

"You are American?" the man asked. "You are American Army?"

"Yes," Battle said, turning only slightly to address the man.

"What happen your friend soldier?" The voice was louder and accompanied by deliberate footsteps. The man said something to the woman, Afifah, and she responded. Battle couldn't understand the exchange. "What happen?" the man repeated. "He's badly hurt," said Battle. "He was shot in his leg. He's lost a lot of blood."

The man stepped to face Battle. He was average height and build. His wiry, short black hair was gray at the temples. His face was peppered with at least a couple of days' worth of stubble. He was wearing jeans and a dark-colored shirt, its collar curled at the ends.

He had a pistol in his hands. Battle guessed it was a GSh-18. It looked Russian and was a pretty common find on Syrian civilians. It could hold nine shots. Battle concluded, without thought, that one was enough given the current circumstances.

The man stood directly in front of Battle and waved the handgun as he spoke. "You talk my daughter?"

Battle stopped himself from reflexively turning around to look at the woman. "Yes. I wished her peace."

"She say that," said the man. He eyed the rifle, his eyes narrowed, and he looked back to Battle. "That gun. Not American Army."

"No," Battle said. "I found it."

The man suppressed a laugh. "Find it? I don't think so, American Army soldier. I hear shoot. I hear lots of shoot."

Battle sighed and flexed his neck and adjusted Buck on his shoulders. The tension sent another jolt of electricity running down his back and through his right leg.

"I no like these men," he said. "I like American Army soldier. I help."

Battle's muscles involuntarily relaxed. "Thank you."

The man motioned to Buck. "You put down. I help. We go my house."

Battle shook his head. "I need to get across the bridge. There's a checkpoint."

The man wagged his finger and pursed his lips. "No. No. Bridge no good. You come my house." He reached again for Buck.

Battle dropped to a knee, and the man helped lower Buck from his shoulders. Together the two of them carried Buck. They quickly followed his daughter and the children west, away from the bridge, and to a three-story building on a dark street.

Battle considered the danger of letting the man help him. He didn't know him. It could be a trap. He might be leading them to nasty, tortuous deaths. Then again, he could have shot them in the street. He hadn't.

This was worth the risk, especially if the bridge was as heavily guarded as the man suggested it was. They reached the battered door to the building, and the woman held it open for her father and Battle to rush Buck inside. The children led them up a narrow set of stairs to a landing on the second floor. They turned down a hallway, sconces lighting their way to its end. The woman rushed past Battle, Buck, and her father to the door, a waft of an organic, earthy, musky scent breezing behind her. She hurriedly jammed a key into the lock and turned it. She shouldered the door open and disappeared inside the apartment, waving the children to join her.

The man led Buck and Battle through the door into a large, warmly lit open room. He guided Battle through the room, along a short hall, and into a sparsely decorated bedroom. The bed wasn't much more than a thin mattress and some sheets. A bedside table held a lamp and a dog-eared copy of the Koran.

The man helped Battle lay Buck on the mattress. Buck was still unconscious and unaffected by the movement of his arms and legs into the bed.

The daughter appeared in the doorway of the room. She stood silently, her hands on the frame as she leaned against it.

The man looked at Buck's wound and his lips curled. He swallowed hard and looked at Battle. "We clean," he said. Then he poked at Battle's left arm, eliciting a wince. "We clean too."

The man turned to his daughter, pointed at her and motioned for her to leave. She disappeared toward the main living area of the apartment. He was speaking with his hands, searching for words in English. "I tell daughter," he said, his eyes turned to the ceiling, "I tell her to get medicine. Clean. Yes?"

Battle nodded. "I'm Captain Battle," he said, offering his hand to the stranger. "Thank you."

The man took Battle's hands with both of his, shaking them vigorously. "Battle is your name?"

"Yes."

"My name is Nizar," he said. "My daughter is Afifah."

Nizar braced himself against the side of the bed and lowered himself to his knees. He hooked his fingers inside the edges of the ragged hole in Buck's pant leg. He pulled the hole wider, ripping the fabric and exposing the wound.

Battle swallowed the bile rising in his throat when he got a clear look at the damage to Buck's leg since they'd evacuated the IED blast site. It was varying shades of red and black, except for the torn pinkish meat climbing angrily outward from inside his leg.

Nizar looked up at Battle, seemingly unfazed by the depth and condition of the filthy wound. "I was doctor," he said. "Before war."

Afifah returned with her arms full. She was carrying a veritable first aid kit of supplies. She sidled up to the bed and dropped the bounty onto the floor next to her father.

Nizar first took a pair of scissors and cut away Buck's pant leg at the groin. He also cut free the tourniquet fashioned above Buck's knee. The wound pooled with blood, and he picked up a clear bottle labeled in Arabic and unscrewed the cap. He held the bottle directly over the leg and then squeezed it, spraying the liquid into and around the wound. The flesh immediately sizzled white, bubbles expanding beyond its edge, draining from Buck's leg onto the sheets.

Buck's eyes popped wide for an instant, and he eked out a semblance of a groan. He tried sitting up.

Nizar looked at Battle. "Help him."

Battle moved to Buck's head and pressed gently on his shoulder, forcing him to lie flat. Buck mumbled something and a stray tear ran from his eye along his cheek.

Nizar then took a pair of large tweezers in one hand and a lighter in the other. He flicked the lighter and ran the tweezer through the flame. He blew on the wound to lessen the still-percolating peroxide and picked through the wound with the tweezers.

His eyes tightened and his jaw set as he pulled out a bullet fragment. He dropped it on the floor and plucked two more pieces from the mess of Buck's lower leg.

Battle turned his attention from the surgery and focused on Buck as Nizar poured sugar into the wound. Battle knew from anecdotal battlefield chatter that sugar liquefied when mixed with any fluid, including blood. If poured into a wound, it pulled the moisture from tissue exposed to bacteria, killing or lessening the chance for infection.

Nizar sprinkled granules around the edges of the injury. "The bone is broken. I cannot fix. I can stop bleeding. It will hurt."

He gave instructions to Afifah. A minute later she returned with what looked like a short-handled branding iron. It was glowing red.

Nizar put his hand on Battle's shoulder and then hugged himself tightly. "You hold him," he told Battle. "Hold him."

Battle's eyes danced between the doctor and the red-hot iron. He laid his torso on top of Buck's to press him into the mattress and turned his head away from Nizar as the doctor pressed the iron onto the wound.

Battle squeezed his eyes shut, hoping to block the sound of skin sizzling, the smell of it burning. With a delayed nervous response, Buck seized and then jerked against Battle's body. A guttural moan crescendoed into a curdled scream. Buck was thrashing in the bed, violently resisting the pain.

Nazir again touched Battle on his shoulder. "Good," he said. Battle, his body still pushing down on Buck's, turned to see Afifah leaving the room with the iron. Buck's flailing diminished, and Battle pushed himself to his feet. Buck's chest was heaving. Sweat pooled on his neck, and his hair was matted flat against his head.

Nazir tore open a square package with his teeth and pulled out what looked like gauze. He separated it into several sheets and, one by one, stuffed them into the gaping, cauterized hole running across Buck's shin and calf.

Once he'd finished packing the wound, Nazir took a wide strip of fabric and wound it around what was left of Buck's lower leg. He called something to Afifah, who appeared a moment later with a glass of water and some pills.

"Kill pain," Nazir said. He cradled Buck's head and force-fed him the medicine. "He live. Foot no good. He live. Now you." Battle nodded and sat on the edge of the bed, ready to be the patient to his newfound doctor friend. "Why are you helping us?"

Nazir shrugged as he cut away Battle's sleeve. "American Army help me. Help my daughter. Help her children."

Battle winced and bit the inside of his cheek as the man probed his injury. It was deeper than a graze. "How?"

"My family like America. Like Army. You help Syria. Some people do not like American Army. They do not like me. They kill my son. Almost kill me and my family. American Army stop them."

"Why not leave?" Battle asked. "If you're in danger."

Nazir laughed and stopped working on the injury. He held Battle's arm with the nimble fingers of a surgeon. His smile faded and his stare intensified. He spoke slowly and clearly. "Syria is my home. A man does not leave his home. I...protect...hide...stay quiet. No people take my home from me. If I die, I die here. My home."

CHAPTER 29

OCTOBER 16, 2037, 7:53 AM
SCOURGE + 5 YEARS
LUBBOCK, TEXAS

It was a Friday. The sun was low on the flat horizon surrounding Lubbock, Texas. Jones Stadium's walls climbed steeply toward the clear pale blue morning. High wisps of clouds floated above an otherwise empty sky.

The stadium could hold sixty thousand people. There were maybe five thousand cluttered along the lower levels near what would have been the field's fifty-yard line.

They were huddled in coats and jackets. Some of them had blankets draped across their shoulders or laps. The collective puffs of breath from the waiting crowd hung in a haze above them.

The field was covered with remnants of artificial turf. It wasn't the bright cheerful green that had greeted football players before the Scourge. It was more of a brownish color, stained in large splotches from the blood of those who'd been forced into the arena and lost.

Battle was standing inside a holding area at one end of the stadium. He was one of twelve gladiators chosen to fight that day. Each of the men carried their own manifestation of fear on their faces. Some were wide-eyed, others were trembling. A few seemed defiant and brimming with testosterone. The group was ripe with body odor and the smell of urine.

Battle didn't fear death; however, the idea of pain, of not knowing how much suffering he might endure, was all consuming. He'd learned in the Army that the threat of pain was far more effective a weapon than the pain itself. It was true.

Battle put his hand on Sawyer's shoulder and whispered into the boy's ear, "Stay with me. Stay close. Do what I tell you to do. We'll make it."

Sawyer nodded and bit his lower lip. He brushed the hair from in front of his eyes. Battle felt the tension in the boy's shoulder as he gripped it and let go.

The large doors that separated the holding area from the stadium floor swung open, sending in the blinding pinkish light of the dawn and the loud rumble of the awaiting crowd. Three grunts powered through the opening and slammed the door behind them. The loud bang sent a shudder through Battle's core.

"All right," one of the grunts announced, "here's how it's gonna work. There are twelve of you. All of you are traitors, thieves, or people we don't like. We could have killed you already."

One of the testosterone-emitting gladiators snarled, "Why didn't you?"

"This is more fun," said the grunt. He licked his teeth. "I mean, I ain't a history student, but this is good for morale. The Romans did it. They was an empire. If it's good enough for the Romans, my guess is the generals think it's good enough for the Cartel."

The same gladiator snickered. "Killing us is good for morale?"

"Seems to be," said the grunt. "We always get good crowds. They come from all over the region. Now shut up and listen."

A grumble rolled through the assembled gladiators. Battle eyed the men he didn't know. None of them looked capable of surviving the Jones. Granted, Battle didn't know exactly what lay ahead, but he couldn't see any of the men faring well in a game designed to kill them.

"There are six from the Cartel that's gonna fight you," said the grunt. "They'll have horses and weapons. You don't. It ain't gonna be a fair fight."

"No weapons?" said one of the gladiators standing behind Battle. "We get nothing?"

"I didn't say that," said the grunt. "You don't walk into the Jones with any weapons. There's a few out there on the ground if you can get 'em. Like I said, it ain't fair. That's not to say we don't want it to be entertaining."

"So there are weapons?" asked another gladiator. "We just have to find them?"

"Yup."

Battle cleared his throat. "What happens when we kill all of the fighters?"

The three grunts laughed. "When?"

"When," Battle stated.

"That's funny," said the leader of the grunts. "You're funny. I can't tell you what would happen *if* you killed 'em all 'cause ain't nobody ever done it."

The grunts laughed again.

"All right," said the grunt leader. "We're gonna open the doors here in a second. Then you run out and you fight. I mean run. Don't walk. Don't be lackadaisical. Run."

The grunt leader planted his hands on his hips. He eyeballed the assembled gladiators and pointed at them. "You can kill each other if you want, but it probably ain't a good idea if you plan on killing *all* of our fighters."

Battle looked at Sawyer, Pico, and Baadal the Dweller. They nodded at each other, acknowledging they'd do what they could to keep each other alive.

From beyond the doors there was a loud roar and the rhythmic thump of feet pounding on the aluminum stadium bleachers.

The doors swung open. "Go now!" yelled the grunts. "Go! Go! Go!"

The dozen men pushed against one another out onto the edge of the field. To their right was a large crowd.

Battle's eyes took a moment to adjust to the light as he ran to the front of the pack. By the time they did, he was a quarter of the way across the field, nearing its center. He scanned the turf, looking for weapons and for his adversaries. He didn't see either.

Then the crowd roared and Battle heard the thunder of horses behind him. He spun around in time to see the slowest of the gladiators knocked to the ground and trampled.

There were six horses and six men atop them. Battle stood frozen with Sawyer at his side. Three of the men had shotguns. One of them had some sort of flail or mace, which he was swinging in a large circle at the end of its chain. One looked to be unarmed, but Battle couldn't be certain. The last was carrying a crossbow, a quiver of bolts strapped to his back. He unwound an arrow right into a gladiator's back and through his chest. The gladiator squeaked, grappled with the arrow as he fell, and collapsed.

The horses were approaching fast and fanning out to attack the gladiators one on one. Battle looked past them toward the doors through which they'd entered. To the left of the doors, pressed against the wall of the stadium, was a small pile of objects. He couldn't tell what they were, but guessed they were the promised weapons. He'd have to get past the horses and their armed riders to reach them. Battle took a deep breath, trying to slow the chaos around him. He gained focus and ran straight at the horses approaching him.

One of the shotgun-carrying grunts took aim at a short gladiator who seemed dumbstruck. An easy target, the man took two in the chest and fell to the ground in a heap. The grunt who killed him didn't adjust his path, and his horse tripped over the dying gladiator. It tumbled to the ground, snorting and neighing as it fell, its fragile legs kicking up into the air. It landed on top of its rider, crushing him. Battle was feet from the horse. He bolted toward it with a quick step and pulled the shotgun from underneath the animal. The rider wouldn't need it anymore.

He knew it was empty from the twin shots that had killed the gladiator. He gripped it like a baseball bat and wrapped both of his hands around the warm barrel. He planted his feet and swung at the next approaching rider. Swinging as hard as he could, he hit the rider across his side, knocking the grunt from his saddle. His shotgun flew to the ground, and Sawyer scrambled to pick it up.

"Run to the doors!" Battle called and moved to the stunned, winded grunt gasping for air on the ground. Battle swung the Browning again, this time like an axe, and drove the butt into the man's chest. He swung again, connected again, and was rewarded with a shallow crack.

Battle tossed the shotgun to the ground and ran, blinders on, toward the pile of weapons. Sawyer beat him there. He was already picking through the offerings.

"This is all junk!" Sawyer said. "A pocketknife, a two-by-four, a can of ball bearings, and a slingshot."

Battle smirked. It was *his* slingshot. "The slingshot will do. You good with that shotgun?"

Sawyer shrugged.

"Point it away from me," Battle said. "You'll be fine."

Battle spun back to gauge the fight's progress. He counted five gladiators on the ground. There were four horsemen still on the attack. Only one of them had a shotgun.

Battle slid the tactical slingshot onto his right wrist and eased the pistol grip into his hand. He uncapped the bottle of ball bearings with his teeth and stood up.

"Let's get back there," he said to Sawyer.

***

Salomon Pico was running for his life. The grunt with the flail was behind him and gaining. Pico tried to dodge him by darting back and forth, but it didn't work. They were at the far end of the field, well past where anyone else had run. Pico turned at the moment the spiked head of the flail swung upward at him. He ducked, lost his balance, and tumbled to the ground. He slid along the stained, aged turf and into the stadium wall.

Pico was done. He backed himself against the wall and tried unsuccessfully to regain his footing. The grunt laughed and pulled his horse to a stop. He dismounted and for effect turned to the crowd a half-stadium away and raised his arms in triumph. The crowd roared its approval.

He swung the flail in circles. Faster and faster it spun, and he walked toward Pico, who cowered against the wall.

Pico buried his head and covered it with his arms. He squeezed his eyes shut, expecting a fatal blow at any second. Worse, he thought, would be a nonfatal blow. Instead he heard a grunt, cursing, and the sound of a scuffle.

He looked up to see Baadal on top of the grunt. He had him pinned to the ground, his legs wrapped around the grunt's neck. The grunt's eyes bulged as he reached for Baadal's thighs, clawing for breath.

Pico saw the flail on the ground a few feet from the struggle. He crawled over to it and picked it up. With one hand he pushed himself to his feet and swung the heavy weapon in a circle, gaining momentum.

He caught Baadal's eyes and shouted, "Move!"

Baadal released his hold and rolled away from the grunt. The grunt clutched his own neck, his chest heaving as he gasped for air. He likely never saw Pico slam the spinning spiked iron ball into his face. Blood, cartilage, and bone exploded outward. Pico let go of the weapon and left it embedded in the grunt.

"Thank you," he called to Baadal.

The Dweller yanked the flail from the dead man, eliciting a sucking sound as he removed it. He nodded and waved Pico to follow him back toward the center of the field.

Pico ran behind Baadal as he worked his way toward the action. The Dweller, Pico surmised, was not afraid. He whipped the flail to his side as he ran, spinning it like a wheel propelling him forward, spitting blood and matter onto Pico. He wiped it from his face and joined the fray, choosing to help one of the gladiators who'd already taken an arrow to his leg. The grunt drew a second bolt from his quiver and set it into the bow. He lowered it at the gladiator who was kneeling on his good leg. His injured one was extended outward as if he were stretching it. He was intermittently squealing in pain and begging for mercy.

The grunt pulled his finger to the trigger, but before he fired, Baadal released the flail. He hurled it, whipping it a short distance through the air until it connected with the bow and knocked it from the grunt's hands.

Pico ran to the side of the horse and dove to the ground. He gathered the bow into his lap, aimed upward, and tugged on the trigger. The bolt shot forty-five degrees and drilled into the grunt's side. The short distance meant the projectile was traveling with a lot of force.

The grunt's mouth dropped open. He blinked rapidly, his nostrils flaring. He reached for the bolt and tried tugging on it as he rode past Pico and Baadal. Baadal ran alongside the horse for a moment and then athletically leapt into the saddle behind the grunt, tossing him from the horse.

Pico held onto the empty crossbow and, crouched low, made his way to the injured grunt as a shotgun blast tore through the man's torso. The rider galloped past, reloading his Browning for another run.

"Get the quiver!" Baadal yelled to Pico. "Get it now!" Baadal turned his horse and ran it toward the entrance to help surviving gladiators on that side of the field.

Pico scurried to the grunt he'd killed with the bolt. Instead of grabbing the quiver, which was trapped underneath the man's body, he drew a single bolt and loaded it into the crossbow. He got to his feet in time to see the shotgun-wielding grunt galloping straight at him. Pico didn't take the time to aim. He fired. He missed.

***

Battle saw three horses with riders. One of them carried Baadal. The Dweller was driving his horse toward him. One of the surviving grunts was farther away and was bearing down on Pico. The other, the one who Battle had thought was unarmed, was circling around for another pass; then Battle realized that the grunt *was* armed. He was flinging throwing stars at his prey. He'd punctured and killed two of the three remaining gladiators.

"Throwing stars?" Battle thought aloud. "Are you kidding me? Does he think he's a ninja?"

The words of the grunt inside the holding area rang in his head. *"Like I said, it ain't fair. But that's not to say we don't want it to be entertaining."*

Battle dumped the ball bearings into a pile on the ground. He knelt, grabbed a pair of them from the turf, fingered them into the leather pouch, and pulled the rubber tubing taut. He aimed at the approaching throwing-star ninja and plucked the fingers of his left hand free, releasing the pouch and firing the ballistic ball bearings with enough force that when they hit the ninja on the bridge of his nose, they shattered it.

The grunt cried out, screaming, "My eyes! I can't see!" He floundered atop the saddle, squirming in pain as his horse maintained its gallop toward Battle.

Battle drew back the leather again.

Pow!

A deafening shotgun blast stopped Battle's draw. The shell exploded into the ninja's chest, making him immediately forget about his nose and eyes. He grunted and moaned, slumping forward.

Battle turned to his left and saw Sawyer with the smoking shotgun pulled to his shoulder. The horse galloped past them and Sawyer anxiously looked at Battle.

"Good job," Battle said with a hint of surprise.

There was one grunt left. He was halfway across the field between Pico and Baadal.

Battle looked over toward the crowd, an indistinguishable mass of people cheering death. In a place rife with decay and pain, they wanted more. Or maybe they wanted others to suffer a fate worse than their own. Human nature was a bitch.

***

Pico's errant shot should have been the end of him. For the second time in as many minutes, Baadal was in the right place at the right time.

The grunt pulled the trigger on his Browning the split second after Baadal dove from his horse and tackled the grunt, knocking both of them to the ground.

The shotgun blast sprayed to the left of Pico, grazing his leg but doing little damage. Baadal, though, was knocked unconscious by the leap and fall.

The grunt was dazed but awake. He rolled over onto Baadal and started pounding him with his fists. Unable to fight back, the Dweller absorbed the beating, unaware of what was happening to him.

Pico scrambled to his feet and ran to the grunt. He pulled back his right leg and drove his foot into the side of the grunt's face. The grunt flew from Baadal's limp body, hitting his head on the ground.

Pico looked around and found the shotgun still loaded with a single shell. As the grunt tried dragging himself away from Pico, the mustachioed Cartel traitor stuck the barrel against the grunt's spine and pulled the trigger.

Pico moved back to Baadal and knelt beside him. He shook the Dweller awake.

Baadal was bleeding from his nose and mouth. He was missing teeth. His jaw was the color of rotten banana: brown and black and bruised. His eyes fluttered open and he tried to speak, though a groan was all he could muster.

"You saved me again," Pico said. "I owe you twice now."

Pico looked across the field, surveying the aftermath.

All six of the grunts were dead. Five of the gladiators lived. At the middle of the field was a gladiator he didn't know. The man was on his knees but alive. Across the other side of the field, walking toward him, were Battle and Lola's boy, Sawyer.

Sawyer carried a shotgun over his shoulder. Battle had something in his left hand. Pico couldn't tell what it was. Pico smiled. His eyes dampened and welled.

They'd survived. They'd beaten the Cartel again.

Pico looked down again at Baadal. The Dweller's pupils were dilated. His breathing was normal.

"Seems like you saved me once," said Baadal, his voice raspier. "So you only owe me once more."

Pico laughed and reached out to help Baadal sit up. He turned his back to the stadium crowd, his hands tucked under the Dweller's arms, and lifted him to his feet.

Salomon Pico didn't see Cyrus Skinner take aim and fire the shot that killed him. However, he heard it. And he felt it. At first he thought someone had punched him in the back. Then the searing heat told him it wasn't a punch. He felt a tear in his abdomen. The heat from the bullet ripping through him evaporated into nothing. His legs went numb and he dropped to his knees, falling into the back of Baadal's legs.

Pico heard a woman's scream from the crowd. He heard Battle calling out to him. He sensed Baadal trying to help him. Pico knew it was futile.

He couldn't feel his legs or move his arms as he lay there on the turf, his blood pooling underneath his paralyzed body and adding to the brown patina of the field.

Pico was on his stomach, his head turned to the side. He tried focusing his vision but couldn't. He saw flashes of his life advancing like a slideshow in front of him. There was the sting of his mother's drunken slap and her prophecy that he would amount to nothing. He relived the confusion and desperation of watching his father wave goodbye and never come back. He smelled the sweet aroma of marijuana and felt the pangs of hunger his first high invoked. Pico felt the rumble of his Camaro's engine as he shifted into third, the squeeze of his girlfriend's hand on his leg. He recalled his fingers spinning the lock on a safe, the satisfaction of sensing he'd hit the combination, and the anticipation of that moment before he pulled it open. He saw himself pouring a shot of Jägermeister for a patron and then downing one himself while looking over his shoulder at the boss's office door. Pico could taste the licorice on his tongue and hear Dusty Hill and Billy Gibbons strumming in the background.

His mind snapped to the day his girlfriend died on the floor of their efficiency apartment above the club where she danced, coughing and wheezing until the fluid in her lungs was too much. He was holding her hand as the warmth dissipated, until she was cold. Pico was growing cold. The warmth of his body was draining from him.

He took his last ragged breath thinking about what he could have done differently, how he could have lived his life more honorably than he had.

The air left his lungs and didn't return. Pico's eyes, still wet with fresh tears of unmitigated joy, fixed. His tongue dropped from his open lips. His fingers twitched and stopped.

Salomon Pico was dead. This time it was for real.

CHAPTER 30

JANUARY 4, 2020, 6:43 AM
SCOURGE -12 YEARS, 9 MONTHS
ALEPPO, SYRIA

Battle opened his eyes to a low hum and cold toes. He was on
the vinyl sofa in Nazir's living room. The sun, peeking above
the horizon, cast a pinkish-orange hue through the open
eastern-facing window. The warmth of the space had given
way to the chill of dawn.

Nazir was kneeling on a prayer rug, his back to the window.
He was reciting the Salat al-Fajr, the first of the five daily
Muslim prayers. Battle closed his eyes and listened to Nazir's
soft voice, his cadence as he recited the words. He opened
them again when Nazir was quiet.

He was rolling up his rug, respectfully tending to its edges.
He looked over at Battle and bowed his head.

"Good morning, Battle," he said, a smile spreading across his
stubbled cheeks. "You sleep good. You snore."

Battle sat up and spun his feet to the floor. He looked at the
bandage cleanly wrapped around his upper arm. "How is
Buck?"

"Sleeping."

"We need to leave," said Battle.

"Too much danger."

"I need to get him back to the checkpoint and back to base.
They can airlift him to Landstuhl from there. You helped him,
but he has to get to a hospital or he loses his foot."

"Landstuhl. American Army hospital?"

"Yes."

"No," Nazir said. "We will wait."

"We can't wait, Nazir," Battle pressed. "We cannot stay here.
We thank you. We hope for peace for you and your family.
We have *got* to go."

"Too much danger."

"Okay," Battle said. "You tell me when there isn't too much danger and we'll go then."

Nazir turned, the prayer rug tucked under his arm, and looked out the window. He took a deep breath and walked to it, staring out above the rooftops. He was looking east, toward the checkpoint on the other side of the canal.

Nazir held his shoulders back, his chest out. His feet were shoulder-width apart, planted firmly on the terrazzo floor. Without turning around, he answered Battle's question. "You are right, Battle. There is no time when danger leaves."

Battle sat forward on the sofa, the vinyl squeaking under his shifting weight. He took as deep a breath as he had in two days and exhaled. His back felt thick with bruising, and his neck throbbed from aching, strained muscles.

"We will go," said Nazir. He turned around, his eyes focused on Battle's. "I will take you."

Battle rose to his feet. "No. You shouldn't do that. We'll make it."

Nazir motioned over his shoulder toward the window. "No. The bridge is too much. You need help."

Battle walked to Nazir and stood in front of him. "Tell us what to do, how to cross the bridge. You cannot leave your daughter and your grandchildren."

"Allah will watch over me," Nazir said, his eyes glossy with emotion. "Allah will provide what is meant to be. I go talk with Afifah. We get you clothing."

Thirty minutes later Battle, Buck, and Nazir left the apartment building, stepping into the crisp winter morning. The streets were mostly empty. It was a Saturday morning. The shops and cafes hadn't yet opened. The late morning hustle was hours away.

All three men were wearing traditional kaftans and white headscarves. Battle and Nazir were armed with handguns. Buck used a snapped broomstick as a cane and leaned on Battle to limp along. He was groggy from the painkillers, and Battle was convinced Buck was only partially aware.

As they moved into the street, Nazir turned to look back at his home. Afifah was standing at the open window, her children flanking her. They waved in unison. The girl was leaning on the sill, rocking back and forth. The boy offered a toothy smile to his grandfather.

Nazir offered a final wave and blew a kiss. His daughter caught it and pulled the children away from the window, sliding it closed.

"She is not my true daughter," said Nazir. "She is my son's wife. I call her daughter. Her parents are also dead."

"You take care of her?" Battle asked.

"She takes care of me," he said. "Her family blessed us with many riches before the war. Praise be to Allah."

They stepped onto the narrow, crumbling sidewalk on the side of the street opposite Nazir's home. Battle helped Buck navigate the curb and they turned the corner to the spot where they'd encountered each other the night before.

"The kaftan helps from a distance," said Nazir. "When we are close to the bridge, it will not help."

"Roger that," said Battle.

They walked opposite oncoming traffic, which was virtually nonexistent, and approached the final intersection before reaching the bridge. They stopped at the corner and Battle looked east to the canal. There were two uniformed, armed guards standing at the stone balustrades that marked either side of the bridge. They were wearing the same paramilitary outfits as the men Battle confronted at the railyard the night before. There was a third walking west across the bridge. All three carried AK rifles.

"You think we can talk our way past?" Battle asked.

Nazir shrugged and started across the street. "I hope. I have idea." He clasped his hands together, the wide draped sleeves of his kaftan hiding his gun. Battle did the same and followed Nazir to the bridge. Buck used the cane and Battle's shoulder for balance while he essentially hopped along.

They were halfway across the street when the guards saw them. The two at the balustrades immediately raised their weapons and pulled them to their shoulders, aiming the muzzles directly at Nazir, who was a couple of steps ahead of Battle and Buck.

The third guard stopped short of the western edge of the canal and leaned on the southern railing, using it for leverage and he too aimed his weapon at Nazir.

Nazir called out to the men in Arabic and kept approaching. The men replied aggressively. Battle was certain they were telling Nazir to stop. He could sense their tension, even from a distance.

Nazir appeared undeterred by the guards. He shuffled forward until he was within a few feet of them. He looked back at Battle and Buck, referencing them with his head as he spoke.

The guards listened but did not lower their weapons. One of them kept glancing over at Battle and Buck as they moved closer. Battle lowered his head and suggested Buck do the same; the less obvious their ethnicity, the better.

Battle watched his sandaled feet move step by step. He glanced up occasionally to make sure he was headed straight for the bridge. He was looking down when he heard Nazir raise his voice. He shouted something in Arabic before calling to Battle, "Run!"

CHAPTER 31

OCTOBER 16, 2037, 8:15 AM
SCOURGE + 5 YEARS
LUBBOCK, TEXAS

Battle heard the shot and saw Pico drop to his knees, falling into Baadal. The sound of it cracked through the air like thunder and silenced the crowd. He ran toward Pico, knowing all the while there was nothing he could do to help him. To his right, standing inside the barrier that separated the field from the bleachers, was Cyrus Skinner. His white hat shadowed his face, but Battle knew it was him.

His six-shooter was aimed at where Pico had stood, a thin trail of smoke drifting upward from the muzzle. He lowered the weapon and holstered it, turning away from the man he'd killed and climbing over the barrier back into the stands.

Battle reached Pico after he took his last breath. He slid to his knees and rolled Pico over onto his back. Battle looked at his friend's dead eyes, his tongue flapping from his open mouth, the broad stain of blood on his shirt.

"Skinner!" he screamed, more of a primal roar than a warning or a threat.

Battle picked up the crossbow from the ground, loaded a bolt, and began a precise march toward the crowd. Skinner had blended into the mass of people in the stands, and Battle couldn't find him. He scanned from left to right, the bow following his gaze as he panned. The crowd shifted, ducked, and screamed as he searched for the target.

He reached the center of the field and was feet from the barrier when he saw the innumerable weapons pointing back at him. Still, he pivoted from left to right to left with his finger on the crossbow's trigger.

"Hold up there," came a voice from the crowd. "Put down the bow before you get hurt, Battle."

Battle swung the bow toward the voice. On the other end of
the bolt was General Roof in his distinctive black hat and
white beard. "I'm not putting this down." Seething anger
dripped with each word.

Roof raised his hands to shoulder height and waved them in
surrender. "Have it your way, Battle. I'm suggesting we have
some folks with itchy trigger fingers. You might be best to say
your piece without the bow."

Battle's eyes darted back and forth, trying to focus. He was
looking for the white hat. He couldn't find it.

"Let me come down there," said General Roof, his hands still
raised. "We can talk about this." The general started moving
through the crowd, people sliding on their seats and making
room for him to navigate the bleachers. He reached the
bottom row and carefully climbed over the barrier. His limp
was pronounced as he walked to within a foot of the bolt.
Battle had it aimed right at his head.

"I want Skinner," said Battle, jabbing the bow closer to the
general's head. He looked into Roof's eyes. There was
something familiar about them. "Give me Skinner. Then you
can do to me whatever you want."

Roof chuckled. "You really aren't in a position to demand
anything right now, Battle. I understand your frustration.
Believe me, I do."

Battle looked past the general's shoulder, looking for the
white hat. He didn't see it.

"What Skinner did was…rude," said Roof. "He seems to have
a penchant for incivility. It's a trait that has its plusses and
minuses, I'll admit."

"We won," said Battle through clenched teeth. "We beat your
men."

The general nodded, unfazed by the weapon aimed between his eyes. "You did. It was impressive. Let's be perfectly honest about this. Salomon Pico was a traitor. He was a rat. There was absolutely no circumstance under which he'd have left the Jones alive. None."

"So you murdered him in cold blood," Battle spat.

Roof's eyes widened underneath an arched brow. "I'm surprised at you, Battle. You're a soldier. You, better than most, know what war is about. This is war. You are the enemy."

"I'm not your enemy," said Battle. "I'm just trying to survive."

Roof shook his head. "Is that all?"

"Yes."

"Then you should have stayed home," Roof said. "Instead you're trying to exact revenge; you're hoping to steal our property and disrupt our business."

"Your property?"

Roof pointed over Battle's shoulder to Sawyer. "That boy is our property. His mother is our property." Roof snapped his fingers. "Bring the woman here!" he yelled without leaving Battle's glare.

Battle looked to the crowd. Standing and moving down the bleachers with Skinner's help was Lola. Battle lost his breath for an instant. The sight of her sent a wave of electricity through his body.

"Lola!" Battle called to her. "Are you okay?"

"She's fine," said Roof. "And I'll let you have her."

"What?"

"Skinner would have her strung up," said Roof. "He'd defile her and then kill her slowly in front of her son. He's that upset."

Skinner climbed over the barrier and yanked Lola by the arm. He dragged her by the elbow until they were standing behind General Roof. Battle lowered the crossbow.

Lola's cheeks were bruised, and there was a cut on her upper lip, though she appeared otherwise okay. Tears streamed down her face. Her nose bubbled with snot as she tried to contain herself. She whimpered softly. She looked even thinner somehow.

"I was telling Battle here that we're going to give him the woman," said Roof.

Skinner's face crumpled into an angry mess. He cursed the general and protested the decision. "You're plain stupid," said Skinner. "And you're weak."

Roof's face transformed and he snarled, quickly turning from Battle and grabbing Skinner by the throat. He squeezed, nearly lifting Skinner from his feet. Skinner's hat dropped to the ground. He let go of Lola and gripped Roof's thick wrist with both of his hands.

"You are the fool," he growled. "Do not question me or I'll put the bolt through your eye myself." He let go and shoved Skinner to the ground. He looked to the crowd and yelled, "Does anyone else have a problem with my authority?" He spread his arms wide. "Does anyone wish to challenge me?" There was no response from the crowd. Roof cleared his throat and turned back to Battle. He let out a deep sigh and forced a smile. "Where was I?"

"You were about to give me Lola," said Battle.

"Yes. I was," Roof said. "I'm giving you a reprieve. It's a reward for surviving today. It's a warning to steer clear of our business. It's a thank you for reminding me of the importance of keeping my people in line."

"What do you mean?"

Roof shrugged. "I'm letting you go," he said. "Take the woman, her boy, and the Dweller. Leave. Don't come back."

"I don't understand."

"I couldn't be more clear, Battle. You are free to go. You have free passage out of Lubbock in whatever direction you choose to travel. Of course, you'll leave that crossbow here. I'm not giving you food, water, or a horse, but you're free."

"That's a death sentence," said Battle. "No supplies and no transportation. You might as well kill us here."

"You said you weren't a warrior," Roof explained. "You said you were trying to survive. So go. Survive."

Battle dropped the crossbow to the ground and reached for Lola's hand. Instead of taking his hand, she dove into his body, wrapping her arms around him and holding him tight. She buried her face in his chest. Then she let go and ran to Sawyer. Battle turned to see them embrace and swallowed past a stubborn ache in his throat.

"What about the other dude?" Battle asked, pointing to the remaining gladiator. "Do we take him?"

"If you wish," said Roof. "He'll only be another mouth to feed, but it's up to you."

"We'll take him," said Battle and waved to the man to join him.

General Roof turned to the crowd, cupped his hands around his mouth, and announced his decision. "I am letting these people go!" he said. "They have earned the right to die on their own. I am banishing them from Lubbock without food, water, weapons, or transportation. None of you is to help them."

Skinner, still on the ground, spat onto the turf. "This is wrong."

Roof pointed a finger at him and then raised it to his lips. He looked back at Battle. "Go. Now. Before I change my mind. You can climb the stands to the first exit. It'll lead you outside of the stadium."

"What about Pico?" asked Battle. "Shouldn't we bury him?"

"Leave that to me," said Roof. "He won't know any different regardless of what I do."

Battle led the others over the barrier and into the stands. The crowd made it difficult for them to push their way upward to the exit. Some were hissing at them. A grunt spat in Battle's face. Others lowered their heads so as not to look Battle in the eye. There was one woman who whispered a prayer of God's speed. The banished five eventually cleared the crowds and found their way to a long concourse that led them down and out of the stadium.

A sentry perched atop the stadium's Spanish Renaissance facade watched them walk across the highway north of the stadium. He signaled down to the general that they were on their way.

The crowd soon followed, filing quietly out of the stadium and back to their post-apocalyptic lives. There would be another group of gladiators to entertain them in a week's time. They'd be back for more, though the chances were the Cartel would assure no gladiator would ever win again.

Skinner stood on the field with his general. Grunts cleared the turf of the bodies and weapons. Bosses led horses back to their stables outside the stadium.

"I don't get you," said Skinner. "Mercy doesn't keep order. It only makes people think they can get away with disobeying."

Roof put his hand on Skinner's shoulder. "Have you ever heard of Sun Tzu?"

"Son who?"

"Sun Tzu. He wrote *The Art of War*."

"I ain't heard of it. Ain't heard of him."

"He was a Chinese general and philosopher. He lived in the fifth and sixth century BC. He was brilliant."

"So?"

"So, Sun Tzu said, '*Opportunities multiply as they are seized.*'"

Skinner rolled his eyes. "What is that supposed to mean?"

Roof reached into Skinner's pocket and removed the box of cigarettes. "It means we have an opportunity to end the Dwellers." He shook loose a cigarette and slid it between his lips.

Skinner pulled out his lighter and offered Roof the flame. Roof tossed the cigarettes back to the captain.

"We haven't been able to get close to the canyon for more than two years," said the general. "The Dwellers' scouts and patrols have cut us off."

Skinner lit his own cigarette and sucked in a drag. He blew the smoke out of the corner of his mouth, away from the general. "We got a treaty with them folks, don't we?"

"Semantics," said Roof. "I want teams following Battle. Chances are they'll die of thirst or starvation before they make it that far north. But if they don't, if Battle is the man I know him to be, they'll expose the Dwellers' defenses as they approach. With a Dweller traveling with them, they'll get through. We'll see where they are strong and where they are weak."

Skinner flicked ash onto the turf. "How do you know they're headed for the canyon?"

"I sent the Dweller with them," Roof said. "They have nowhere else to go. We'll observe, keep our distance. When the time is right, we attack. We take control of the canyon."

"Why don't you send a mess of men to take the canyon? Why play these games? That's what got us into this mess with Battle to start with."

"This isn't a game," said Roof. "If we send a large army, even one that far outnumbers their population, we will lose if we don't know where they are vulnerable. They'd funnel us into ambush after ambush until the remaining men are demoralized and mutinous. I know this."

Skinner drew in another breath of smoke. "So you knew they'd survive the Jones? That was your plan all along?"

Roof laughed. "Of course not. When they somehow survived, I saw an opportunity. I seized it. You almost blew it with your fractious impulsivity."

Skinner tossed the butt to the ground. He stomped it out on the turf and turned to leave. "I don't know what you're saying. I don't care. You got a plan. I hope it works. I want to see that Battle fellow dead. Period. I want to see that woman and her boy dead. Period. If I'da been quicker, they would be."

"I want you in charge of the surveillance," said the general. "Keep your men back. Send three teams of three each. You pick a couple of men and you go too. Have one team follow them now. They'll rotate with the other teams. They are not to engage. You are not to engage. Simply observe."

Skinner nodded over his shoulder. He picked his hat up off the turf and put it on his head. He had work to do.

CHAPTER 32

JANUARY 4, 2020, 7:58 AM
SCOURGE -12 YEARS, 9 MONTHS
ALEPPO, SYRIA

Nazir drew his handgun and put a bullet in each of the two balustrade guards.

Battle pulled his weapon from beneath his sleeves and immediately took aim at the guard running along the bridge. Leaving Buck behind, he darted forward, both hands on the gun.

Pop! Pop! Pop!

Two of the three shots were true, and in his peripheral vision he saw three more flashes from Nazir's weapon. Certain he'd dropped his target to the ground, Battle stopped running and swiveled toward Nazir. He was leaning over one of the guards, picking up the AK.

"Battle, we hurry now," he called.

Battle turned back and ran to Buck. "Get on my back," Battle insisted. "Piggyback."

"What? I don't—"

"Just do it!"

Buck climbed onto Battle's back, aggravating the electricity running down his right leg. Battle slid off his sandals, wrapped his arms under Buck's legs, and ran barefoot toward the bridge, trying to catch up with Nazir. He could hear voices behind him.

He reached the balustrades and turned. There were a dozen armed men racing toward them. Some of them were in uniforms, some in street clothes.

"Go. Go. Go. Go!" Battle called to Nazir, hoping the repetition might elevate the urgency of his suggestion.

Nazir kept running, the AK in his hands. He jumped over the guard's body and stopped. He was halfway across the bridge, standing above the effective middle of the canal. He edged to the southern balustrade and leaned against it. He pulled the AK to his shoulder and aimed it straight at Battle.

Nazir's eyes widened, his neck strained. "Move!"

Battle leaned to his left and his momentum carried him away from Nazir's line of sight an instant before he felt the shudder of the AK unleashing its magazine in a rumbling, cracking hail of heavy 7.62x39 bullets rocketing past him at twenty-four hundred feet per second.

Clearly unaccustomed to the physics of the weapon, Nazir had trouble with its recoil. While his spray of bullets was effective at unloading a deadly swath at the oncoming horde, it also caused him to lose his balance. Despite leaning against the balustrade for support, he tripped backward.

In the time it took for him to regain his composure, the seemingly dead guard lying in a heap on the bridge raised his own AK and managed a quick pull of the trigger. A short burst found Nazir's midsection, and the doctor dropped his weapon over the balustrade and into the canal below.

Battle reacted and ran toward the guard. He reached the dying man and stepped onto his neck, exerting his full weight until he heard a snap and the man's tongue hung from his open mouth.

He stomped on it for good measure and then bolted to Nazir, who was sitting upright on the bridge. His arms were limp in his lap. His gaze was distant, his chest heaving. Blood was pooling on the stone underneath him.

Battle dropped Buck onto his good leg, knelt, and looked back at the approaching enemy. They'd slowed. Some of them were dead. The others had taken defensive positions some hundred feet from the bridge.

Nazir's bravery and foolhardy attempt at machine gunnery had given the horde pause. They were yelling instructions to one another. Their advance was measured.

Battle focused on them and then back on Nazir, whose lungs rattled with each raspy breath. Blood was leaking from the corners of his mouth. His olive skin was draining to the color of the gray stubble in his beard.

Battle couldn't carry both men across the bridge to its safer, eastern side. But he didn't want to leave Nazir alone either. The man had given his life to save theirs.

Battle clenched his jaw. The sight of his new friend gasping his final breaths pressed the angry adrenaline through his body. He looked up at the enemy and then back at Nazir. He glanced behind him at the eastern side of the bridge. Beyond it was the checkpoint. He could see the offset rows of concrete barriers protecting its entrance.

Battle put his hand on Nazir's shoulder. "I'll come back for you."

Nazir's eyes drifted toward Battle but couldn't find their focus. His shoulders shuddered.

Battle motioned to Buck. "Let's go." He resumed the piggyback carry and ran as fast as he could, Buck bouncing up and down with each stride, until he reached the end of the bridge. He could hear the intermittent staccato of automatic gunfire. Some of it pinged against the bridge, but missed the men as they reached the barriers.

By the time Battle had entered the serpentine arrangement, he had four HKs pointed at him and MPs were yelling at him to stop.

He did. He offloaded Buck, dropped his sidearm, and raised his hands. "Captain Marcus Battle. US Army!" The words couldn't escape quickly enough. "I'm with Sergeant First Class Buck. He's injured and needs immediate medical attention."

"To your knees, soldier!" one of the MPs called and approached with the HK leveled at Battle's head.

Battle dropped to his knees. "Sergeant Buck cannot follow the command. Please get him help."

With the MP barking commands, two others lowered their weapons and jumped the barricades. They each grabbed an arm and helped balance Buck. A third approached Battle, his weapon trained on him.

"We were hit with an IED," said Battle. "We got trapped. A Syrian local helped us."

"So that explains the getup?" asked the MP closest to Battle. Battle nodded. "He's dying on that bridge. We need to get him."

"Not gonna happen," said the MP in charge of the group. Battle pointed a finger at the MP. "Now wait a minute, soldier. I—"

The MP tightened his grip on the HK. "Do not confuse your rank with my authority, Captain. There are hostiles on the other end of that bridge. I am not sending men into a firefight over a dying local."

"Give me a weapon, then," Battle snapped. "Take care of Buck; I'll go get him."

"Relax, Captain," the MP ordered. "Not gonna happen. You're gonna come with me. We'll sort this out."

Battle cursed at the MP. "Give me a rifle!" He pushed himself to his feet and started toward the MP when he felt the poke of an HK muzzle at his bruised ribs.

The MP at the other end of the rifle pressed it into his side. "Easy there, Captain."

Battle cursed again but raised his hands as high above his head as he could hold them. His bruised side, his pinging right leg, his aching neck, his throbbing shoulders, and his wounded arm all contributed to his lack of flexibility. He looked over his shoulder at the bridge and quietly begged Nazir for forgiveness.

"We need to get inside," said the ranking MP. "This situation is about to get unruly."

The four MPs, Buck, and Battle wound their way past the remaining concrete barriers and beyond the raised manual gate arm. The trailing MP closed the arm. Battle stopped beside him and turned to watch the horror unfolding on the bridge.

A half dozen of the enemy, some in uniform, reached the middle of the bridge. They were calling out in Arabic, yelling in Battle's direction.

Two of the men picked up Nazir's body, holding him up by his armpits. They turned him to face the checkpoint. From the distance between them, Battle couldn't tell if Nazir was still alive or if Allah had mercifully hastened his death.

It appeared not to matter to the men holding up his body. They dragged him forward, the tops of his sandaled feet scraping along the ground. A third man came up from behind them and gripped the top of Nazir's head, yanking it backward. He then wielded a large reflective blade and sliced it across Nazir's neck, a fountain of blood spraying outward. Battle closed his eyes to the sound of the men cheering their baseness. He opened them again to see Nazir's head held high by the swordsman's hand.

The man shook the head, screamed something at Battle, and then heaved it into the canal. The two men holding the headless body dropped it on the bridge and kicked it. Another man spat on it. A fourth and a fifth did the same.

Battle's fists clenched and he gnashed his teeth. His pain evaporated. It was replaced with a seething he'd never felt. It was the desire for revenge, the guilt-fueled need to exact torture on the men who needlessly killed a selfless doctor, father, and grandfather.

As the MPs led Battle back to the confines of a small military installation inside what used to be Maysaloun Park, he tried to rationalize what he'd witnessed. He came to the conclusion, as much because of its truth as its ability to help Battle cope, that Nazir died because he'd left his home.

The doctor's world had ceased to exist as he knew it. War, famine, and disease had decayed Aleppo. All he had left was his family. He chose to expose that family to risk and danger by allowing them to venture outside. Had they never left home, they'd have never encountered two injured American soldiers they felt compelled to help.

Their selflessness in the face of a post-apocalyptic landscape had ruined them. Nazir was dead. Afifiah would never know what became of the man she called father. Her children would wonder about him the entirety of their lives, however long they may be.

Battle resolved he would prepare for the end of days. He would make a home worth defending, one from which he would never have to stray. That was the way to survive.

It was the *only* way.

CHAPTER 33

OCTOBER 16, 2037, 4:30 PM
SCOURGE +5 YEARS
ABERNATHY, TEXAS

Baadal leading the group, they walked silently north on Interstate 27.

"The canyon is about a hundred miles from here," he explained. "The first scout is maybe seventy or eighty miles. We need to find water or we won't make it. We've been walking for six hours."

"We need to keep moving or we won't make it," said Battle. "They're not letting us get away as easy as the general made it sound."

"I'm dehydrated too," said the gladiator. His name was Charlie Pierce. He told them he was a grass farmer who'd refused to increase his crop supply to the Cartel. They'd punished him, killing his wife and taking his farm. He was sent to the Jones to die.

"I hear you," said Battle. He licked his dry lips. The cracks told him he needed water. All of them did. "We'll figure it out."

Lola and Sawyer dragged behind. They were talking to each other in hushed voices, and Battle didn't want to interrupt. As long as they kept pace, they were fine.

Ahead on the right, there was a mobile home. Even from a distance, Battle could see it was a wreck. It was the first house they'd passed outside of Lubbock.

"I'm gonna run ahead," Battle said. "Meet me outside that house."

Battle jogged ahead, his head throbbing. He pushed his way into the trailer, kicking in the thin, hollow-core door.

He was immediately hit with the odor of urine and feces. A pair of rats scurried past him, diving into holes at the baseboards. He covered his mouth and nose with the crook of his arm, his eyes burning from the acidity in the air. He shuffled his way through what he imagined was the living area and found the kitchenette. With one hand he flung open cabinet doors above and below the laminate countertops that ran the length of the galley.

From the cabinets he pulled three large plastic cups, an open box of sandwich bags, and some pipe cleaners. He stuffed the findings into a plastic grocery bag he found on the floor. He looked for utensils but didn't find any.

Battle opened the refrigerator but instantly closed it when he found a nest of rodents chirping back at him, their eyes reflecting what little light had seeped into the box. He didn't bother with the freezer.

Nauseated, he hopscotched his way to the bedroom on the opposite side of the trailer. On a bare mattress in the corner of the room, there was a body. It was shriveled and decaying. A rat was chewing on the corpse's arm. Battle couldn't tell if the body belonged to a man or a woman.

He inched his way to the dresser opposite the mattress and pulled open one drawer after the next. There were some clothes—shirts and jeans mostly. There were undergarments, which told Battle the body belonged to a woman. And there was a knife. It was a small jackknife with a three-inch blade, but it was something. He stuffed it into his pocket and bolted.

He emerged from the home to find his four companions waiting for him. Baadal was bent over, hands on his knees. Charlie Pierce was sitting in the dirt. Lola and Sawyer were leaning on each other.

"All right," Battle said and pointed across the interstate. "We stay here for now. See that clump of trees on the other side of the highway?"

Baadal looked up, his hands still on his knees. "Yeah," he said.

"We'll make camp over there," Battle said. "Right by those trees. We'll chill until it's dark. Then we go again."

"We can't go again if we don't get some water," said Charlie Pierce.

Battle held up the plastic bag and shook it. "Leave it to me." He led the foursome across the highway to the grouping of shinnery oaks. They plopped into the dirt and weeds while Battle opened up the bag.

He pulled out a sandwich bag and opened it wide. He yanked on a low branch of the oak and stuffed its broad leaves into the bag, then took a pipe cleaner and twisted it around the top of the bag. He repeated the process six times.

"What is that?" asked Sawyer when Battle was twisting closed the final bag.

"I'm making water," Battle said. "The leaves sweat like we do. I'm trapping it in the bag. At nightfall we should have a cup of water each. That'll be a start."

"It's called transpiration," said Charlie Pierce. "Hadn't thought of doing that. It's smart. It'll work."

"So we stay here until dark?" asked Lola. "Just sit here?"

"For now," Battle said. He motioned to Baadal. "Since we have some time, tell us more about the canyon."

Baadal sat up, arching his back. He was holding onto a large branch he'd fashioned into a walking stick and leaned on it.

"We are strong people," he said. "We didn't succumb to the Cartel. Even as the government failed us, we fought for our freedom. We are doctors, farmers, honest politicians, lawyers, firefighters—"

Battle laughed. "Honest politicians?"

"There are not many of them, I'll admit. But yes, there are some among us. Our leader, Paagal, says it is important to include all types. Every perspective is needed to effectively run a free society."

"This Paagal," said Battle. "How did he become leader?"

"*She* became leader because we chose her," said Baadal. "She is forceful but merciful, intelligent but inquisitive. She believes the time is drawing near that we can disrupt the Cartel and lead an uprising. They are losing focus. We are gaining clarity."

"You're Baadal," said Charlie Pierce. "She's Paagal. What's with the names?"

Battle looked over at Charlie. The farmer was enraptured, fully focused on the story Baadal was weaving. He'd pulled his knees up to his chest and had his arms wrapped around them, his right hand holding his left wrist for balance.

"They are Hindi," said Baadal. "We all take Hindi names. They represent a rebirth, a cleansing from the filth of the Scourge and what it bore. Before I joined the Dwellers, my name was Felipe. Paagal's was Juliana."

"What do your new names mean?" asked Sawyer. He was playing with a large, straight branch he'd found on the ground, drawing circles with it in the dirt.

"Baadal means *cloud*."

"And Paagal?" asked Battle.

A smile spread across Baadal's face. "It means *crazy*."

CHAPTER 34

OCTOBER 16, 2037, 4:50 PM
SCOURGE +5 YEARS
LUBBOCK, TEXAS

Cyrus Skinner tapped the last cigarette out of the box. He'd smoked one after another since he'd left the Jones.

He was in a building adjacent to the stables outside the stadium, pacing back and forth. Though he was furious with the general, there wasn't anything he could do about it. He was only a captain, a white hat. General Roof was a black hat. There was no arguing with a black hat. He dragged his fingers across his neck and winced at the tenderness along his windpipe.

He'd thought about killing Roof right there in the stadium. He could have drawn his pistol and shot him in the chest before the general knew what hit him. Cyrus Skinner's life was a series of regrets and miscalculations. Not killing the general when he had the chance was one of them.

Cyrus thought the plan was flawed. He believed the Dwellers were constantly changing and shifting their defenses, and that was why they were virtually impenetrable. The Dwellers also knew every Godforsaken inch of Palo Duro Canyon and its vicinity.

They had the advantage, no matter what kind of surveillance the Cartel undertook. Brute force would have been smart, Skinner thought. Send in everyone at once and end it.

Skinner thumbed his lighter and held it to the cigarette. He inhaled deeply and held the smoke in his lungs. Sometimes the generals were too smart for their own good.

Porky walked into Skinner's office, knocking on the open door. "Captain?"

"What?" Skinner spun on his boot heel to look Porky in the eyes.

Porky immediately averted his gaze and stared at the floor. "The first team is on its way," Porky said. "I sent the Dalton brothers and another grunt. They're on horseback."

"So they're a few hours behind Battle and his friends," said Skinner.

"Yes, sir. They'll catch up by nightfall. They're headed straight north on the interstate. I told them to keep their distance. I said you don't want Battle to know he's being followed."

"Fine," said Skinner. "When's the next team leaving?"

"In a minute," said Porky. "They're in an SUV. They're gonna move east on 62 and then take it north until they connect with 70. That'll take them into Plainview ahead of when Battle should get there. They can set up a watch there."

"Good."

"Captain," said Porky, his eyes still on the floor, "can I ask what they're doing? What are the men looking for?"

"The canyon," said Skinner. "They're looking for a way into the canyon and how the Dwellers are set up to protect it."

Porky looked up from the floor, his mouth agape. "The Dwellers? I thought they were gone. I thought the Cartel—"

"You thought wrong, Porky," said Skinner. "The Dwellers are alive. They hold the canyon."

"But—"

"But nothing," said Skinner. "The generals made a truce with them. Now it seems the generals don't want the truce no more."

Porky shook his head. "So we don't... I mean, the Cartel don't control everything this side of the wall?"

"No."

"What would happen if that got out? I mean, if people knew—"

"That's why we got to put an end to the Dwellers," said Skinner. "They been quiet since the truce two years ago. If they decided to make noise, it could be trouble."

Porky drew in a deep breath and slowly exhaled.
"Dwellers…"

Skinner flicked the remains of his last cigarette to the floor.
"You ain't got no idea, Porky. Dwellers ain't the half of it," he
said. He flicked his tongue across his teeth and made a high-
pitched squeaking sound. He pointed at Porky and shooed
him away,

"Go get me some more smokes," he ordered. "I'm out and I'm
gonna need 'em for the trip."

CHAPTER 35

OCTOBER 16, 2037, 7:00 PM
SCOURGE +5 YEARS
ABERNATHY, TEXAS

The sun hung low on the horizon, obscured by the distant line of scrub oaks at the edge of the dirt plain on which Battle stood. It dipped lower, clouds filling the dark blue sky. The clouds would trap what little heat was left from the day. It wouldn't be quite as cold overnight.

He touched the bottom of one of the plastic bags hanging on the tree beside him. It was heavy with water.

"Everybody take a bag," he said, passing out the cups. "We got a cup of water each. Drink it slow. Sip it. Take turns with the cups. Sawyer gets two bags."

The group was sluggish. They were smart to have stopped and taken a break for a few hours. If they'd kept going, Battle's head would be throbbing more than it was, and there was a good chance more than one of them would have collapsed.

Battle unwound the pipe cleaner from his bag and carefully pulled the plastic from around the perspiring evergreen leaves. He zipped the bag three-quarters of the way and then drew the opening to his lips. The water was cold. He licked it across his lips, feeling it moisten the cracks, and then swallowed successive sips until he'd finished the bag.

Battle dipped his hand inside the plastic and ran his damp hand across his forehead and cheeks. The others were finishing their allotment. Baadal had his bag turned inside out and was licking the remaining moisture from the plastic.

"That was a smart idea," said Charlie Pierce. "You probably saved us from getting sick."

"Saw a video online about it before the Scourge," Battle said. "I tried it out a couple of times with the oaks on my land. It worked pretty well."

"Where was your land?"

"Near Abilene," Battle said, taking the plastic bags from everyone to save them for later use. "You?"

"Seguin," he said. "Near San Antonio."

"Grass farmer, you said?"

"Yeah," he said. "Hay, alfalfa, that sort of stuff. Kept the livestock fed."

"We should hit the road. The clouds are gonna cover up that moon and make it pretty dark."

"How far are we gonna walk?" Sawyer asked.

"If we walk at a good pace," said Baadal, "we should reach the first scouts before sunset tomorrow."

"I'm hungry." Sawyer sounded every bit the teenager that he was. "My legs hurt."

"We'll find something," said Battle.

"What?" asked Lola. "There's nothing."

"We'll find something."

They left the trees and headed north along Highway 27. Battle walked behind the group, making sure everyone stayed together. Baadal was in front, marching like a soldier. Charlie was a step behind him. Lola and Sawyer walked together. She held his hand. Both were using walking sticks. Sawyer took Baadal's lead and picked the dead leaves off a pair of branches, keeping one for himself and giving one to his mother. Battle noticed her limp was less pronounced. She was improving. That was good.

They'd walked for close to an hour when Sylvia's voice filled Battle's head. "You like her."

Battle tried to ignore it. He didn't want to have a conversation. He was too tired.

"It's okay," she said. "You've been alone a long time."

"I'm not interested," he mumbled under his breath.

"Don't lie to me, Marcus Battle," Sylvia's voice countered. "I know when you're lying. I see the way you look at her. I see the way *she* looks at *you*."

Battle looked up at the sky at the first stars twinkling between the clouds. He exhaled through his mouth, puffing his cheeks.

"Marcus," she said, "you can't be alone forever. You've left our home. You've moved on."

Battle gritted his teeth. "I haven't moved on. You're wrong."

Lola turned around and looked at Battle over her shoulder. "Did you say something?"

Battle waved her off. "No," he said. "Just thinking aloud."

Lola's eyes lingered as she kept walking. The corner of her mouth curled into a knowing smile. It looked like pity to Battle.

"She knows," he whispered. "She knows I talk to you."

"All the more reason to like her," said Sylvia. "She knows about it and doesn't think you're crazy."

"I *am* crazy," Battle whispered. "I've been hanging onto my sanity by an unwinding thread since you left me."

"It's okay with me too, Dad," Wesson said, joining the conversation. "She has a son who needs a father."

"He does," Sylvia added. "You're such a good father."

Battle stopped walking and clenched his fists. He drew in a long, steady breath and exhaled, trying to slow his pulse. He turned south, away from the group, and bent over with his hands clasped behind his neck. He needed to clear the voices. He squeezed his eyes shut and held his breath. The group had walked far enough he couldn't hear their footsteps. It was quiet, save the distant, high-pitched chirp of cicadas.

He stood there motionless for a moment. The voices in his head stopped. He opened his eyes and looked south along the highway they'd already walked. Battle was about to catch up with the group when he saw something reflected in the moonlight. It was a flash more than a true reflection. He waited. There it was again. Then he heard a noise. No. It was more of a song. Somebody was singing. Somebody was following them. Battle spun around and sprinted to catch up to the group. They needed to get off of the road.

***

The last thing Grat Dalton wanted to do was sit in a saddle. His rear and his thighs were rubbed raw from the subtle slide back and forth on the leather. Orders were orders, though, even if they came thirdhand through the hefty grunt called "Porky".

Porky told them their mission was direct from General Roof. Captain Skinner had seen to it they picked the best teams to head north. Their job was simple: ride and observe. That was it.

Emmett Dalton told his brother it was worth the saddle sores for the five days' worth of fresh rations, a bottle each of Tito's Vodka, and cold water in their canteens. Emmett was halfway through the Tito's, relishing the hint of corn in every fiery swig, as he, his brother, and a third grunt named Jack Vermillion neared Abernathy. Abernathy was a nothing town even in the daylight. The Daltons had ridden past it before, both north and south along the interstate. They joked the town marker read "Now Leaving Abernathy" on both sides of the sign.

Grat wasn't joking with Emmett this trip. He was frustrated by his own aches and his brother's drunken serenade. Jack Vermillion wasn't doing anything to help. He was encouraging it by humming along.

"C'mon now," Grat said loudly enough for his brother to hear him over his own wail, "enough singing. My ears hurt." Vermillion unscrewed his own half-empty bottle and raised it in a toast to Grat. "Give your brother a break. He's just having fun."

Grat didn't know Vermillion well, but he could tell from the man's slur and his slack in the saddle, he was drunk. Grat would have loved to toss back some of the liquor himself. But with both companions already wasted, he couldn't take the risk. They had a job to do.

He leaned forward to get a better handle on his reins. His horse was as undisciplined as Emmett.

He was looking down at the animal's crest. He rested a hand on its coarse black mane. When he looked up again, he almost fell off the horse. Three men were standing in the middle of the highway. The building clouds had obscured the moon enough that he couldn't see much more than their forms. The men looked big, and each of them looked to be holding a long gun of some kind. Grat couldn't tell if they were rifles or shotguns. It didn't matter much. The men had the drop on them. Grat tugged on the reins and slowed his horse to a stop. "Stop there," one of the men ordered. "Get off your horses and drop your weapons to the ground."

***

Battle used the dark to his advantage. When he'd seen the approaching grunts, he'd run back to the group to get Charlie Pierce and Baadal. He borrowed the long walking sticks from Sawyer and Lola and handed one of them to Charlie. Baadal already had his own. Lola and Charlie stayed back and off to the side, ducking into a shallow culvert.

"Hold these like rifles," Battle told them and led them south toward the approaching horsemen. "It's so dark, they might not know the difference."

He was right. The first of the men didn't hesitate to raise his hands and dismount.

"I'm gonna reach to my side," the grunt said, "and pull my revolver. I'm gonna toss it."

"Do it slowly," said Battle, aiming the stick at the grunt. "What's your name?"

"Grat Dalton," he said. "You know you're being stupid."

"Real stupid," slurred one of the two grunts who hadn't yet dismounted. "You're gonna get yourself killed."

"Shut up, Emmett," said Grat. "We ain't in a position to be makin' threats."

"I ain't givin' up my guns," said Emmett. "Ain't takin' my Tito's neither." The drunkard laughed.

"This isn't a joke," said Battle, his eyes darting amongst the trio of dark figures forty feet in front of them. "Get off your horses and step off the road."

"Seriously?" Charlie whispered into Battle's ear. "We don't have any *real* weapons. These are *sticks*."

"We'll be fine," Battle whispered back. Charlie had reminded Battle of the jackknife in his pocket. Still holding aim on the grunts, he fished out the knife and flipped it open with his thumb. "Get off the horses now, or you're going to need another gallon of Tito's to dull the pain."

Vermillion reached out and pushed Emmett in the shoulder. "I reckon we listen to the—"

Emmett pushed him back. "I ain't listening to these fools," he spat. He hopped off his horse, dropping the near empty bottle, which shattered on the asphalt. "Now see, that's just infuriating." He stomped his foot and started marching toward Battle.

Emmett shoved his way past his brother and reached to his hip to pull his revolver. He was twenty feet from them when he pulled the trigger.

Pow!

Drunk as he was, Emmett couldn't have hit a barn from three feet. The shot was errant and missed all three men. Battle's aim was true.

At the instant the shot was fired, he'd flung the knife, end over end, at the growing target in front of him. It hit Emmett above his heart on the left side of his chest. The blade carved into him to its hilt.

Emmett dropped his pistol and staggered backward. He looked down at the knife handle protruding from him and gripped it, wrenching it from his body. That was a bad move. Blood coursed from the wound, draining faster than Emmett could plug the hole with his fingers. He looked back at his brother, mumbled, and fell over onto the interstate, the knife still in his hand.

Grat backed away from his dying brother and moved deliberately to the shoulder of the road. He didn't say anything, but his eyes stayed glued to Emmett struggling and twitching on the asphalt.

Vermillion raised his hands and jumped from his horse. He dropped his pistol and quickly joined Grat at the edge of the highway.

Battle advanced quickly and picked up Emmett's pistol, aiming it at Grat. He tossed the stick to the ground, pulled the knife from Emmett's hand, and watched the horror envelop Grat's face as the grunt realized he'd been had by a man armed only with a knife.

"You gotta be kidding me," Grat said. He swallowed hard, his eyes drifting to his brother. He looked back at Battle, cursed him and spat in his face. Battle could see the man's fear morphing into defiant anger.

"I know who you are," Grat said through clenched teeth. "You're that fella from the Jones. Skinner shoulda shot you dead instead of Pico."

"Shoulda killed both of you," Vermillion said. "That's what I woulda done."

Battle wiped the spit from his forehead. "Coulda, woulda, shoulda. Too late now." He raised the pistol and pressed it against Grat's forehead.

Grat squeezed his eyes shut. "Just do it. Get it over with." Battle stood with the weapon at Grat's head until the grunt opened his eyes. Then he lowered it.

"C'mon, guys," he called to Baadal and Charlie. "Get the horses." He walked backward to the horse Grat had been riding and took the reins with one hand. The other trained the pistol on the grunts. "Mount up."

Each of the men heaved themselves into their saddles. Baadal and Charlie started their horses north.

"Looks like we got some food here," said Battle. "And a full canteen of water." He reached into the saddlebag and pulled out Grat's unopened bottle of vodka. He tossed it to the grunt and spurred the horse north to join the others.

Grat juggled the bottle, but caught it before it hit the ground. "Wait," he said. "You gonna leave us here?" Grat snarled. "You kill my brother for nothin' and then leave us in the middle of nowhere? No food? No water?"

"We walked here from Lubbock," said Battle. "No food. No water."

Vermillion called out, "You can't leave us here. We walk back to town, we're as good as dead."

"Better drink up, then, fellas," Battle said over his shoulder. He slid the pistol onto his hip and controlled the horse with one hand.

He brought the horse to a canter until he reached Lola. He offered her a hand and pulled her onto the saddle behind him. Sawyer climbed aboard Charlie's horse. Baadal led the way north.

"We can be there before sunrise," he said to the others. He pulled his canteen and drew a long drink before coaxing his horse to a gallop. "We'll probably reach a scout not long after midnight."

Lola wrapped her arms around Battle's waist, her hands pressed flat against his chest. He turned his head toward hers as his horse picked up speed. "You okay?"

"For now," she said. "I've got Sawyer. I've got you. And we're going to a place the Cartel can't touch us."

Battle took one of her hands and squeezed. She leaned into his back, resting her head against his neck. It was the most human contact Battle had experienced in five years. It felt alien yet comforting. It took his breath away. He allowed himself to enjoy it.

Lola was right about two things. She had Sawyer. She had him. He didn't want to tell her that deep down he believed the Cartel's arms were long enough to always reach them, even in the canyon.

CHAPTER 36

OCTOBER 17, 2037, 1:00 AM
SCOURGE +5 YEARS
LUBBOCK, TEXAS

General Roof stood in front of a panel of large monitors on the wall of the Lubbock HQ office. He was alone. He'd shooed away the grunts and bosses who were hanging around drinking and smoking. He poured himself a cup of coffee. It was black and like mud, but he was tired and needed the jolt of caffeine.

The power in Lubbock was better than in some of the less populated areas. It was necessary, given Lubbock's importance to their drug trade, that the electricity be more stable. Roof was thankful for that as he pressed a remote on the desk to activate the office computer.

"Computer on," he said. The trio of wide screens flickered to life. "Conference Generals. Live chat."

A series of numbers and letters moved across the center screen. It went black and then turned on again. Roof's mirror image filled the screen. The monitors to either side buzzed to life. A bald man appeared in the screen to the left, and a leathery one was visible on the right.

"We need to talk," said Roof. "You have a minute?"

"It's late," said the bald general. General Harvey Logan. Roof could hear a woman in the background. She was complaining about the interruption. Logan ignored her.

"I'm good," said the leathery one, Parrott Manuse. "What do you need?"

"I think I've found a way to deal with the Dwellers," said Roof.

"We dealt with them two years ago," said Manuse. "We signed a truce. We told everyone we'd eliminated them. What's the problem?"

"It's only a matter of time before their influence spreads," said Roof. "We've caught their scouts farther and farther away from the canyon. They're planning something. We need to be proactive."

"So what is this proactive approach?" asked Logan. "What have you concocted this time?"

"You know about the man they called Mad Max."

Both generals nodded and acknowledged they knew of him.

"What about him?" asked Logan, rubbing his head.

"He survived the Jones," said Roof. "He and four others."

Logan cursed. "How?"

"He's a warrior," said Roof, looking directly into the camera at the top of the center monitor. "He survived. I let him go."

Manuse leaned into his camera, his face growing large and out of focus on the screen. "What? Who gave you that sole authority? We have rules, Roof. We have three generals for a reason."

"We had four generals," said Logan. "Your last plan to end the Dwellers and take the canyon left us with three. You recall that, Roof?"

"I recall that," said Roof. "That's why it's imperative we take care of them now."

Manuse sat back in his chair. His face pulled into focus. "What does Mad Max have to do with the Dwellers?"

"One of the men traveling with him is a Dweller. He survived too. He's going to lead Mad Max and a couple of others straight to the canyon. I've got teams following them, looking for defense strategy."

"That's not enough," said Logan. "They shift their defenses constantly. That's why we can't defeat them. Surveillance won't be good for more than a day. It's a waste."

"You better have something else," said Manuse.

Roof smiled. "I do."

"What is it?" asked Logan. "Stop being coy."

"One of the men traveling with Mad Max is one of ours," said Roof. "A captain from Houston. I brought him with me to Lubbock. I put him in the Jones and told the fighters not to touch him. His name is Charlie Pierce. He's smart. And he's going to be on the inside."

Logan nodded. "So the surveillance is a decoy?"

"Exactly," said Roof. "It's a distraction. Mad Max, whose name is Battle by the way, will spot them. He'll probably kill some of them. Pierce will work hard to gain Battle's confidence. Pierce is our real weapon. He'll walk right into the canyon with a friendly escort and a badass warrior at his side."

The generals congratulated Roof on his brilliance and they agreed to talk soon. Roof ended the call and shut down the computers.

He walked over to the desk in the corner of the room and sat on its edge. He picked up the mug of coffee and took a healthy swig, wincing at the bitterness of it. It was cold too, but it was coffee. He finished it and wiped his mouth with the back of his hand.

Roof pinched the bridge of his nose and rubbed his eyes with his fingers. It would be a long few nights waiting for word from Charlie Pierce. It would be worth it in the end.

They'd rid themselves of the threat from the Dwellers. They'd truly establish dominion over the two hundred and seventy-thousand square miles they'd fought hard to control in the months after the Scourge.

The best part of it was that an old friend was unwittingly doing his bidding for him. Marcus Battle, the war hero, was under his command. He laughed thinking about how Battle hadn't recognized him. Maybe it was the ponytail or the beard. Maybe too many years had passed. It didn't matter. It was better that Battle was clueless.

General Roof reached inside his shirt and pulled out a pair of dog tags that hung around his neck on a thin ball chain. He'd worn them every day since his enlistment more than twenty-five years earlier; before earning his E-7 stripes, before Syria, before Landstuhl and Walter Reed, the meth and the heroine, the riches, the Scourge, the Cartel, the depravity, before...
The chain was long enough that he could read the stamped lettering on the tags. He ran his thumb across it, reminding himself of who he'd once been.

BUCK
RUFUS
000-11-0200
O NEG
CHRISTIAN

EXCERPT FROM WALL:

BOOK THREE OF THE TRAVELER SERIES

CHAPTER ONE

OCTOBER 25, 2037 2:00 AM
SCOURGE +5 YEARS
PALO DURO CANYON, TEXAS

Dragging a fresh corpse across the Canyon's floor wasn't part of the plan. Not much that had happened in the week since he'd arrived had gone as Charlie Pierce expected, but there was a job to do.

Regardless of the obstacles or the unforeseen circumstances, Pierce had to deliver. General Roof was relying on his surveillance for the coming assault.

Pierce was bent over at the waist, slugging backwards on his heels as he pulled the body through brush, over rock, and across dry creek beds. He didn't know how far he'd have to go to find the right spot to dump the man he was forced to execute. He'd know it when we found it.

Lightning flashed in the sky above, illuminating the steep jagged walls of the Canyon. Thunder followed and reverberated as it traveled the wide valley of Palo Duro. Pierce stopped and dropped the body. He stood erect and put his hands on his hips. He was winded and, despite near freezing temperatures, was sweating through his shirt. He could feel the perspiration chill as it dripped from the nape of his neck down his back.

Another fork of light jabbed the black sky, pulsing as the thunder cracked and rumbled before the afterglow was gone. The storm was getting closer.

Pierce wondered if the turn in the weather was a good thing. A heavy rain would wash away the impression of the body from having it pulled it through the dirt.

He'd snapped the man's neck during a brief struggle. The man, a sentry for The Dwellers, had asked too many questions. He'd pressed to hard about Pierce's intentions. Pierce had tried to talk his way out of the predicament. It hadn't worked.

Pierce had found a communications bunker on the Canyon's floor. It was two miles from The Dwellers' central encampment. The bunker wasn't much more than a small grotto nature had carved into the mesa walls. There were several two-way radio base stations running on a small gas powered generator. It was the rumble and hum of that generator that had led Pierce to the grotto.

A thin wire, serving as an antenna extension ran up the steep wall as far as Pierce had been able to see in the dark. The Dwellers' communication system was a fortunate but critical find for the spy. If he were couldn't disable the two-way system as the attack occurred, he could, at the very least, relay frequencies to The Cartel so they could monitor The Dwellers' tactical positions. The sentry had surprised him as he was checking those frequencies.

"Hey," the sentry had called out from beyond the bunker's entrance, his voice echoing inside the small cave. "What are you doing? You're not supposed to be in there."

"I just stumbled in here," Pierce had lied. "I was out for a walk…"

The sentry had stepped into the cave, aiming a small pen light at Pierce's face. It had been otherwise dark save the glowing green and blue lights on the two-way tranceivers. "It's two o'clock in the morning."

"Yeah," Pierce had shrugged before making his deadly move. Now he found himself dragging a body along the canyon floor.

The canyon was immense in its size. It ran seventy miles long and, at it's widest, twenty miles across. Its walls stretched skyward close to nine-hundred feet from the floor. Pierce had learned in his brief stay that The Dwellers were experts at navigating it and protecting it. Pierce had done everything he could to soak in as much information as possible. He'd listened to conversations, observed patterns of movement and behavior, and he'd absorbed the bizarre philosophical bent of the bellicose pacifists who gave themselves Hindi names in a freakish ritual that, to Pierce's limited theological education, bore no resemblance to Hinduism.

Pierce had done his job invisibly until he'd killed the sentry. He'd performed exactly as the General had instructed.

"Be a fly on the wall," General Roof had said the night before he put him in The Jones. "Learn as much as you can about how they work. Then, as we attack, damage whatever defensive systems you can and run."

They were broad orders with little assurance of survival. But Pierce gladly accepted the challenge. He had no family. He'd grown tired of his monotonous and sour post-scourge existence. This was an adventure with the promise of greater things to come should he succeed and live.

Pierce blinked against another flash of lightning and shivered at the first icy drops of rain that smacked against his head and shoulders. The storm was coming.

He was running out of time to dispose of the body in a way that made the sentry's death look like an accident. He needed to finish the job and return to the camp before anyone knew he was missing.

Pierce looked around his surroundings. He couldn't see much beyond a few feet except when the lightning flashed. He decided this spot was as good as any. The ache in his lower back made the choice as much as his brain.

He lifted up his shirt and reached into his baggy, sweat and dirt stained pants. Strapped to his leg was a gift General Roof had given him. He flipped it open and pressed a series of numbers before pulling the satellite phone to his ear. It took a couple of minutes for the satellite to acquire his signal. When it did, he heard a series of warbling rings.

The General answered with a voice more gravelly than usual. "It's two in the morning," he said.

The rain was intensifying. The drops were heavier and just as cold. Pierce wiped the water from his eyes. "I found their communications hub. They're working with two way radios. I've got the frequencies."

"Go ahead," said the General. "Give them to me."

"Four sixty seven point fifty eight seventy five," Pierce answered, "and four sixty two fifty eight seventy five."

"Just two frequencies?"

"That I could tell."

"So they've got a two mile range."

"I don't know."

"And they're operational?"

Pierce squatted, resting his weight on his heels. He shielded his face from the rain and tried to cup the phone tight to his ear. The rain was making it difficult to hear. "What?"

"They're operational?"

"They seem to be," said Pierce. "They've got a generator running it."

The signal was beginning to weaken. "Are they on to you?" Pierce turned his back to the gusts of wind blowing through the canyon. "No."

"You sure?"

"I had to kill a guy," Pierce admitted. His body involuntarily trembled from the cold.

"That changes things."

"I'll be f-f-fine," Pierce stammered. His jaw was beginning to ache from his chattering teeth. The temperature had dropped what felt like fifteen degrees in a few seconds. The rain was beating down, slapping Pierce's neck and arms with a cold sting.

The General's voice was hollow and digitally distorted. "Hello?"

"Hello?" Pierce pulled the phone from his ear and looked at the signal. It was almost non-existent. He pressed a button to end the call, wiped the screen with the tail of his shirt, and stood to stuff it back into his pants.

"Pierce?" A voice called from behind him.

Pierce spun as thunder shuddered through his shivering body. A flash of lightning revealed a dark figure standing a few feet from him. Pierce couldn't make out the man's features, but he knew who it was and saw the gun in his hand.

"What are you doing, Pierce?" Marcus Battle asked the question as if he already knew the answer.

39946566R00154

Made in the USA
Middletown, DE
21 March 2019